MW00624984

BLOOD FOR MOLASSES:

A Mississippi Massacre

Based on a True Story

Rick Ward

http://www.springmorningpublishing.org

Blood for Molasses: A Mississippi Massacre
Copyright © 2010 by Rick Ward
Spring Morning Publishing, Inc.

All rights reserved. No part of this book may be reproduced (except for inclusion in reviews), disseminated or utilized in any form or by any means, electronic or mechanical, including photocopying, recording, or in any information storage and retrieval system, or the Internet/World Wide Web without written permission from the author or publisher.

For more information please contact:
info@springmorningpublishing.org

Cover design by Scribe Freelance of New York
http://www.scribefreelance.com

2nd Edition, printed November 2010

Blood for Molasses: A Mississippi Massacre
Rick Ward

1. Title 2. Author 3. Historical fiction
Library of Congress Control Number: 2010912641

ISBN-10: 0-9828099-1-3 (Paperback)
ISBN-13: 9780982809914

ISBN-10: 0-9828099-0-5 (Hardcover)
ISBN-13: 9780982809907

ISBN-10: 0-9828099-2-1 (E-book)
ISBN-13: 9780982809921

Printed in the United States of America

"Those who do not remember the past are condemned to repeat it."
- George Santayana

Pre-Publication Comments
On Draft Material to the Author

"You have a deeply heartfelt connection to your characters and their electrifying and unusual moment in our tumultuous history. Please keep up your remarkable quest."

- Stephen Molton,
novelist, screenwriter, professor, playwright,
painter, and former HBO, MTV Networks,
and Showtime executive.

"It is rare when someone has a real story and real research. My gut tells me you will meet a great collaborator who knows screenwriting and will help clear the road for an epic historical film."

-Bob Morris,
novelist, screenwriter,
former New York Times columnist and
contributing editor to numerous magazines.

ACKNOWLEDGEMENT

Elizabeth Spencer published *The Voice at the Back Door* in 1955. She maintains that the book was purely fiction. However, it has a scene that clearly is a reminder of the courtroom massacre that occurred in her childhood hometown. Her book earned a nomination for a Pulitzer Prize in the same year Emmett Till was murdered near Carroll County, Mississippi. We should all be thankful that she had the courage to write what she did even though, for the most part, it alienated her from her family and hometown friends for telling a story they did not want told.

In the mid-1990s, Carrollton freelance writer Susie James conducted research locally and exposed the real story of the courthouse massacre in the *Greenwood Commonwealth* and *Clarion Ledger* newspapers. That was the first time it had been public since the newspapers of 1886, giving our generations a real look at this incident.

In the early 2000s, Professor Sally Greene of the University of North Carolina published an essay that compared Elizabeth Spencer's novel with the real life incident that occurred. Dr. Greene conducted an exhaustive search for newspaper accounts of the incident all over the United States and in other countries. When my work started, Dr. Greene provided me with all her work documents and put me in touch with Elizabeth Spencer to enlighten her on new facts I had found about the incident. Ms. Spencer and I discussed the matter over the next year or so.

I am deeply indebted to these ladies for their groundwork that led to my book. I am also most appreciative to the kind citizens of Carrollton and the various Carroll County offices. I am especially thankful to Carroll County Chancery Clerk Stanley "Sugar" Mullins and his entire, helpful staff of wonderful ladies who always stopped what they were doing to help me.

However, that does not suggest that they were aware of, or would endorse or concur with the fictional dialogue or scenes in this book.

I would also like to thank the many friends and family members, too numerous to name, that helped with the edits, comments and reviews of the various versions of the manuscript before it was finalized. I am also grateful to the media contacts that helped promote the book.

Preface

"History is written by the victors."
-Winston Churchill

T his book is profoundly based on a true story. I originally wrote this manuscript as nonfiction. However, to make the story more interesting, it became necessary to insert dialogue and occasional fictional characters and scenes, making it more consistent with a fictional format. Therefore, I reclassified it as fiction. In the case of railroad detectives mentioned herein, I used real characters in fictional scenes. That does not take away from the fact that the central theme of this story is true. What happened in and around the Carrollton, Mississippi, Courthouse grounds in October 1875 and the months of February and March of 1886 happened as stated in this book. I made up the dialogue between characters throughout this book, but did so with a great deal of knowledge about the characters' personalities, beliefs, and methodologies, based on extensive research. I have not changed the names of any real character in this book for any reason, nor have I altered their positions within the local, state or federal governments.

Wherever possible, historical documents and/or copies of newspaper articles from the times and sometimes pictures are included to refer to and keep the reader in tune with the reality that the facts listed are true. A few of the pictures are from that era, not necessarily from Carrollton, but most are. All documents and articles are genuine. Documents written in text other than those copied as images appear as italic text. I transcribed them as accurately as possible from handwriting of that day and our copying capability of today.

Some of the text, but primarily author comments at the end, include quotes and comments taken from sources listed. I used those quotes and comments to inform the reader again of the realism. By today's standards, these comments sometimes reflect negatively on the person portrayed. However, they are not intended to distract from the good for which these people were responsible – most of which has been well documented in history books and other forms of media. I intended to show today's reader a side of those persons' habits, attitudes, and actions most likely unknown to them and how they relate to this book. They are in no way a reflection on the descendants of these people.

The terms "nigger," "nigga," "niggah" and "negro" appear in this book not as an insult to the African American race, rather as an attempt at being historically accurate and in some cases showing actual quotes from politicians. If you are offended by the term as I have proposed it in this book, you should not read further.

I have made an exhaustive attempt to make this story as historically accurate as possible. If you find any errors, they were unintentional and you should report them via the book's website at info@bloodformolassses.com for review, confirmation, and possible correction in future editions.

Introduction

*"God alone knows the future, but only an
historian can alter the past."*
-Ambrose Bierce

This story is about the fate of three young men, one black and two half-black/half-Choctaw Indians, who lived in north Mississippi during the late 1880s. Although virtually unknown to the world, the white people on the periphery of their lives that made them what they were and resulted in their demise, are more well-known now than during their own lifetimes. These individuals represented a much larger group of people—an entire Indian nation and former slaves who outnumbered their white counterparts five to one, each suffering many of the pitfalls shared by the other. The hardships they suffered and pain they endured symbolized the oppression of both races.

In order to tell the story of these young and determined men, we must first go back in time and look at their ancestors' lifestyles from a sociological perspective. In the early 1800s, Indians in the Southeast were, for the most part, a peaceful race favoring farming and trade over savage acts of violence. As the European settlers, discontent with the East Coast, began to move west, they encroached on the Indian lands. This sometimes resulted in individual fights but often erupted into family, if not tribal, feuds. Local American lawyers would try to settle the lesser of the disputes. However, some larger altercations brought the congressional lawyers out of the woodwork to settle matters using brutal military force. In doing so, they usually took as a prize for the many victories, land belonging to the Indians with promises of protecting them from foreign invading enemies.

By the mid-1830s, there was no more land to take and many red men had died in battles along the way. Many of those that survived would also die on the long walk to their new promised land. Few stayed, but those who did eventually became subservient to Caucasians. White men really did not care what happened to them, viewing them as savages, unwilling to adapt to lifestyles from the mother country, so they had to go and settle elsewhere. After all, the white man considered himself the dominant, supreme race and barely regarded the Indians as animals.

Now that all this rich soil once owned by the Indians was in the hands of American citizens, it needed clearing to raise large commercial crops that would bring millions of dollars in the open market with fair trade from Europe and Asia, to name a few. The age of mechanization had not yet come about so the only way of clearing this land was brute strength in numbers. Opportunists would bring in black slaves by the thousands from Africa at the point of a saber and sell them in open markets. Our ancestors considered them property and did not allow them to assimilate into the white supremacist society, but gave them the necessities and forcibly oppressed them in order to maintain control. They also separated and sold them on a regular basis. Slave "massers" (masters) often used the wives and daughters of the slave men for sexual pleasure, and they regularly sold their off springs. Many states, as well as individual plantation owners, had laws or rules that prohibited slaves from learning to read and write, although many did, in secrecy by candlelight.

In the early 1860s, the slaves were in such high numbers that many were escaping or their bounties were being paid. As a result, many were finding their way up North to tell their stories. The entrepreneurial men from the North that had come down South to make riches often told these stories as well. However told, many Northerners did not want the blacks taking the jobs of their working force in the coming age of mechanization. Others saw it purely from a moral view and did not believe in people owning other people regardless of their skin color. This attitude of economic indifference and moral persuasion broke the country apart as states in the South began to secede from the Union, ultimately leading to the Civil War and the freeing of all black men. However, once free, they had no jobs, nobody to furnish them with the necessities of life, and nobody in the South that wanted them as a part of the lawmaking government. Like the ethnic cleansing of the Indians thirty years before, an effort began at the hands of Abraham Lincoln to colonize them into an African country known as Liberia. That effort failed to obtain funding through Congress.

The men responsible for the Indian removal became heroes and most of the Indians were of little concern. The few that remained were common laborers or very low-scale businessmen, supplying the needs of the white man. A few within the Indian circles became rich for their assistance in the ethnic cleansing but those common Indians left behind became a burden on society, stereotyped as drunkards, fighters and lowly members of society.

Lincoln, the one single man credited with freeing the blacks, died at the end of the Civil War. He left behind no plan to deal with the freed slaves' futures or any program to assist the former slave owners with re-employing them. His only plan to send them back to Africa had failed when a group he sent to Haiti started an uprising, infuriating Congress. They made him take the last one-hundred-thousand-dollar budget for colonization in Liberia and bring the colonized group back from Haiti. Congress disestablished the program after that. Therefore, the blacks, too, became a "burden" on society in much higher numbers than the Indians had because most of the Indians were now on their sovereign land in Oklahoma—out of sight, out of mind.

The two oppressed societies often intermingled and the result was offspring of mixed race, rejected by most. They had to earn their living any way they could and bow down to the white man. All the while, the white man accepted their goods and services but still saw them as rejects in society, highly suspicious of their conduct and motives.

That brings us to the story of half-Indian, half-black Ed and Charley Brown of Carrollton, Mississippi. They were hardworking young men in their twenties whose father was black and had been killed by a local newspaper editor. Their mother was once an Indian slave paid for by their father to gain her freedom. They raised sugar cane to make and sell sorghum molasses. They might have been boisterous loudmouths with chips on their shoulders, unyielding to the white supremacists' mentality, but unlike their white counterparts, they complied with the law. Their faults were minor compared to the politicians at the time that, uncontroverted by history, either personally participated in or used paramilitary groups to terrorize, maim, and murder blacks attempting to vote.

Chapter One:

The Outskirts of Town

"When sorrows come, they come not as single spies, but in battalions!"
-William Shakespeare

Carroll County, Mississippi, 1867

S creams, bone-chilling screams, echoed throughout the woods; louder and louder, they came in the dark, unmistakably a woman in trouble. "Help me, please help me" could be heard coming from the small, unpainted wooden shack.

Smoke rose from the chimney of the dimly lit house that cold February morning. The plain but well-built sharecropper tenant house, surrounded by empty fields of harvested crops on all sides, had a small garden in the back. Only tiny heads of cabbage peeking through for spring consumption would be edible any time soon. No sign of life at first, except a black and white cow. An immense red rooster paced back and forth, startled by the continuous screams and what might be lurking in the dark. Nearby in a plum tree were hens still roosting from the night before, not yet yielding to the morning light.

If only the animals could talk. Maybe they could reveal the source of the screams, maybe even what caused them.

The sun was by now rising through a dense fog as the twinkling lights in the distance slowly disappeared with daybreak. The blast from a shotgun echoing from the wood line just minutes after daylight came from only a short distance away. A hunter was taking the last of the white tail deer for the season. A hardworking freed man, William McKinney was bringing fresh game home to his wife. The big guns had become silent almost two years prior. The war had ended in 1865. Many of the slaves had moved on, exercising their freedom. The McKinney's' loyalty remained with their "masser," since they knew no other life and had no place else to go. This was a common practice in their Carroll County, Mississippi, community.

The sun, now high in the sky, was melting the fog. A figure was seen racing towards the house where the screams had now subsided. The Negro man with gun in hand approached the front porch; a dog tagged along behind him. As he threw the gutted deer carcass on to the porch, blood still dripping, he heard a sound, a faint cry coming from inside the house. He rushed in, calling to his wife, "Lucindy, Lucindy, you okay?"

Not a sound except for creaking boards as he moved about, knocking over a cane back chair, quickly making it to the rear of the house. The back door stood wide open, revealing a sight he hoped never to find, a sight he could not even imagine. Her lifeless body lay covered with blood on the bed of patchwork quilts. Her eyes had been beaten shut and her throat cut slightly, but not through the windpipe. Her legs were wide-open, left foot dangling to the floor and right ankle wedged against the wall.

As he turned away to vomit, he heard another faint cry. He looked back and saw movement through the several layers of quilt, blanket, and blood-soaked sheets. Pulling the covers back, he found a kicking, prematurely born baby boy. She had delivered two months early before losing her own life. Perfect in every way except fingernails not yet developed, the miracle child mewed softly until he found his father's eyes and then started wailing uncontrollably.

As William gathered the newborn into his arms, he whispered tearfully, "Yo ma'ama wanted you to be named after your daddy. We gonna call you Will."

William summoned the doctor, who said his wife's struggling before she died must have put her into early labor. He also presumed she used the last strength she had in her body to see to it that the baby survived with no need to lay in a pine box along with her.

"She fought real hard," the doctor said. "Both arms are broken, most likely in an attempt to defend herself from the blows of that ole fire poker. Indentions in her arms showed traces of ash."

Even the doctor could not tell her husband about some of the unspeakable abuse that had been perpetrated against her. However, the obvious was undeniable: The assailants had carefully removed her nipples with a sharp knife.

Word of the attack spread quickly throughout the small town. What kind of sick, perverted man or men could launch such a violent, deadly attack? The community suspected it was the work of Indians. Judging from the food and whiskey taken from the house, it would have taken at least two.

The Choctaw were indigenous to the area. They were normally agriculturist and had given up most of the nearby land some forty years before. Some of their descendants, especially young males unable to handle their liquor, would commit crimes of violence and steal whatever they could get to eat. This was more prevalent in the winter months. Ironically, there was no sign of forced entry into the house. Over the next several months, similar murders occurred in the small towns nearby, including Coffeeville, Grenada and Pickens, where patches of some bitter Indian families remained.

William would forever grieve for his beloved Lucindy, convinced his wife's murder had to do with politics. William was a gentle man, small in stature, slightly bent, not from age, but from many years of bending over to pick cotton. He used whiskey only as a medicine for pain. He never bothered anyone, kept his place clean, and believed in doing what white people told him to do. William always walked behind the masser's family down an old dirt road to church, where he sat on the back row peeping over the heads of white folks in front of him. The small community of Carrollton had its share of churches of all denominations. Gazing occasionally out the window of the old Baptist church at the cemetery, William longed for the day he could join his old friends and family in heaven.

William considered the white McKinneys his family. Masser Bud and his wife, Mrs. Emma, came from a long line of Christian people always extending a helping hand to those in need regardless of their race. Mrs. Emma was the daughter of a missionary to Africa and had grown up around black children, always helping them and their families. Bud McKinney was the son of a Baptist preacher and began his education in a seminary. He and Emma married and settled in Carrollton on McKinney family land just east of town.

William was content living on the white McKinney plantation and raising his child alone with only occasional assistance from the white family.

Chapter Two:

Railroad Detectives

"The real art of conversation is not only to say the right thing in the right place but to leave unsaid the wrong thing at the tempting moment."
-Dorothy Nevill

On November 6, 1867, the deafening, smoke-bellowing, iron locomotive with steam rising around the mighty wheels, screeched into the nearly empty station at Winona, Mississippi. Hanging at an angle to an outside handle by one hand was a highly astute young man with a custom-made derby barely covering his head full of unruly brown curls. Well-dressed and cleanly shaven, this young man was obviously from the North. Not even waiting for the train to come to a complete stop, he jumped onto the station platform and ran into the depot to buy a newspaper.

On his way from the City of New Orleans to Memphis, Tennessee, the young man began to read the local paper to catch up on the news of the district he had recently taken over for his company. Unlike most of the small-town papers, with their advertisements for things like cure-all tonics taking

up more space than the news of the day, this
newspaper had startling headlines.

"UNSOLVED MURDERS STILL A MYSTERY"
was the headline for the weekly edition. He
continued to read as the paper described the murder
of Lucinda McKinney, survived by her husband,
William Sr., and newborn son, Will McKinney, the
first of the mysterious murders. Three other
gruesome murders had occurred in the last nine
months in nearby towns of Grenada, Coffeeville, and
Pickens. All victims were black females, former
slaves, freed but still living and working on their
plantations. Sickeningly enough all had their nipples
removed.

As he continued to read, a heavyset black
porter, dapper in his black pinstriped suit with a
matching vest, interrupted and handed him a note.
As he read the note, the young man smiled from
cheek to cheek. The note read, "I understand we have
a distinguished gentleman as a guest on our train this
morning. Please be my honored guest in the first
class dinning car at precisely 11:30 a.m. Signed,
Albert Morgan, Vice-President, Illinois Central
Railroad." The man quickly scribbled on the note, "It
would be my honor, sir." He then signed the
embossed ivory notecard and handed it back to the
porter with a smile.

The young man looked forward to it. With
more than two hours until his lunch meeting, he had
time to study the newspaper articles concerning the
recent murders. He removed a railway county map
of the Southern states to familiarize himself with the
communities mentioned in the paper and was most

intrigued when he noticed that each of the towns was on, or very close by, the railroad line on which he was traveling. He made notes of the towns, dates of the murders and particulars of the savage torture of the victims.

****

At 11:20, the gentleman left his seat and made his way to the first-class dining car, where the same porter greeted him and escorted him to his seat. Upon arrival, a very nicely dressed middle-aged gentleman rose to his feet with his hand out.

"Al Morgan," he said with a hearty handshake.

"I am Robert Allan Pinkerton of the National Detective Agency, sir, at your service."

"I am sorry. I thought you were with the Pinkerton Detectives. Is it one and the same?" asked Morgan.

"No worries, it is one and the same. With our expansion in many major cities across the nation, we have assumed the name of the National Detective Agency, still run by us Pinkertons. I am also a sworn deputy by the New Orleans Provost Marshal," Robert said.

"Yes, indeed you are. It is my honor to meet not only an employee of the famous detective agency, but a family member as well. Go ahead drink your tea. What brings you aboard today if I might ask, Mr. Pinkerton?"

"Oh, just traveling on business and finding your train must faster and more comfortable than that of an old hack." Pinkerton laughed.

"I would love to hear about your organization. Although our company has worked closely with your agency for a number of years, this is the first opportunity I have had to meet such a celebrity!" Morgan said.

"My father, Allan J. Pinkerton, started the company in the 1850s and was first hired by the railroad to examine vouchers of train conductors who were suspected of stealing money. He became somewhat famous with his investigative innovations, known as the 'rouge galleries,' a method of investigation that he developed that displays characteristics of known criminals. In addition, he uncovered a plot to kill President Lincoln on his way to Washington and took a sabbatical from the company while serving as Officer in Charge of Civil War Operations under General George B. McClelland until 1863."

"You mean you can track and analyze criminals?" asked Morgan.

"That is one of our functions, sir, but rest assured I have no knowledge of a traveling criminal onboard your train today. I have studied recently at Scotland Yard learning modern-day techniques of death investigation but expect most of our efforts will be focused on thieves and train robbers…just outlaws," said Pinkerton.

"Well, that is reassuring, especially coming from a man of your stature," Morgan said. "Let's have a helping of this fine pheasant along with mashed potatoes and bread. George, bring our guest another tea, please."

As they started to eat, Pinkerton began talking about his family.

"I have plans for a son to follow along my footsteps someday and he will carry this company into the next century," Pinkerton said.

"Let me guess...he, too, will carry the name of Robert Allan Pinkerton. Am I correct?" asked Morgan.

"That you are, but as for now, my brother William Allan and I are taking over the affairs as my father has fallen ill," Robert said.

"I'm sorry to hear that. Is your brother William Allan a twin?" asked Morgan.

"No, but funny you should ask that. I am a twin. I have a twin sister named Joan. We were born in Chicago," Robert said. "She is not a detective, though. My brother William, Willie, as we call him, had the distinct honor of being an observer in a balloon overlooking the battlefields with my father at the Seven Days Campaign working out of the Department of Mississippi. That was the first aerial reconnaissance in the history of warfare. Hopefully, it will not be the last."

Robert paused for a moment as he could see his host devouring the pheasant concerned that his might be cold before ending the conversation. He placed one leg of the pheasant all the way in his mouth, pulling back a mere bone, following that with a spoonful of mashed potatoes before continuing. His host only grunted with a mouth full of bread but was very interested.

"You might surmise that our experience is not indicative of our age. However, we grew up in the agency. Willie is twenty-one years of age and I am only nineteen. We are quite proud of our family, sir," Robert said thoughtfully.

"As you should be, my dear man; few could boast of your accomplishments and expertise many times over your age," Morgan said.

"Sir, I am sorry to bore you with my family and company matters," Robert said.

Morgan interrupted, "Oh no, no, no, you are not boring me at all. I see how your energy and professionalism can make a good partner as we progress across the country."

"Well, thank you, sir, for the fine food. I look forward to seeing you in the future. I will retire to my seat and review some of my materials, if you will excuse me," Robert said.

Resting comfortably back at his seat, Robert just couldn't get the murders out of his mind. He recalled his training at Scotland Yard in death investigation and remembered the discussions of potential serial killers, not yet seen in the United States.

"Hmmmm," he mumbled to himself, "Not a sign of torture. They would have left the nipples. This was the work of someone who wanted to keep a trophy, a psychopath, maybe two men—a small trophy each. Either that or the killers had to deliver proof to somebody."

***

Upon arrival in Memphis, Robert sent a telegram to the heads of the police courts in the four towns of Mississippi that had recently experienced the violent murders of four former black female slaves. He asked to examine records and witnesses, citing that he would return to New Orleans late the following week and planned to stop off in each town.

"To what do we owe the honor of a member of the Pinkerton Detective Agency visiting our small town?" asked the president of the police court in Coffeeville as they met privately in the small courthouse conference room normally used for their meetings.

"Sir, I have reason to believe the murders are in some way associated with the railroad. All four murders occurred within twenty miles of the main line from Jackson, Mississippi, to Memphis, Tennessee. I have studied similar murders in other countries and this may be the work of a single serial killer traveling our trains. We keep track and conduct plain-clothes surveillance of suspected traveling criminals. To date, we have no open case or reason to suspect anyone. I became interested from a Winona newspaper account linking the four murders together in such a close area and looked on the map to find all of them along the railroad. The methodology of the criminal is quite interesting," Robert explained. "There seems to be no rhyme or reason why these murders occurred. The only similarities of the victims are that they are all black females and former slaves who willingly stayed on with their masters following the war. Maybe this criminal has a hatred for those who have betrayed the South and they are unhappy that the Negroes are now paid members of our society rather than freed men who moved on to the North. What intrigues and excites me the most from an investigative standpoint is the fact that the killer is taking souvenirs from the bodies. Since those 'trophies,' if you will, are female nipples, this could be some sort of sexual perversion."

One other man in the back of the room raised his hand. "Mr. Pinkerton, we have lynchings all the time where men, women, and children cut off ears, penises, fingers, toes and even pieces of skin from the dead as souvenirs. That may sound perverted to you but it even happens at the legal hangings. Are you saying if one of our family members do that, as sick as you may think it is, that they are some kind of sexual perverts?"

"No, sir, I am not saying that at all. Even though I would not condone that activity, what I am talking about is a person that murders another person and takes away a trophy. From a psychological standpoint, that tells me the person needs a reason to feel important and may feel weak or unimportant now. He exhibits his weakness by attacking women, and then cuts off their nipples to show his friends what he has accomplished. This is his way of bragging about it.

"Before I say this, I do not want you to think I am of the opinion that people who hunt for food are perverts. However, people who hunt for trophies, although not likely perverts, do share the same characteristics. They kill a large bear or antlered animal and take pride in the length of the bear's claws, size of his head or even the spread of the antlers on an antlered animal such as a deer. They will in some way display that trophy and show it off to their friends to feel important. The same is true with murderers who take trophies. The problem arises when they have to plan that next hunt and get a large number of kills behind them or a spectacular specimen that happens to be a human," Robert explained, gravely.

"Well, I hope you don't investigate us," the president of the police court said. "We will all be suspects with antlers hanging on our walls."

"No, what I ask your help on is your knowledge of anybody out there bragging or showing off nipples as trophies. It could be somebody from as far away as Chicago, for all we know. However, I suspect it is a local person with a group of friends or relatives they feel a need to impress. These murders are very close together, especially by train ride. This person or persons could be from a prominent family but likely lives in or around one of the towns where the crimes are occurring and using the railroad as his means of travel. I plan to meet with the other three police courts over the next few days. If you should hear anything, please contact me through my Chicago office by telegram and they will reach me. Thank you very much for allowing me to give this presentation," Robert said in conclusion.

****

Weeks passed as Robert continued to investigate the case. He got his first break while examining ticket purchases of everyone traveling back and forth to the towns affected by the murders. Only one traveler had visited all of the towns where the murders had occurred. A Mr. "John Smith" was on the reservation list of travelers during the times of all of the murders. A local conductor described the man he knew as John Smith but told Pinkerton he did not think that was the man's real name.

"So why would he be traveling back and forth in an assumed name if he weren't up to something?" asked Robert.

"I don't know," the conductor said. "He just always introduced himself that way. But one day, I heard a lady refer to him as Paul and he got visibly upset."

Robert began to ride those lines on a regular basis hoping one day to find this John Smith and question him. One day after a brief stop in Water Valley, a man meeting the description of John Smith came aboard. As he went to take a seat only one row in front of Pinkerton, he tipped his hat and greeted a lovely lady sitting there. He introduced himself as John Smith. Strangely enough, Robert noticed, he carried a leather case with the initials P.L.W. on it. Robert sat behind his newspaper and strained to hear the conversation, but due to the rumble of the train, he could barely make out the man's softly spoken words. All he could hear was that the man was going to Memphis.

"Sir, I couldn't help but hear you say you were going to Memphis. Do you know the city well?" asked Robert as he introduced himself as Rudy Hayes.

"Why no, no, I don't, Mr. Hayes, but allow me to introduce myself. I am …John Smith. I live near Water Valley and just visiting friends in Memphis."

"Sorry to interrupt you and the lady, sir, I'll return to my seat and read awhile," Robert said.

Throughout the entire trip, questions filled Robert's mind. He wondered if this guy had finished his handy work and was leaving the state. He wanted to know his real name and more about him. He just could not decide how to approach him. As the train began to offload in Memphis, the crowd began to walk away. Robert kept his eyes on Smith in the crowd but he was about to disappear. All of the sudden he just had to do something. "Paul!" he yelled out. The man known as John Smith turned instantly to look at him. He appeared upset, frightened, and anxiously walked away quickly without responding.

Holding up his badge, Robert pursued him just as quickly and yelled out, "Paul, John or whatever your name is, I am Robert Allen Pinkerton with the National Detective Agency, and I need to talk to you."

The suspect took off running, not into the depot but across the myriad of tracks at the busy station as Robert ran behind him telling him to stop. It appeared he was about to jump up onto the locomotive of one train when he diverted quickly and ran in front of it. Just as he rounded the locomotive, another train was only a few feet from him heading directly for him. He panicked, looked back at Robert, then back at the train, and started to run. He got his foot hung in the crossties and fell with his right cheek against the opposite track. Robert watched as the man disappeared under the churning wheel of the locomotive. When the trained had passed, the man's bloody remains were scattered across the track. Robert rushed to examine the body before the officials arrived. He found no form of identification—only an odd-looking, oyster-shucking knife in his black leather bag.

****

As months passed without another attack, Robert concluded that the train got his man rather than him. He went on to investigate other railroad-related crimes, still wondering if this was the right man and not knowing who his accomplice could possibly be. One thing he knew for sure: the force used in the murders had to have taken more than one person.

Chapter Three:

Without a Mother

"We're born alone, we live alone, we die alone.
Only through our love and friendship can we create the
illusion for the moment that we're not alone."
-Orson Welles

Masser Bud McKinney had given young Will's parents a job, a roof over their heads and a little garden spot to tend to their own rows after the war. After all, they had both been his slaves. He freed them at the end of the war and even arranged for their marriage. They might as well have stayed there with the same last name as their masser anyway.

After Lucinda's death, Masser Bud gave William a milk cow and a couple of goats so that the new baby would not have to want for milk. Will's daddy tied them out on ropes behind their shack and moved them around every so often so they could eat fresh grass. Old metal barrels up against the back of the house caught rainwater dripping from the slanted tin roof above.

Will was very lucky to grow up around a family like that. The white McKinneys really did treat him like family. Years later, he would learn how some massers were very mean and beat their slaves even though they had become free men. They would threaten to kill them if they ran off. Some of them kept old red bone bloodhounds just for tracking.

Masser Bud's beautiful wife, Emma, had long blonde hair that fell to her shoulders in big curls when she released the hairpins that held it in a tight bun at the nape of her neck. She said she did that so she could lean down over the baby's bed and play with Will without her hair getting in his face. She wanted to see Will reared properly and helped in every way she could.

They were good people with two children of their own – a daughter named Gracie, who was one year older than Will, and a son named Pinckney, three years older than Will. Pinckney and Will were about the same size but Will was growing fast and was big for his age.

Will's dad never had to buy clothes for him. Mrs. Emma said little Pinckney grew so quickly that the clothes that fit him today were too little by next month. Will ended up with just about every little suit of clothes Pinckney started with. They played together just as if Will was a white boy. He was the best-dressed little Negro in all of Carrollton. He also got all the storybooks he wanted from his white neighbors when they were finished with them. In his earliest years, Will would have no black mother or black nanny influence. His real nanny was Mrs. Emma.

Everything was going just fine, that is for the first couple of years. However, Bud never really did recover from his losses during the war. The Union army destroyed all his equipment during their raids, burned his barns, and stole his mules, which forced him to buy more after the war. The problem was, he had no money to rebuild or buy new equipment or livestock. All the money he had saved was Confederate currency and it was no good after the war. In order to keep his farm, he had to reduce the size of it. He sold off acreage and used that income for his new payroll of the freed slaves and other purchases necessary to keep the farm operational.

Masser Bud made William his foreman to justify paying him more money since he was raising young Will with only the help from Mrs. Emma. He was still a young man around thirty, although he had never celebrated a birthday and was not certain of his age. Everyone encouraged him to remarry but he just couldn't think of anyone but his Lucindy. William was what the typical white society wanted him to be – a "good Negro." He did what he was told, more than what he was asked to do, and was always respectful to white people. He learned the basics of reading and writing in secrecy while still a slave. However, with the help of Mrs. Emma and Masser Bud, he became proficient within a year or so after the war.

Working around the other Negroes, it was hard for him to speak like a white man, still using the vernacular of the Negro race. However, he insisted that young Will learn to talk just like white people. He wanted to see Will get a college education.

From the very beginning, the whole town was distraught over what happened to Will's mother.

They were equally concerned about Will's father being able to take care of him. It was no secret that Mrs. Emma was helping to raise a black child. Given the circumstances, everyone was in favor of it. On his first birthday, shopkeepers and ladies' organizations brought gifts for Will and offered any assistance they could. This was unheard of in a white community during those days. Will became the "miracle child" but it really did not catch on until after his birthday. There was some concern that he may have sustained internal injuries or complications from the premature birth and that he wouldn't live. But, his first birthday proved how strong he was and how much he had to live for.

****

Before anyone even realized it, another year went by and Will was as healthy as could be, actually big for his age.

"Will, sweetie, tomorrow is your birthday and Nanny is going to take you to town. You will be all dressed up and the prettiest two-year-old around. Hey, that rhymes. I'll just make a little song out of it for you and sing it to you anytime you like," said Mrs. Emma.

"Take him and our other two to the drug store and get them an ice cream, Nanny," Masser Bud said as he held Will up over his head, making him laugh.

Will was the talk of the town. The ladies of the local garden club came over to the drug store and helped him celebrate his second birthday, again unusual for a small Southern community.

The celebration was short-lived, though. A few days later while Masser Bud was out working on the plantation, the local banker came by to see him.

"Evening, Mrs. Emma. Is Mr. Bud around?"

"Well, no, he is out on the farm somewhere. May I help you?"

"No ma'am, that's alright, but would you ask him to come see me in the morning?" the banker asked.

"Sure, I will," she said with a confused look.

A little while later Bud came in from working in the field and Mrs. Emma had supper prepared.

"Honey, the bank president came by here today looking for you. He said it was very important for you to get in touch with him tomorrow morning. What's that all about, dear?" asked Emma, with a slight frown wrinkling her smooth forehead.

Bud dropped his spoon and paused for a moment as if he had seen a ghost. Then he broke the dreadful news.

"Sweetheart, I didn't want to burden you with that. I was not altogether truthful about selling off that land a little over a year ago. I did sell some, probably too much, and now I don't have enough land to raise the crops I need for a profit. I borrowed the money from the bank and put our property up as collateral on the loan. The repayment was due at the end of a year. That was three months ago and we just haven't had enough money," Bud said with his head down, ashamed of what he had done.

After only the slightest hesitation, Emma got up from the table, went around, and hugged her husband.

"You are doing the best you can, honey. You have always taken good care of us and you always will. We will make it somehow. I believe the bank will work with you, don't you?"

"I don't know, this is prime property and a lot of people would like to get their hands on it," Bud said.

"Well, which piece of property is it?" asked Emma with a confused look.

Bud raised his eyes up from the spot he stared at on the floor and looked straight into Emma's eyes with tears in his own, his hands trembling.

"Honey, the land by itself was not enough collateral. It had to be property with a house of some value, don't you see?" he asked reluctantly.

"Oh, for heaven's sake, you mean they may take our house?" she gasped, now in tears herself.

"I am afraid that is a possibility," Bud said with his hands cupped over his face, his elbows on the dining room table.

Emma ran for the bedroom, fell face down on the old brass bed, and sobbed. She had never been so devastated.

Chapter Four:

The Bank

*"Wilt thou seal up the avenues of ill?
Pay every debt as if God wrote the bill!"*
-Ralph Waldo Emerson

Early Tuesday morning, Bud hitched up the mules and drove his buggy into town. It was only a two-mile stretch but it seemed like a hundred to him. He arrived out front of the bank, just north of the square, and pulled his buggy over to the right side of the road. As he dismounted, he saw the president of the bank in the window across the street peering out at him with a look on his face that would scare an Indian warrior. The walk across the street was just as gloomy as the ride into town.

If it had not been for his children born late in his life and his lovely wife Emma, he may have cast himself under the wheels of a horse-drawn logging wagon. He felt like he was moving in slow motion, certain when he turned that brass knob on that old wooden bank door, it would be like turning the lock on his old mansion door as he left it for the last time.

"Well, Mr. Bud, come on in," Bank President B.W. Holmes said with his hand reached out, exposing his gold watch chain as it drooped across his vest.

"Thank, you," Bud said as he sat down in the wooden chair while Mr. Holmes dropped down proudly into his beautifully upholstered high back executive chair.

They exchanged small talk about the weather, politics and the economy, all the while Holmes struggled to keep the fake smile plastered across his broad face.

"Mr. Bud, you know we are going to have to call the note very soon on your land. You are not the only one that has experienced the losses the war brought on us. If the North really wanted reconstruction, they should have brought their factories down here and hired our people to build them and work in them. They left us in a boat without a paddle!" he said loudly.

"Yes, you are right, but I just need a little more time, that's all," Bud said.

"Time, what's time gonna do for you other than put you deeper in debt?" the bank president asked.

"I don't know. I have always been a farmer. We had plenty of money before the war and I never had to worry about managing money, just the farm. Things are different now, though. You have to manage everything," Bud said.

"Mr. Bud, I'm gonna see if there's a chance to save your farm," Holmes said as he pulled a piece of paper from the desk drawer and drew a pen from the well on his desk. "You owe the bank $89,817.12. Now, we need to see how much cash you have on hand and how much your assets are worth. Tell me first of all how much cash you have," said the banker.

Bud flipped open a worn leather ledger and began to read. "Well, let's see, I have thirty four thousand, give or take some change, to pay overhead. I have ten thousand each for the children's college funds for a total of thirty thousand dollars. That's all the cash we got. Do you want to know about the livestock and equipment?" Bud asked, peering over his financial bible.

"Yes, yes, sure, but let's back up a minute. Are you sure you have thirty thousand in your children's college funds?"

"That I am certain, sir," Bud said slowly with a confused look on his face.

"Well, I thought you and Mrs. Emma only had a little boy and girl. That would only be twenty thousand dollars if you have ten thousand each in their funds," Holmes said.

"No, no, you might as well say we are raising little three-year-old Will McKinney like our own and we are providing for him just like our other children," Bud explained.

The banker paused, darting his eyes around the room. "You talking about that little Negro child whose ma'ama got killed a few years ago out back of your place?" he asked curiously.

"That's right." Bud answered, quickly and affirmatively.

"Well," demanded the banker, "we may have to talk about that."

"What do you mean talk about it?" Bud asked.

"We will come back to that. Let's move on and talk about your expenses starting with payroll. Let's start at the top. Here, I tell you what, take this paper and write down your employees beginning with the highest paid at the top. I will be back in a few minutes. I need to step outside," the banker said hurriedly as he mumbled to himself in indignant disbelief over a college fund for that little Negro.

Bud took the paper and made a neat list of the payroll then gave it back to the banker when he returned. Holmes removed a monicle and placed it against his right eye. Looking down at the paper, his eyebrows popped wide open, causing the monicle to fall from his eye and hit the floor.

"My dear man, you can't be serious!" said Holmes as he jumped from his seat, hands on his desk, arms stretched out almost face to face with Bud.

"I am very serious. I have not lied to you to obtain funds, sir!" Bud exclaimed.

"I am not suggesting you have lied. I am suggesting that your payments to yesterday's slaves are outrageous, one in particular, this William McKinney. He earns twice what the others make. No wonder your farm is going under," Holmes shouted.

"I will not sit and be ridiculed by you, sir. I will be on my way. Good day, sir," Bud said as he stood up and reached for the office door.

"Wait a minute. Sit down. I beg your pardon. I apologize for being so hasty to pass judgment on your efforts. Please sit down. I think there is a possibility I would like to discuss with you," the banker said.

Hesitatingly, Bud took his seat casting a stone-faced look at Holmes. "Tell me what is on your mind, sir," Bud said.

"You cannot continue to run the farm this way and survive. You are going to have to increase production and cut costs. I would like to offer a few suggestions. First, paying your overseer twice as much as the others will not continue if we are to help you. In addition, the others' pay must be cut by fifty percent. I suggest you do away with the overseer position and start performing that function yourself. Getting rid of him would most likely mean getting rid of that little darkie, too and you could apply that ten thousand dollars you have towards the loan. We are going to have to have some cash, if for nothing else to pay the interest on the loan. In addition..."

"You hold on right there, you shyster of a man. I will not have you speak of them that way and I will do no such thing. Do not summon me again!" Bud said as he rushed out the door, slamming it so hard, the shade fell off.

He stomped across the street back to his awaiting buggy as puffs of dirt flew up from each heel.

Chapter Five:

The Discussion

*"Every area of trouble gives out a ray of hope,
and the one unchangeable certainty is that
nothing is certain or unchangeable."*
-John F. Kennedy

B ud returned home both angry and
distraught. He just couldn't see himself
cutting the workers' wages in half, firing
William or taking little Will's college fund.

"How did it go with the banker, dear?" asked
Emma as he entered the house.

Bud paused without a word, trying to hold his
temper. Then he went into an outrage, slamming his
fist on the table, knocking things off shelves and
yelling to the top of his voice.

William was out back fetching water when he
heard the commotion. Unsure of what was going on;
he cautiously eased in the back door and listened for
a moment. He had never heard a fight between
Masser Bud and Mrs. Emma.

"Emma, he wants me to cut the workers' wages
in half, dismiss William as the highest paid with me
taking his place," explained William.

"And what honey, what else does he want?" interrupted Emma with anger now in her voice.

"He wants me to take the money we have in Will's college fund and apply it towards interest on the loan and maybe give up some amount of what we have for overhead. I don't care about anything else but he belittled me for taking care of our people, especially little Will, calling him names!" Bud said as he paced back and forth across the floor. Little did he know that William was in the next room eavesdropping, something he would have never done before if he had not been worried about Mrs. Emma. He heard the whole discussion.

"Oh, my dear, maybe we just need to sell out before they take the property. Maybe we could sell the farm for a profit and use that as a start on a new life. We could move to New York and stay for a while with my sister. You could get a job," she said, hands shaking violently.

William couldn't believe what he was hearing. With fear and caution, he reluctantly and quietly knocked on the door. He opened it and stuck his head through the opening.

"Masser Bud, Mrs. Emma, could I speak with y'all for a minute?" he asked in a trembling voice, wringing his cap in his hands as if wringing out a wet rag.

"Of course you can, William. Come in," Mrs. Emma said, grabbing his shirtsleeves and pulling him into the room.

"You folks been mighty good to me and my family, but I think it is time for us'in to move on," he said.

"Jesus, no, you heard us talking, didn't you?" she asked in a panic.

"Yes, ma'm. I ain't meant to. You know me, I couldn't help it," William said. "I didn't even know y'all was savin' for my little Will to go to college. That's a long time away. You got to do what you got to do ra't now. Take that money on down there and give it to the bank."

"I'll do no such thing, William!" Bud yelled out.

"Yes, sir, you got to, Masser Bud. I'll find something else to do and some other place to stay. You go on down there now, take the man the money," he said as he walked back out to his shack, the first time he had ever told Mr. Bud or any other white man what to do.

"What are we going to do, honey?" asked Emma.

"I am going to try to re-work these figures the banker gave me and make up a new plan. He seems like he wants to help but he is being too harsh. I will go back to see him but I will not bow down to his terms," Bud insisted.

The next morning Bud mounted his horse and rode down to the bank bright and early. He took with him a plan he felt would work and would be acceptable to the bank.

"I want to apologize for storming out of here like I did yesterday," he told the banker." I have a counter offer I would like to discuss with you."

"I am not pleased with the way you left me yesterday, any more than I am pleased with the way you have conducted yourself on that farm. As I look over this document, I see William McKinney still on the payroll in high dollars and I see no effort on your part to withdraw the money from the little pickaninny's college account," the banker said.

"Why you no good son-of-a..." Bud growled as he grabbed Holmes by the collar across the desk and began shaking him. "Will McKinney's college fund is not negotiable!"

Suddenly Bud's hands let go of the banker and his left arm first fell to the desk, then curled towards his body as his head leaned to the left. Gurgling a few times, his arm jerking wildly, Bud McKinney fell backwards to the floor.

Chapter Six:

Bed Rest

*"Come unto me, all ye that labor and are heavy
laden, and I will give you rest."*
- Matthew

T he doctor gave Bud had a fifty-fifty chance of
survival, warning Emma that he would
probably never walk again and would suffer
with permanently impaired speech. There was also
no guarantee that he wouldn't suffer another stroke.
Emma took him home and cared for him through
constant bed rest.

The banker, concerned he may have been to
blame for Bud's condition, began to worry. He
suddenly became overly nice and put the note on
hold for the time being. He would monitor Bud's
condition and then make a decision about the debt.

Emma had been at Bud's beside for only a few
days when he began to mumble a few words that she
could barely understand. She thought she could
understand the word "bank" but was unsure as to
what he was actually saying.

Within a week or so, he began speaking clearly
enough to understand but very impaired. Emma

finally understood what her husband was trying to say. He wanted to know how Holmes was doing and how badly he had hurt him. He remembered grabbing the banker by the collar and shaking him but couldn't remember anything beyond that. Bud didn't realize that he had collapsed with the stroke immediately after grabbing Holmes. As he struggled with worry about what he had done, he seemed to be having another mild stroke. Emma noticed his discomfort and sat beside him, holding his hand.

"Honey, you are not going to be well enough to work again for a long time," Emma told Bud, as she lovingly wiped his forehead with a damp cloth. "We are not going to be able to keep this farm. But, I don't want you to worry about that. It doesn't matter. The only thing that matters is your getting better."

A large tear slipped from the outside corner of his eye, followed by another, and another until the pillow was drenched with tears.

"God is punishing me," he mumbled as he stared towards the ceiling.

"Honey, God doesn't punish His children," whispered Emma. "Don't say that."

"I know the wrath of God," Bud insisted.

"Look, sweetheart, you need to get some rest. Don't strain yourself," Emma said, gently tracing the frown lines on his forehead with her neatly manicured finger.

"Wanna see William tomorrow," Bud said as he closed his eyes.

The next day Emma brought William into the bedroom. At first Bud just looked at William as if he didn't know who he was. Then he insisted that Emma leave them alone while he talked to William.

That's highly unusual, Emma thought as she quietly closed the door to the bedroom leaving William and Bud to talk. *What could be so important?*

"William, I'm dying," Bud said emphatically.

"No, sir, Masser Bud, you done got much better. Don't be talkin no hogwash like that. You gone be just fine," William said.

"No, I'm dying. Maybe not today, maybe not tomorrow, but my life on this earth is just about gone. Please listen to me. It is very hard to talk. Can you understand me?" asked Bud.

"Masser Bud, don't you worry about this place and Mrs. Emma. You just get you plenty rest. I'm gonna make sure everything gets done," William said pleadingly.

"No, William. Look in the top drawer over there and get out some of that letter writing paper. My cousin in Natchez was good friends with Mayor Hiram Revels. I saw him in Jackson just before he got the job as US senator. He told me if I ever needed anything to be sure and let him know. I want him to help you for me. There's not much more help I can give. I am going to tell you what to write," Bud said with a worried look on his face.

Will carefully and neatly wrote down every word Masser Bud spoke.

August 2, 1870
Honorable Hyram Revels
U.S. Senator
Washington, DC

Dear Mr. Revels:
I hope this letter finds you in good health. I trust
you remember me as I met you in Jackson in the
presence of my brother, your dear friend, John. R.
McKinney from Natchez. You said to me if I ever
needed anything, to contact you. I am asking you to
stand up to your word.
    Mr. William McKinney, a colored man on my
plantation, is in need of a job due to my failing health.
He would make a fine candidate for the postmaster
position vacant here in Carroll County. Like you, he
too, is a man of God and a man of his word. He can
read and write very well; he can decipher and knows
the county and its people. He is well liked by all.
    This request comes to you from my deathbed.
Sincerely,
James P. "Bud" McKinney
Carrollton, Mississippi

"Now, William, you get that letter off to
Washington just as soon as you can. You hear me?"
Bud asked his old friend.

"Yes, sir, Masser Bud, but I ain't never had no
job but with you," he said.

Bud stared quietly at William letting him know
with his eyes what he wanted him to do.

"Yes, sir," William said obediently as he turned
to walk away.

"Come back," Bud said as he breathed in deeply. "That's not all. Give me a minute to rest."

"You just rest, Masser Bud." William said.

"No, William, I did a very bad thing a few years ago. I never told anybody about it but the good Lord knows. I haven't been the good man you thought I was all this time. I did the unspeakable. I…I," he broke into tears. "I have a confession to make to you and my Lord."

"Masser Bud, you don't have to say nothing to me. I was afraid this day may come. I got sumpin in my pocket I been carryin around for you a long time. You'll understand evathang here directly. I have saved it to give you at the right time. I reckon this must be the right time."

William reached into his pants pocket and pulled out an object wrapped in an old piece of flower sack.

"What is it William?" he asked.

"Just open it, Masser Bud. You will understand then," William said as he handed it to Masser Bud with tears in his eyes, turning away as the wrapping material fell to the floor.

"Oh, my God," Bud said. "Where did you get this? How long have you had it?" He paused for a moment. "You knew all along didn't you?" He continued to fire questions at William without waiting for a response.

Then William told him what he knew.

Bud reached for Willliam's hand and held it as he told him the worst story he had ever told. He started to jerk and gasp for breath and William ran for Emma.

She rushed immediately to her husband's side to hold his hand and calm him down but his hand was closed tightly around the object William had given him. He rolled his head towards her, making a pucker motion with his lips. She bent down and kissed him as one last tear ran down the side of his face. His mouth fell open and his breathing stopped. William's Masser Bud was gone forever.

Chapter Seven:

The Farm

"To die: - to sleep: no more; and, by a sleep to say we end the heartache and the thousand natural shocks that flesh is heir to, 'tis a consummation devoutly to be wished."
- William Shakespeare

The black McKinney family had a family cemetery laid out on the old home place. Bud McKinney was laid to rest in the town cemetery. The bank had made it perfectly clear by then that the old home place did not belong to the McKinneys any longer. William asked and received permission to dig his Masser Bud's grave himself. So, on a blustery fall morning, William pulled on his bib overalls, grabbed a shovel and went out to dig the grave. He had a rhythm for each shovel load as he soulfully sang one old Baptist hymnal after another.

When he finished the last task he would ever perform for his masser, William changed into one of Bud's old hand-me-down dark suits and stood with Mrs. Emma and the children at the funeral. More than 100 friends – both black and white – crowded into the small Southern Baptist church to honor the memory of Bud and show love and concern for Emma.

When the funeral was over the bank president sheepishly approached Emma, offering his deepest sorrows and regrets. At least he made it appear that way. He explained that he held no grudge against Bud either before or after their encounter at the bank.

"Mrs. Emma, don't you go making any plans about leaving here yet. I understand you are considering moving to New York with your sister. I also know how fond you are of little Will McKinney," Holmes said earnestly.

Emma was in too much grief to try to sort between his true feelings but accepted his comments as they were.

"You also have your own children to worry about and you might want to ask yourself which is the best place to raise them. I have been discussing your farm with some friends out of Grenada and over in Tallahatchie County. Both have indicated a possible arrangement that I believe you would be quite pleased with if you decide to stay. Why don't you come see me in a few days and let's talk about it?" Holmes asked.

Mrs. Emma just nodded as she wiped her eyes, a child clinging to both legs.

"Does that mean you will consider it?" Holmes pleaded as he wiped sweat from his brow.

"We will be along directly," she said with a quick smile, leaving the banker with uncertainty.

After a week of grief and worry, Emma decided it was time to go and see the banker.

"William, please hook my buggy up for me and drive me into town," she said.

"Yes, ma'm, I will be ready in just a minute, don't you worry," William said cheerfully, happy to see Mrs. Emma up and around.

Emma dressed carefully for her business trip to the bank and was standing by her front door when William brought the buggy around to pick her up. William hurriedly helped her up into the buggy as he eyed the dark cloud that was forming in the west. After making sure Emma was safely inside, he jumped into the driver's seat, clucked his tongue against the roof of his mouth and steered the horses in the direction of town.

Just as he rounded the big curve in the dirt road, he spotted a familiar buggy approaching driven by a Negro man from a neighboring farm. As was customary during those times, the man pulled over to the side of the road when he saw that it was Mrs. Emma's buggy approaching to allow her to pass without a cloud of dust. As her buggy slipped past the neighbor's buggy, Emma saw the Negro man standing at attention on the side of the road, hat over his heart in honor of her late husband. Confused at first as to what the man was doing, tears once again welled up in her eyes as she realized the meaning of the gesture.

Not aware that she was coming but pleasantly surprised to see her pull up out front, the bank president jumped out of his chair and rushed out to the buggy, extending his hand to help her down.

"I am pleased to see you, Mrs. Emma. Please come on in before it starts to rain and feel free to bring William if you like. Who is taking care of those wonderful children today?" he asked, almost suspiciously.

"They are with one of our hands today, doing just fine," she said as she threw back her shoulders and bravely walked across the street to the bank.

"I have no issues with William attending our meeting, sir. He was with my Bud for the last hour of his life. He knows as much about the farm and what Bud would have wanted me to do as I do," she said with a slight smile. "Come along, William."

"Yes ma'am, I'm right here, Mrs. Emma. You be careful going up them steps though," William said with concern.

Getting directly to the matter at hand, Holmes asked, "Mrs. Emma have you made any plans as of yet?"

"No. Why no, I expected to hear your offer first," she said affirmatively.

"I have an offer on the farm from a nearby landowner. He says he only needs farmland and not the mansion or the house William lives in. He is willing to pay the farm off for the balance owed on it, leaving your funds intact. He understands you are not a charity case nor are you looking for a handout," said Holmes. "His offer is in exchange for the farm equipment and livestock used for farming, he will allow you to keep both houses as long as you like."

Big tears welled up in her eyes again as Emma dropped her head. She could not believe she was in the bank talking business without her husband.

"Give me a moment, please," she said.

"Absolutely," the banker responded.

After a short pause, she regained her composure and asked him to continue.

"As I said ma'am, those are the terms. I don't think you could beat them given the circumstances. The money will be paid to you, and the bank so you will not suffer the embarrassment of a foreclosure. This is a winning situation for all concerned. We get our money and you keep yours to live on. We can help you with some investments of that money that will most likely earn you enough to live on and you don't have to use your principal. Of course, it will be there if you decide to relocate to New York or elsewhere. You keep your home, William here keeps his home, and you continue to help with the raising of little Will. How does that sound to you?" Holmes asked, beaming with pride for the deal he had manipulated.

"Well, if the alternative is foreclosure and putting us out, I guess I have no choice," Emma sighed.

"What do you think, William?" she asked.

"Now Mrs. Emma, you know it ain't up to me, but if you wanna know what Masser Bud wanted, you know he always wanted you in that house. You know too, all our time is coming when the Lawd's gonna call us home. When yo time comes, Masser Bud ain't gonna want you way up yonder in New York. He gone want you rat out there beside him, em hmh. I know that's right. He ain't even had to tell me that," William lamented with a voice of authority, before looking away as if he were talking to himself.

He would never dare to speak so directly to a white person for fear of appearing too "uppity."

"Well, I guess that's that, Mr. Holmes. When can we complete this transaction?" she asked, ready for the banking arrangements to be finished.

"There is one thing I want you to understand, Mrs. Emma. We believe in a man's word here but as of now that is all we have. I will notify the gentleman that you are willing to accept his offer and it will be up to him to provide payment for the farm. If he does so, we will all be just fine. I just want you to know that right now, all we have is a verbal offer," Holmes clarified in a very businesslike tone. He knew he had another taker if this one failed.

"Let's get along, William," said Emma. "We need to attend to those children."

"Y'all have a very fine day," Holmes said extending his hand to take Emma's gloved one. I'll be in touch."

Filled with relief, Holmes closed his door and sat down at his desk, convinced he was off the hook for Bud's death and the bank debt.

Chapter Eight:

The News

"Undertake not what you cannot perform but be careful to keep your promise."
- George Washington

O nly a week had passed since the meeting when the banker pulled up out front of the old McKinney mansion.

"Mrs. Emma, you in there? I got some news for you," Holmes said loudly after rapping softly on the front door of the McKinney home.

Emma wiped the biscuit dough from her hands onto her old apron as she walked out on the porch to greet the bank president. She hid a slight smile as she saw Old Joe, Bud's blue tick hound, jumping up on Holmes soiling his clothes with dirty paws and growling as if he knew something the humans didn't. William came around the corner of the house and yelled at the dog.

"Git on outta here, you old hound. Leave that white man alone. Git on round yonder under that porch and behave yo self. Go on, now. You gone make me have to tie you out there on a chain, you old crazy mutt, you," William yelled, as if he expected the dog to understand his every word.

"Oh, it's alright William, but I am glad you are here too, 'cause I got news for both of y'all," said Holmes, as he gently removed large, dirty paws from his custom tailored suit. "Mrs. Emma, we have the funds deposited in our bank for the purchase and all we need you to do is sign this paper and we will transfer the money from the buyer's account to the bank's funds just as soon as your husband's estate clears in probate. You don't have to worry about it in the meantime. Y'all just stay put."

"Thank you so much. I know Bud would have really appreciated what you have done. He was a kind man and I hope you know that he didn't mean you any harm that day at the bank. He was just upset. That's all. He wouldn't hurt a flea on that hound's back," Emma said sympathetically.

"I know, you don't worry about that, Mrs. Emma. That's all in the past. By the way, where did William go? I got something for him," the banker said, looking around for William.

"Oh?" she said curiously. "Let me get him for you. William, oh, William, come on back around here," she said as she rounded the side of her house.

"Yes, ma'm, I'm coming, just putting that old dog up," he said.

"Mr. Holmes said he needs to talk to you," she said.

"Yes, sir," William said as he approached the banker, dusting himself off.

"William, I was having coffee this morning at the drug store and the telegraph operator overheard me saying I was coming out to the McKinney place. He said he had a telegram to deliver out here and wanted to know if I would bring it for him. It's addressed to you," Holmes said cheerfully, digging a crumpled yellow envelope out of his pocket and handing it to William.

"A telegram for me? Must be some kind of mistake. Ain't nobody ever sent me no telegram before. I ain't hardly ever got no mail, much less no telegram. I ain't never been important enough for that," William said, as he wiped his hands off on his pants before accepting it.

"No, William, this is not a mistake and I'm not supposed to know what it says but you know how small towns are," Holmes admitted. "You must be real important. This telegram is from the United States Congress, just for you,"

"Well, for heaven's sake, William, go ahead and open it before I do," Mrs. Emma said excitedly.

Will's hands were shaking so badly, he couldn't open it.

"Let me help you," Mrs. Emma said as she reached for it while the banker stood by, watching the two with a grin.

She began to read it as she burst out in tears of happiness. "William, I am so proud of you!" she said. "Listen to this."

FROM: United States Congress
TO: William McKinney
Report to Postmaster, Jackson, Mississippi, 1 September 1870 to take oath of office and receive training to assume responsibilities of Carrollton,

*Mississippi   postmaster   upon   completion.
Congratulations on your appointment.*
    Very Truly Yours,
    Hiram Revels, United States Congressman

William's eyes popped open wide in disbelief. All he could do after the initial shock was yell to the top of his voice, "Halleluiah, thank you Jesus, thank you Lawd!" He had a smile on his face as big as Texas.

"Wait, William, I have even more good news for you." Holmes said.

Chapter Nine:

The Resting Place

"Oh, how a small portion of earth will hold us when we
are dead, who ambitiously seek after the whole world
while we are living!"
- Henry Philip

T he probate closing went as expected, as did the funds transfer to purchase the McKinney place. The buyer, aware that Lucinda McKinney was buried on the property, had one acre of land surrounding her grave surveyed and granted the property through deed, paid in full to William McKinney and his heirs. In addition, in order to ensure that William and other friends and family members would have access to the gravesite and future graves within the plot, he also granted a right of way through the property in William McKinney's name. William celebrated by posting a sign at the entrance officially naming it the "McKinney Cemetery."

A permanent marker of stone was already in place on Lucinda's grave but William wanted to make sure there would be no fuss made over him after his death so he went ahead and made one for himself. He figured all anybody had to do was inscribe the date of death when the time came. He pulled out a clean hanky from his back pocket and carefully cleaned off the cold, smooth slab of stone. He rummaged through his old toolbox until he found the sharpest chisel he could find. After thinking about what he wanted to say, he simply carved these words into the stone:

William McKinney
Born a slave about 1840
Made a freedman
Became
a
Husband, Father and Postmaster

He placed it two graves over from Lucinda's grave with a spot between them for their son, Will McKinney. William was proud of what he had made of his life. He collected flat stones for years down at the old Sandy Creek bed to build a fence around the one-acre plot that he and his family would have as a final resting place. He stacked them one by one until it was built.

The time had come for William to make his long journey to Jackson for postmaster training. Emma had taken several suits of clothes that belonged to Bud and tailored them the best she could to fit him. He was complete with a vest, even an old gold pocket watch. He wasn't too sure about that, though, expressing a little doubt to Mrs. Emma.

"William, you need to look nice traveling down there on the train," Emma said. "We want you to look like an aristocrat."

"Yes ma'am, whatever you say. I don't know nuttin bout no ris, ah ris, risa. Well you know, I don't know nuttin bout them kind of peoples," William said shyly.

"It is 'Ah RIS toe crat,' aristocrat. You remember to use your best English too now! You are an important man now, William," she said with a big smile.

"Yes, ma'am, I'll do my best. I don't want to embarrass nobody. Least ways, I hope I don't," he said as he looked down, straightening the brim of his hat.

"You'll do just fine, William. I bet you graduate at the top of your class," she said proudly. "Now come on and let's go before we are too late and you miss the train in Winona."

As they rode along in the buggy towards Winona, Emma could tell he was very nervous.

"You are not nervous about the train are you, William? Have you ever ridden a train before?" she asked expecting to hear a quick "no."

"Yes, ma'am, twice before. Me and my Lucindy was tied together in a cattle car from Mobile to New Orleans. We was sold in New Orleans and our first master brought us up here to Grenada. We rode in a boxcar then. That was before Masser Bud bought us," he said sadly.

"Well, those days are gone, William. You are going to sit in a seat and look out the window at the countryside. Nobody is going to mistreat you again," she said as they pulled up to the depot at Winona.

The train was puffing smoke about ready to take off. William jumped out, pushed his hat down on his head so far he collapsed his ears. He ran around and got that old hand-me-down bag out of the buggy that Emma gave him and ran for the train with the ticket in his other hand. Not realizing he hadn't told Emma goodbye, he turned around in a dead run, yelling, "Good-bye, Mrs. Emma, I'll see you in two weeks," as his voice was drowned out by the train's whistle.

She just waved her handkerchief in his direction as he climbed aboard the train.

William's head was turned on most of the trip. He was trying to see everything on the way to Jackson. When he got there, it was worse. Many of the old buildings in town were still demolished from the fires of the war with the chimneys still visible. The train off loaded at Capitol Street, a long but wide dirt road with a straight line view from the station to the State Capitol Building. There were brick buildings on both sides of the street that were two or more stories tall.

A postal employee picked him up outside the station to take him to the training site. William was in awe of the beautiful Governor's Mansion they passed a few minutes after leaving the train station. They traveled straight for the Capitol.

"If we don't turn up here pretty quick, we gone run right up in that big old Capitol building," William told the driver.

"No, we'll be fine." he said.

William spent the next two weeks in training and was proud to have had a nice place to stay with food and transportation furnished. He was really looking forward to getting back home and telling Emma all about his adventures, but most of all standing behind that counter in the post office with the title "Postmaster."

After his training in Jackson, Will assumed his new position as postmaster of the Carrollton Post Office, but was still nervous about his new job. He had never worked inside an office before and wasn't sure if he wanted the responsibility this new position would bring. Mrs. Emma kept reassuring him that he could do the job and that it would be the best thing for him and his son, Will.

Although Emma volunteered to keep Will at home with her while William worked, after a while, William decided to take little Will to the post office with him occasionally. The three-year-old could make toys out of about anything, often playing with the newspapers that were to be sent out as subscriptions. With his active imagination, the newspaper became a telescope as Will rolled up the paper and peeped through one end, watching his dad work.

Extremely intelligent and inquisitive for his age, Will was the center of attention wherever they went. William felt very comfortable taking Will to work with him and letting him play during those times.

William enjoyed his job and the comforts it afforded him. Although he was appointed by an important congressman at the recommendation of Mr. Bud, that did not mean that everyone was happy about his newfound opportunity. As times changed, so did the comfort zones he and other black people enjoyed. Before long, notices arrived for all postmasters to read, especially those who happened to be black. One such notice said national newspapers were reporting that black postmasters across the country were facing intimidation, threats, even murder – scare tactics aimed at intimidating them out of the jobs. William McKinney's job was no exception. It was just a matter of time before he faced similar threats.

Chapter Ten:

The Editor

"Opinions founded on prejudice are always sustained with the greatest violence."
- Lord Francis Jeffrey

Newspaper headlines in the early 1870s told the story of a peaceful existence in the Mississippi. Things were fairly peaceful, with the exception of political uprisings that popped up here and there across the South. Many blacks, especially nearby in the Mississippi delta, were forming black farmer alliances and some of the black men who now owned businesses were forming their own alliances. As long as they didn't prosper much or pose a threat to the white businesses, nothing was said. However, if a black man was doing well in business or even hinted at organizing a boycott through the alliances to keep blacks from buying goods from the white storekeepers, that is when the trouble started. Though free and often business owners themselves, black people were still expected by the white community to act a certain way - subservient to the white man.

In 1872, Tandy Oury, editor and co-owner of the *Carrollton Conservative Newspaper*, along with his brother, printed a story about a black businessman named Adam Brown. Brown was a freedman from Tennessee who moved to Mississippi after the Civil War and married a Choctaw woman. Brown had two small plantations, a store, and a blacksmith shop. Oury, who was not only a newspaper editor but also part-time town marshal, wrote of him and his efforts to monopolize in the county and organize boycotts against white business owners. Adam Brown, a very proud man, was furious. He hunted Oury down just as everyone expected. He found him in his newspaper office late one afternoon.

"Mr. Oury, I don't mean no harm to you, but you done lied in yo paper bout me and I'm aiming to see that you set the record straight," Brown said insistently.

"Well, just how do you think you are gonna get me to do that, you Injun-lovin niggah?" Oury shouted.

"Now you take that back, Mr. Oury. I aint got no fight to pick with you. Take it back, I said," Brown yelled as he moved closer to Oury.

Oury eased his desk drawer open and reached inside. Grabbing his pistol and dropping behind the desk to take cover, scared and alone, Oury just knew it was the end of his time.

A gunfight ensued. Adam Brown had the upper hand on Oury when he drew his Colt .45 double action revolver, one of the finest, if not the finest, handguns available. In moments, the dispute ended tragically.

Chapter Eleven:

Loss of a Father

*"Let us so live that when we come to die even the
undertaker will be sorry."*
- Mark Twain

B rown had the drop on Oury and had the best gun of the two. However, Brown made one mistake. The ammunition he used was cheap, old, and defective. When he pulled the trigger and the hammer came back, it fell to a clicking sound rather than a blast. Oury took advantage of the situation, drew a much-inferior handgun, and pulled the trigger. He deposited a .36 caliber round of hot lead into the stomach of Adam Brown that left him in misery for almost two years. The wound, known as a "gut shot," usually proved fatal, often-bringing months of pain and infection before death. He died in the early spring of 1874 of complications from that wound, leaving behind his wife, Juliet, two young teenage sons, Ed and Charley, as well as three older beautiful daughters.

Many feared retribution by the Brown family but the boys were young and the older girls were less likely to start any trouble. Everyone said the older of the boys, Ed, would be the one if either went after his dad's killer. However, their mother, who remembered many stories of what the white men did to their families when she was only a child, knew she had to keep the focus on survival. The plantations and store they owned failed not long after Adam's death and succumbed to the white man's greed. The blacksmith shop, on the other hand, required too much hard labor for the white men of Carrollton. They didn't bother the Browns as the boys continued to run that business.

The Brown sisters and their mother made molasses. As the years went on, the boys would make a living peddling jugs of molasses around town either before or after work at the blacksmith shop. Although they were hard workers who stayed to themselves, they were often picked on because of their color and half-breed status. Ed grew less tolerant with age.

****

As the mid-1870s approached, times were changing for the worse for black people. Many Whites developed the attitude that the blacks were taking over in offices, businesses and everywhere in between. Whites were attempting to regain the political positions filled by many blacks after the Civil War due to the freed slaves' right to vote and their population, which now outnumbered the white folks in the county. When the whites knew they couldn't swing the elections in their favor because of sheer numbers, they began intimidating the blacks to keep them from showing up at the polls. When that didn't work, they started physically shoving blacks at the polls and blaming them for starting fights. These incidents later led to lynchings and sometimes-burning blacks at the stake. When their efforts proved successful, they started looking at the federally appointed positions occupied by many blacks.

William McKinney feared the greed of the white supremacy groups in the state and the terror imposed by the Democratic Party's left wing paramilitary group of enforcers and regulators known as the Ku Klux Klan, Red Shirts and other organizations. He knew what they were capable of. He got into a discussion with Adam Brown's widow about that when she came to the post office to pick up mail one day. Unaware of whom she was, he questioned her about picking up Adam Brown's mail. He sympathized with her as Juliet explained how her husband had been killed, leaving her to raise two young boys, one not quite a teenager yet.

Finally, William had met somebody who shared common losses as him. The post office was about to close and he asked if he could accompany her back to her buggy.

Chapter Twelve:

Christmas 1874

"Marriage is not a ritual or an end. It is a long, intricate, intimate dance together and nothing matters more than your own sense of balance and your choice of partner."
- Amy Bloom

"William," his dad, said. "Come on in here and let me talk to you, son."

Will came into the room with a string wrapped around his fingers, trying to learn some tricks the white McKinney children had shown him.

"How did you learn to do that?" asked William.

"Pinckney showed me, Dad," Will grinned.

"Well, how would you like to learn a lot of new things from older boys, even some old Indian tricks?" William asked.

"Wow, I would like that, Daddy," he said.

"Son, yo daddy is getting married," William said, watching carefully to get Will's reaction.

Caught off guard, Will appeared confused. "What do you mean, Daddy?" he asked inquisitively.

"I mean there is a real pretty Indian woman who used to be married to another colored fellow, but he died. She has some older girls but she got two boys, too, older than you that might could help teach you some things and keep you outta trouble. You almost eight years old now and I figured you could use some older brothers. One of them is almost twelve and the other one is about fifteen or sixteen," William said with a smile.

William hugged little Will before he went to sleep that night and promised him that he would meet his big brothers very soon. He could hardly wait.

The next morning, just as he always had since losing Lucinda, William went into the kitchen and started breakfast on the old cast iron wood stove. Little Will ran into the kitchen yelling, "Daddy, Daddy!"

"What is it, son, what are you so doggone excited about?" William asked.

"Daddy, does this mean I'm gonna get a new mama, too?" he shouted hopefully.

William just smiled and hugged his son, swinging him back and forth, comforting him as he always had being both the mother and father.

"Yes, son, it does mean you will have a new mother. She will never replace your real mother to me, but since you never knew your real mother, she will be like your own," William explained.

Later that day William decided it was time to break the news to Mrs. Emma. She was speechless, but overjoyed that William was happy. Her main thought was Will. All she could think about was how little Will would be treated and whether or not the new mother would replace her.

****

Christmas Eve had come, and so did the day of William and Juliet's marriage. Both were excited as Emma made all the necessary plans at the Baptist church. William had promised Will two new brothers and a mother by Christmas Day and he wasn't going to let him down.

William and Juliet were married in a small ceremony with only immediate family members attending. Within hours they made their way home. Emma kept Will that night. The other boys had not yet moved in. William and Juliet celebrated their first night of marriage on Christmas Eve. Santa Claus brought Will a new family for Christmas.

Plans were made for the three older Brown girls to continue to live in their mother's house while Juliet and her two sons, Ed and Charley, moved in with William and Will. The Brown brothers didn't say much, especially Ed, but they were glad to have a new home and a younger brother. Will had something the Brown brothers would never have. That was full blood, albeit that of a Negro. They cherished that. However, they vowed to make young Will their "blood brother."

In a backyard ceremony, the Brown brothers solemnly promised to protect their new little brother as they made jagged cuts on their wrists with their ma'ama's old kitchen knife and squeezed blood into each other's wounds. Will bravely allowed the older boys to perform this painful Indian ceremony because he was eager to learn the Indian way of life.

Chapter 13

The Elections of 1875

"Non-violence is a powerful and just weapon. It is a weapon unique in history, which cuts without wounding and enobles the man who wields it. It is a sword that heals."
- Martin Luther King, Jr.

William and Juliet made the perfect couple. He loved her and her children about as much as he loved his own child. Not only had she taken to Will like a fish in the water, so had her boys. They spent a great deal of time showing him the ways of their ancestors that had once owned the vast lands that surrounded them.

Juliet fixed meals uncommon to the black race. Old William himself was a good cook, and shared the Negro recipes that were passed down from generation to generation in his family.

The new family was settling in nicely at home in Carrollton, but in the outside world tensions between blacks and whites began to surface again. These feelings came on the heels of the upcoming election of 1875. The Klan and other groups of regulators were constantly intimidating and injuring the black families. There were even some reports of murder but the lack of bodies gave no proof and officials dismissed the claims. Only the rivers could yield the evidence of the tragedies.

It wouldn't be long though as the election neared in November that the white offenders became more blatant with their harassment and murders of black voters and office holders.

The people of the South began to see horrors beyond their wildest dreams. Bodies had been found tied up in trees, not only hanged but also riddled with bullet holes. Sometimes they bore crudely made signs reading, "Stay away from the polls, Nigger." Because of the sheer numbers of freed blacks after the Civil War, they far outnumbered the whites. Since they now had the right to vote, they posed a threat to the hateful white supremacy groups. The only way these white supremacy groups could win the majority of the vote was through murder or intimidation. If those efforts failed, they would even steal the ballot boxes and dump the results in the river.

By November 1, with the election only days away, the whites were confident that they would win by a landslide, not just a few positions, but all positions, including those currently held by blacks. They would stop at nothing to make that happen. Carroll County had 5,000 registered black voters, all Republican. However, one newspaper reporter at the polls turning in an early news report said, "You can count the number of Negroes here tonight on one hand and have fingers left over." Blacks were just too afraid to go vote.

William had suffered threats himself as a black federally appointed postmaster, but he stood proudly around the courthouse that night, listening as the election results were called out under the watchful eyes of the regulators.

The light of flaming torches on the courthouse lawn illuminated anxious faces on election night as the votes in the election of 1875 were counted and announced. As white candidates were declared victors, groups of white men, encouraged by the election outcome, started pushing the blacks and accusing them of starting fights to justify beating their heads in with pistol butts. As the night worn on, the crowd soon become an angry mob of white supremacists looking to make examples out of any black man within reach.

In fear of his life at that point, William started to make his way to the back of the courthouse out of sight and leave as quickly and as quietly as possible. As he rounded the corner looking over his shoulder to see if he was being followed, he felt the heat of a flaming torch touch the side of his face. The brightness of the flame prevented him from seeing little more than figures in the dark, but he clearly heard their threats as they moved closer. William started to run as the crazed group of men ran after him crying, "Come on! Let's get that Nigger!"

William glanced back just in time to see one of the mobsters drop a large lighted torch onto the dry autumn leaves as he grabbed the back of William's shirt.

Chapter 14:

The Morning After

"The weakest and most timorous are the most revengeful and implacable."
- Thomas Fuller

The morning after the election brought the first cold snap of the season. A slow, steady rain helped squelch the smoldering rubble where the Carroll County Courthouse once stood. In less than three hours following the dropping of a torch, the stately old wooden courthouse had burned to the ground.

The election of 1875 would long be remembered as the one where the white democrats took back the seats from Negro republicans.

Ed and Charley Brown were among the crowd gathered at the courthouse to gawk at the smoky mess. William did not make it home the night before and they were looking for their stepfather. A neighbor stopped by earlier that morning to tell Juliet that he had seen William in the courthouse corridor before the fire started, but had not seen him coming back out. Juliet sent her older sons into town to look for William while she and Will started home in case he returned before the boys got back.

The boys went around town asking about the father they had known for less than a year, but had grown to love. Nobody had seen him. Around noon, Ed noticed that an old Negro man appeared to be following them. Finally, Ed turned and asked the man if he knew where William might be.

"Boys, we been havin to keep to ourselves all us'ins lives," he said, quietly. "You go outside of town a little ways and you run into the cane brakes. They too thick for a hound dog. That's where we always went when there was trouble with the white man. He wouldn't go in there and neither would them old dogs of his'in. Can't stay in there too long though. Good a hideout as it is, man gotta eat and drank sometimes. I say give it a few days, yo daddy will most likely come home when thangs settle down and he gets houngry."

The boys took the old man's advice and went on back home. They calmed their mother down and insisted that William had probably been threatened causing him to hide out in the woods until things about the election settled down. That was the best advice they could give her, although they had their own doubts as to whether or not that was true.

Two days later the boys heard word that a body had been found just off the east side of the square in the Wilson's back yard. Nobody would go near it, but people who had been close enough to get a glimpse said it looked like a fat black man whose face had been beaten beyond recognition. The coroner would not even go around there. "If he has been dead that long," said the coroner, "then old Mr. Wilson ought to just dig a hole and push him over in it. If he don't want to do that, then the buzzards will do the job pretty soon anyway."

Two young white boys who lived next door had seen the body and also described it as a heavy black man. That really didn't fit William's description as he was really pretty skinny, but the Browns felt the man deserved a decent burial. When Ed asked the boys where he could find the body, they pointed past a house towards a large vacant lot. On the back of the lot was a split rail fence and the top two rails of the fence were broken down. They said the body lay just on the other side of the fence.

Chapter 15:

A Body Discovered

*"How many roads must a man walk down
before you call him a man?"*
- Bob Dylan

E d and Charley jumped over the fence and walked slowly toward the bloated, putrid body. With the tip of his boot, Ed gently rolled the body over until he could make out a face. Ed knelt down on one knee to get a closer look as Charley loomed over him, fist over his nose, casting a thin shadow over the body. As described by others, the face was beaten in beyond recognition. For a moment, Ed felt a flash of relief as he did not recognize the dead man.

From behind he saw Charley lift his finger and point toward something he saw on the body. As Ed's eyes followed his brother's glaze, his heart sank. He recognized the cattle brand that had been burned into the man's skin, a sign that he was a former slave. He grabbed a small stick and lifted up the dead man's hand to find that the tip of his little finger was missing. He knew that finger had been the victim of an old steel hunting trap. The body was obviously bloated from lying in the field but there was no mistaking the identity. Grief-stricken, both boys were brokenhearted for their mother, their little brother and for themselves. Ed stayed to watch over William's body while he sent younger brother Charley to get a wagon.

Heavy-hearted, Charley arrived home wiping his eyes, dreading the conversation he would have to have with his mother. Juliet was in the kitchen when she heard Charley's steps come slowly into the house and pause before opening the kitchen door. One look at his anguished face and she knew that the worst possible thing had happened.

"What happened, son, did you find him? Did you? Did you? Answer me!" she screamed.

"Yes, mama," Juliet's younger son answered. "I gotta borrow Mrs. Emma's wagon to get him so we can bury him."

His mother began to scream as Mrs. Emma came out on the back porch to see what was wrong.

"What is it? What's going on?" she exclaimed.

"We need to borrow yo wagon, Mrs. Emma, so we can bring our daddy home to bury him," Charley said quietly.

"Oh, no, not William...please God, not William," Emma cried and cried as Charley hooked up the wagon.

"I'll be bringing him home directly," Charley said. He stopped long enough to grab the old wedding ring quilt from atop the bed to wrap around William.

Will was in bed sick and did not know what was going on.

Charley and Ed carefully lifted the body of their father and placed it in the back of the wagon. Tears of grief mixed with sweat burned their eyes as they silently paid their respect to the man who had loved them and cared for them as his own. Before leaving town, they stopped at Smith's Cabinet Shop and choose a wooden coffin that would be placed in the McKinney Cemetery alongside Lucinda.

"Just carry him on out yonder on y'alls place and bury him before he stinks the whole place up," the coroner yelled out as they passed the general store in town, where he sat spitting tobacco juice into the dirt street.

The Brown brothers just looked at each other in disbelief that a man could be so cruel. All they wanted to do was see to it that he got a decent burial.

When they arrived home, their mother was dressed in Choctaw clothes and was chanting some Choctaw song that the boys didn't even understand. Mrs. Emma was trying to console Juliet even though she was hardly in any shape to help take care of anyone else. In William, she had found a true and loyal friend and would miss him terribly.

Awakened from all the commotion, Will ran outside on the porch. He recognized his daddy's shoes sticking out of the blanket that covered the rest of his body on the back of the wagon. He looked from Juliet to Ed and finally to Emma's tear-soaked face before he realized what he was seeing. He began screaming and running toward the wagon. Mrs. Emma grabbed him and told him everything would be okay, but Will was hysterical.

****

William McKinney was laid to rest on a cold dreary day beside his first wife, Lucinda. The Brown boys dug the grave and finished off his headstone noting that he died in November 1875. On a blank spot below the date they chiseled, "He was our father, too."

William would have wanted no greater honor.

Chapter 16:

The Arsonist

"'Cause I's wicked, - I is. I's mighty wicked,
anyhow, I can't help it."
- Harriet Beecher Stowe

Everybody knew William was a good man. However, Tandy Oury, town marshal, coroner, and newspaper editor, tried to paint a different story. He wrote an article that appeared in the newspaper the week following William's murder that explained his death this way: *"William McKinney, postmaster, a Negro, angered about the election results, set the courthouse on fire. Observed running from the scene, he was pursued by a group of citizens doing their duty, but McKinney fell over a fence in the dark. He broke his leg in the fall and died of his injuries."*

****

"Juliet, I can't believe the death and destruction we have seen in our lifetime. Aside from the war, your first husband was murdered, Will's mother was murdered, my husband died, leaving me and these young children. Now your William, our William, was murdered, too. I just don't know how much more I can stand," Emma said as she crumpled up the newspaper and threw it into the fireplace.

"You are right, Mrs. Emma. It seems as though it will never end. My family before me died at the hand of white men. I just pray for my sons that they will never cross a white man. Now I have young Will, another prayer I must pray," Juliet said stoically.

"Do you intend to stay here on the McKinney place or move back home with your daughters?" Emma asked the young widow. "I would be willing to keep Will."

"No, I think I will stay here next to William so I can visit his grave often," Juliet replied.

"Mrs. Emma, my brother and I have a new brother, Will. He is not up for adoption. We will see to his every need," Ed said. As the new man of the family, he felt the weight of responsibility, not only for his mother, but also for his younger brothers and his sisters.

During the past few months, Ed Brown had grown from a carefree, adventure-seeking youngster into a man. Although he felt a sense of pride about this, he also held a bit of anger and resentment in his heart also.

"I know you will, Ed. I didn't mean anything by that. He has just been in this family so long," Mrs. Emma said.

"We will stay here and help you do all those things around here that Daddy did for you. Don't worry about us or anything else," Ed said quietly to Mrs. Emma.

"Yes, ma'am, I will help, too," Charley said shyly, nodding his head.

"Me, too," Will said as he ran into the room. "I will be nine years old in a couple of months."

Emma gathered her rather diverse and unusual family close and held on tightly, afraid to let any of them get out of her sight for very long.

****

The next two years went by without incident as the family went on with their lives without William.

Will had become somewhat of a clown. He would mock white men and their way of speech, but he knew not to do it in the presence of anyone white, not even Mrs. Emma. Just as Ed and Charley would stop laughing at one of his antics, he would then mock black men with the deepest dialect that he could muster. His brothers would continue to be amused. They grew to love him as their own blood brother, listening to him read the newspaper from front to back without missing a word.

"I'm gonna be a doctor someday," Will said in a confident tone. "I am really. I'm gonna go to college too! You just wait and see!"

"We hope you do, baby brother, so you don't have to work in an old blacksmith shop like us and peddle molasses all over the place," Ed said, as he grabbed Will in a headlock and ruffled his head with his knuckles. "But you are only nine years old. You have a long way to go. You will have to make and save a lot of money to go to college."

"Ed, would you take me into town and let me see if I can get a job?" Will pleaded. "I want to start right now saving money for college."

"Who in the world would hire a little rascal like you?" Ed teased his little brother.

"Come on, jump in the wagon with me. I have some work to do on the square. You can check around some of the businesses there. You could be a stock boy or something, I guess."

Chapter 17:

Pete and Re-Pete

Friendship is the only cure for hatred,
the only guarantee of peace.
- Buddha

Will's daddy taught him to fear nothing, so he marched boldly into the hotel restaurant and asked the manager about a job.

"What can you do?" asked the manager, inquisitively.

"I can do anything, sir. I can wash dishes, mop the floor, clean off tables, wash windows, just anything you want. I just need a job so I can save for college," Will said politely.

Struck by Will's insistence and demeanor, the man handed him a rag and an apron. "Is that so? Well, go over there and clean off those tables. Show me what you can do."

Will put on the apron, went over and cleaned off the stains and spilled food from two tables. As he was finishing, another couple got up from the table next to him. Will lifted up the bottom of his apron and put the dirty dishes in it holding them tightly until he got back to the kitchen. When he returned, the manager was standing there waiting for him.

"You are hired. You start Saturday morning at six. Don't be late," the manager said in a firm but friendly tone.

Will ran out the door cheering, with the apron still on. Halfway down the street he realized what he had done and ran back to return the apron.

"Keep it," the manager said. "Bring it back clean. By the way, the pay is thirty cents a day."

He would keep a nickel and give the rest to his mom to help buy groceries and supplies. He wanted to save his nickel so he could go to college one day.

****

One Saturday when he was cleaning up tables, a big fat white man was sitting there eating. He was reading a thick book while wiping his double chin with a white cloth napkin. He saw what a good job Will was doing. He couldn't help but notice, though, that Will kept looking curiously at the book he had brought from home.

"Boy, you know how to read?" asked the man.

"Yes, sir, I can even read big words now like in the newspaper. I can talk just like you, I mean, like a white man, too," Will said with a big smile on his face. "My daddy used to like for me to do that."

The man laughed hysterically, almost choking on his cornbread.

Will ran his finger across one line of the book the man was reading and read it aloud in the manner of an astute gentleman. When he finished that line, he read another and another. The man was delightfully surprised.

"Boy, do you work here all the time?" the man asked.

"No, sir, just on Saturdays," Will said.

"My wife died last year and my house ain't been cleaned since then," the man said.

"Hasn't," Will said, without thinking.

"Hasn't what?" asked the man.

"You used the word 'ain't' and that's not a word. You should say my house 'hasn't' been cleaned since then," Will said, laughingly.

"Well, aren't you something? How would you like to come over to my place and clean some for me and you can take any book you want from my library to read? I will even pay you two bits. I just live right over yonder in that big old white house with the columns on it," the man said, pointing out the window in the direction of his house.

Will was not only good at reading, he was no pushover when it came to math, either.

"Two bits," Will said, "That's only twenty-five cents. I get paid thirty cents a day working here and I am gonna keep this job."

Impressed by the boy's cleverness, the man made the deal for thirty cents a day, one day a week. Will rushed home that day to tell Juliet. At first, she was very happy, not only that he would be making more money but also that Will had negotiated another job by himself. Then she started thinking about all the chores around the house and wondered if Will could do them and the two jobs. After a short but serious deliberation, she told him no.

Will was devastated and he begged her to no avail. She knew how important it was to study and she knew all of the other things Will had to do. Will dreaded having to go back and tell the man he could not do it but knew he had no choice. He had to take the responsibility and his first responsibility was at home. Will reluctantly told the man he could not accept the job and the man assured him it was okay.

Determined to work in a place that was filled with all kinds of books to read, Will set out to prove he could do more. He started getting up an hour early, long before that old big red rooster of theirs crowed. He would gather the eggs the hens laid, milk the cow, and nanny goat with only the light of a coal oil lamp he carried with him. He would then read until time to go to school.

Juliet realized what a special child he was.

****

Cool spring mornings soon gave way to hot summer days and Will was out of school with a lot more time on his hands. Juliet told him if he wanted to go help that white man, he could. Will was overjoyed.

At almost eleven years old, he towered over other children his age in both height and intelligence. He worked and cleaned until the man's house was almost spotless and came back every now and then just to do a touch-up. Will's new employer told him to just call him "Pete." Will and Pete became fast friends. Pete fondly referred to his new friend as "Re-Pete."

Before long, Will had read many of Pete's books. Pete was amazed at how quickly the young black boy learned and how much he already knew with very little formal education. Will loved spending as much time as possible with Pete, discussing books, politics, and learning to play chess. The two were inseparable. Will enjoyed being with his two older brothers but they were always working, too. They often walked by the restaurant and peeped in the window with their hands cupped around their faces to get a glimpse of Will cleaning tables. He would just look up and smile. They were the best family he could have since the loss of his dad.

Many times Pete invited Ed and Charley to visit along with Will. He thrilled the boys with stories of his days on the high seas as a sea captain. They never were really sure if he had been a sea captain but the stories were exciting.

The Brown brothers felt comfortable with Pete but they could easily see the attachment he had to their little brother. They stayed and helped Pete with some of the more strenuous things he needed to do around the house. They wouldn't take a penny for the work they did. They just thanked him for taking care of their little brother and giving him a job.

Pete told Will how lucky he was to be part of a large family with older brothers after being born an only child. Pete explained that he too had been an only child and now he was the only surviving member of his family. Pete had been married but he and his wife could never have children. With the death of his wife, Pete was all alone – until he met Will and his whole life began to change. Will was the son he never had. He had a reason to stay clean-shaven and to dress neatly - to set a good example for Will.

He thought to himself one day, *I don't know what it is about that child but he has a certain magnetism that you can't resist. He is funny, smart, polite, ambitious, and works hard. He is everything I would have wanted in a son. I don't even see his color. I am going to make a New Year resolution this brand new year, 1878. I'm going to treat that child as if he were my own.*

Chapter 18

An Epidemic

*"Disease is an experience of so-called mortal
mind. It is fear made manifest on the body."*
- Mary Baker Eddy

O ne day just before his birthday, while Will
was helping Pete, his mother pulled up in a
buggy.

"Oh, no, I wonder what's wrong," Will said.

Juliet hurriedly explained to Will that his oldest
sister, who had gotten married and moved to
Grenada, was about to have a baby. She was going to
Grenada to stay with her and help with the delivery
and should be back within a week.

"Let me drive you up there, Mrs. McKinney,"
offered Pete. "That's twenty-five miles away.

"Oh, no, thank you, Mr. Pete. I will be okay. I'll
stop by the blacksmith shop and tell Ed and Charley
and make sure they check on you, Will," Juliet said.

She arrived at her daughter Eve's house later
that day and found her to be bedridden. She was
running a fever and could not keep any food down.
Juliet went to the hospital to see if she could get some
medicine or get a doctor to come out and check on

her daughter. The entire nursing staff and all the doctors were treating sick people and nobody could attend. Juliet was insistent. She walked through the wards and begged every doctor she could find to come see about her daughter. The doctors refused to leave the unusually number of sick they were attending to.

When Juliet got back to the house, her son-in-law Jordan had come in from work. He was washing her daughter's face with a cold rag, trying to get the temperature down. Not knowing what else to do, they finally resorted to taking her clothes off and wrapping her in a sheet that had been soaked in cold water. Eve was delirious at that point and didn't know what was happening. They fanned her and watched her all night. The temperature would seem to subside, then come right back. Her husband, intent on getting a doctor, left on his horse and told Juliet he would not come back without a doctor.

Two hours later Jordan walked back into the house with a stunned look of disbelief and fear on his face.

"The hospital is being quarantined. They are talking about quarantining the whole town. It is an outbreak of yellow fever," he whispered. "We have all been exposed. People are dying by the dozens and the whole town is in a panic. They are burning sheets and clothes, anything touched by anyone known to have the disease. It is nothing but chaos in town."

Jordan demanded that Juliet go back to Carrollton to attend to her own children. Aware that she was exposed to the dreaded fever, she feared exposing them to the disease as well. Juliet chose to stay with her daughter. There was so much panic nobody believed it was transmitted only by mosquitos. Many feared it was on their clothes, skin, even the air they breathed.

Juliet and her son-in-law concentrated their efforts on making Eve comfortable. Aside from the disease that was killing her, she was going into labor. Juliet and Jordan attended to her and prayed for her all the next night a part of the next day. Early the next afternoon, Eve delivered a stillborn son.

Jordan took his firstborn child, a son, and wrapped him in a patchwork quilt. He held him and admired his high cheekbones like his mother's. He chose to bury the child out back of their house. As he was throwing dirt on top of the grave, he heard a scream from inside the house. He threw the shovel down and ran as fast as he could back to the house.

Juliet, now deathly sick, was rocking her daughter's lifeless body back and forth, crying and singing a Choctaw chant, refusing to let go of her daughter. Although temperatures were nearing 100 degrees, Juliet was shaking violently as if stuck in a snowstorm in the dead of winter. When Jordan saw the look of desperation on his mother-in-law's face, he just dropped to his knees and prayed.

Within hours, Juliet was dead and Jordan was experiencing many of the same symptoms as the women had experienced: nausea, vomiting, chills, profuse sweating, and weakness. He knew it was just a matter of time before he, too, would be gone. Too weak to bury his wife and mother-in-law and aware that his life would be over soon, he chose to suffer no more. He also wanted to prevent the spread of the disease.

Jordan removed a coal oil lamp from the wall and set the curtains on fire then threw it across the small wood frame house, spreading the fuel and fire as quickly as he could. He went to the corner of the bedroom and removed his old .50 caliber muzzle loader rifle, placed the stock on the floor in front of his chair and leaned his head over the end of the barrel. After placing his mouth over the barrel, he reached down and cocked the hammer with his thumb inside the trigger guard.

Chapter 19:

Will and His Brothers

"Who of us is mature enough for offspring before the offspring themselves arrive? The value of marriage is not that adults produce children but that children produce adults."
- Peter de Vries

J uliet never got to see her children again. However, they were honored that she chose to spare them from potential exposure and gave her own life trying to save their older sister.

News of the yellow fever epidemic spread quickly and became a horrendous threat from Memphis to New Orleans and all sites between. Carrollton was only about twenty-five miles from Grenada, where the epidemic was worse, but Carrollton was off the beaten path with no thruway to other towns. If a traveler had no need to go to Carrollton, he probably would not end up there since few roads connected it to other towns. With few people coming into the small town and even fewer people leaving it, Carrollton did not experience the multitude of deaths that other small towns in Mississippi suffered.

The Baptist Church was filled to the balcony when the preacher told his congregation that God's hand was on the people of Carrollton and it was by His grace that they had been saved from the yellow fever epidemic of 1878.

****

Will, almost twelve years old now, was still the center of attention in the town, especially by church groups and some of the old gossiping ladies. Old Mrs. Peggy Lawrence clucked to Mrs. Sally Houston that he probably shouldn't be raised by two young half-breed stepbrothers in their teens. It just wasn't right, they whispered.

Most of the people in town were unaware of the good deeds the Brown brothers did. They had helped Mrs. Emma fill in where William left off, doing chores for her and keeping up the two houses without any expectation for money. They treated Will like their own, protected him from bullies and encouraged him to work for Mr. Pete and save his money for college, a lifelong ambition of his.

In addition to running the blacksmith shop left behind by their father, they helped their two remaining sisters by selling the molasses they made and giving them all of the money. They sold molasses to individuals, restaurants for biscuits and saloons to cut whiskey. They gave molasses to young mothers to sweeten the goat milk given to their babies. The boys kept to themselves and many people never knew what good boys Juliet had raised.

Ed and Charley had suffered many tragedies in their short lives. They had lost their father, their mother, their stepfather and their sister. Hard times coupled with the treatment of blacks, Indians and half-breeds caused them to withdraw from society. The local whites really didn't know how to take them. Charley had almost withdrawn into a depressed shell, barely speaking. Ed, though not a troublemaker, was quick to respond defensively if mistreated or abused.

Even with all the bad things that clouded their lives, Ed and Charley had a bright spot in their brother, Will. Will was loved by everyone and smarter than kids twice his age. But ladies of the church were talking to the preacher, who was talking to the judge—and issues were being raised to take him away from them.

The Brown brothers didn't want to fight with the ladies of town or the church, and especially not the judges or the law. They only wanted Will to be happy.

Ed and Charley had a long discussion with Will and asked him what he wanted to do. He didn't feel comfortable moving in the same house with Mrs. Emma and he didn't want to leave his brothers. He knew the ladies were concerned about him having adult supervision and they didn't think his older brothers were yet adults themselves. They were facing a dilemma they didn't know how to deal with. Even though they were responsible business owners and worked two jobs, many people did not consider them appropriate guardians to young Will.

On Thanksgiving Day in 1878, Pete invited the boys to join him for dinner. Ed and Charley had their sister bake a Southern pecan pie especially for the occasion and they brought a jug of their own sorghum molasses. Pete cooked a twelve-pound turkey and Will helped with the cornbread dressing.

Pete approached the sensitive subject of Will's guardianship after dinner. He told Ed and Charley that he had been hearing the rumors that Will was going to be taken from his home and placed with a family from church.

"I don't know how you feel about it but Will is welcome to stay here with me. At sixty-eight years old, I think I qualify as being an adult. How would y'all feel about that?" asked Pete.

Ed and Charley just looked at each other. Charley shrugged his shoulders and raised his eyebrows as he looked over at Will. Before Charley could speak, Ed asked Will what he thought about that idea.

Without speaking, Will jumped up with a mouthful of pecan pie and ran around the table, hugging Pete as hard as he could and almost choked on the pie.

"Well, I guess that is that!" Pete said as he pinched both sides of Will's cheeks. "You boys and your sisters are welcome here any time."

The next day Will visited Mrs. Emma to get her approval. As much as he wanted to live in the big white house with Pete, he would never do anything to hurt his Mrs. Emma.

He waited until he knew the other children were out playing and found Mrs. Emma in her sewing room.

"Mrs. Emma, you have always been so good to me, I hate to talk with you about this." Will said shyly.

"What is it Will? You know you can talk to me anytime about anything. Is something wrong?" she asked curiously.

"No, nothing is wrong and I want you to know I love you like I would have my own mother but.... I would like to move into town and stay with Mr. Pete. He is a good man and lives by himself with health problems. I would like to help him. That don't mean I don't care for you." he said.

To his delight, she was thrilled with the idea. She knew how much Will liked Pete. She was equally impressed with Pete's regular church attendance and belief in a well-stocked library and daily reading.

Emma told Will, "Oh, Will, is that all that was worrying you? Don't you worry at all. I think that is a great idea. I am sure Mr. Pete will enjoy the company. I will 'call off the dogs' in the church and ask the ladies to leave you be and let you live your life."

Will just hugged her and thanked her for being so understanding.

Chapter 20:

The Productive Years

"When one door of happiness closes, another opens; but often we look so long at the closed door that we do not see the one which has been opened for us."
- Helen Keller

I n early 1879, when adjusting to life together in the big Carrollton mansion, Pete treasured every day with his little Re-Pete. The town folk joked that where you saw one of them, the other one must not be too far behind.

Most people accepted their "salt-pepper" relationship with the exception of one mean and bitter man – the coroner who had killed Will's stepfather seven years before. Everybody around town knew the coroner as a hate monger and white supremacist. Will just tried to stay out of his way.

Five years – from 1880 to 1884 – passed without incident. Will and Pete's relationship grew as strong as any father-son relationship could be. In his mid-seventies, Pete was still as spry as ever when Will was around and he hoped Will didn't notice but his health was failing. Will was a very smart and polite, well-read young man who had just graduated top in his class from high school and wasn't fooled easily.

One day as they were talking, Pete began to cough profusely. His eyes got glossy and his face turned red. Will handed him a handkerchief. Pete coughed in it and later dropped it. Will picked it up and saw that it was partially covered in blood.

"Pete, is your mouth bleeding?" asked Will.

"Oh yeah, Re-Pete, it's nothing, just got an old tooth that's been bothering me. It bleeds every now and then, especially when I cough," Pete said, trying to show little concern.

"Well, I was wondering about that this morning when I was making up your bed. I didn't say anything because there was blood on the pillow and some nasty-looking brown stuff, too," Will said, making a face as if it was grotesque.

"Probably just some of my old snuff, Re-Pete. I am sorry about that," Pete said as he continued to try and keep from coughing.

"Are you sure you're okay?" Will asked as he noticed Pete still struggling to keep from coughing and by then noticed blood between Pete's fingers.

"I said I am okay, Will, now leave it alone," Pete scoffed.

Will was convinced something more serious was wrong because Pete was getting angry. That was not like him and he had not called him "Will" since the first week he met him. Still, against his better judgment, he left it alone so as not to anger Pete any more.

Will had taken on a full-time summer job working in the library the summer between his

junior and senior year. He saved every dime he made
to apply to his college fund. By then he had over
three thousand dollars in the fund. Following his
graduation, he was offered a job as a mail carrier in
honor of his father. He gladly accepted the position
but told the postmaster as soon as he earned enough
money for college he would leave. The postmaster
told him he would expect nothing less of him and
highly encouraged him to go to college. Will knew he
would probably have to work a year or so full-time
before going to college but he kept up his studies and
reading while deciding for sure on his major.

Will thought back to the day he had told Master
Bud that he wanted to become a doctor. Bud told him
he would have to read " a whole lot of books" to be a
doctor. That coment only challanged him more as he
thought about it over the years. He read every book
Pete had in his own library plus scores of other books
anywhere he could get them. He had a genuine desire
to help other people. Besides that, he was beginning
to worry about Pete's age and health. He felt if he
became a doctor, he could at least take care of his
family. However, Will was not only a dreamer but a
realist too. He knew blacks weren't allowed at the
University of Mississippi and had decisions to make.

One day in the summer of 1885, Will was
invited to an open house at Alcorn Agricultural and
Mechanical College. He wanted to go but still had in
the back of his mind that he wanted to be a doctor.
Unfortunately, the University of Mississippi was the
only school offering a medical degree and it was only
open to whites. He decided to see what Alcorn
College had to offer.

"Go with me, Pete," Will said. "We can stay a few days and take a look around Jackson."

"Now, Will," Pete replied. "It is time for you to be on your own and make your own decisions. I'll be just fine right here at home." He turned and left the room just before he started one of the coughing fits that kept him awake at night.

Will was gone for two days.

After being on the college campus, Will could not wait to tell Pete about his adventures. As he walked onto the porch of the mansion and opened the heavy ornate, he smelled a strong odor coming from inside.

"Whew…must be an old dead dog around here or something. Hope it hasn't gotten up under the porch," Will muttered to himself.

As he climbed the concrete steps, he noticed that the door was slightly ajar. Thinking how strange it was for Pete to leave the door open, he gave it a little push. Swarms of flies filled the entry hall and the smell was much worse.

"Pete, you in here?" yelled Will as he walked from room to room.

Worried and a little sick to his stomach, he stumbled through the house until he came to Pete's bedroom. Will found Pete dead on the floor next to his bed. He had a bloody gash in his forehead and an array of pills scattered across the rug beside his bed. He must have been trying to take medicine and had fallen onto small table, which was now covered with blood and skin tissue.

Will broke into tears as he held his hand over his face, pinching his nose to avoid the smell. He ran out of the house to the sheriff's department. He knew it was too late for the doctor. He figured Pete had died about the time he left for Alcorn College.

Will ran as fast as he could to the courthouse in search of the sheriff. Unfortunately, the sheriff was not in but he found the old long time coroner, Tandy Oury.

"You better know what you are talking about, boy, dragging me away from my lunch. I got important business to take care of here," he warned Will in a condescending voice.

Oury locked the door and walked over to Pete's house with Will. When he went in and saw the body, he asked Will what he was doing in the white man's house. Will told him he had been living with the man for several years.

"Oh, yeah, that's right, I forgot about that. Salt and pepper team and all that," the coroner smirked.

Suddenly Will remembered something Pete had always told him. He grabbed the old cookie tin from atop the dresser.

"Here," Will said, thrusting the tin toward the coroner. "He told me if anything ever happened to him to give this to the sheriff or a doctor."

The coroner snatched it from Will, opened it and pulled out a handwritten note: "This is my final will and testament. My old house can go to the ladies of the garden club. They always wanted to dress up the yard anyway. I want to leave what cash I have, about five thousand dollars, under my mattress to young Will McKinney as a college fund. He is going to be a fine doctor one day."

Will's face lit up. Thanks to his friend Pete, he would go to college. He stuffed his hand under Pete's bed mattress and felt around until he found the large brown envelope containing his college fund.

"Give me that money, boy, ain't no nigger going to get this money for no college. You just keep your mouth shut about this or I'll take you in for killing this man. Looks like somebody hit him in the head. Now you get on out of here and go home," the coroner yelled as he crumbled up the will and put it in one pocket while cramming the money into the other.

Devastated, Will ran straight to the blacksmith shop to talk to Ed and Charley. He told his brothers what had happened.

"I came home and found Pete dead," he cried. "I did what I was supposed to do. I ran to get the sheriff and the coroner was the only one in the office. He came with me but he couldn't help Pete. All he could do was to steal the money Pete left for me!" Will sobbed.

"Hold on, hold, Will. Now, you listen to me," said Ed. "Will, you don't open your mouth and even think about accusing no white lawman of stealing money. They'll put the blame on you and next thing you know you will be hanging up on a big old gallows up there on 'hang hill' with everybody looking at you. They ain't gone worry about your innocence. They will kill you dead without a blink of the eye. Then they will come around with pocketknives and cut pieces off you, like your ears for souvenirs. Don't you ever, and I mean ever, breathe a word of this. The war has been over twenty years but more of our people are being lynched now than ever before."

Will had never seen his big brother more serious.

Will, now barely nineteen years old, moved back in with his brothers in their new rental house in the edge of the town limits. He grieved for weeks but knew Ed was right. He listened and just kept on doing what he had done.

His demeanor and pleasant personality gained him respect of most of the town. Only occasionally would he run into a disrespectful white person and that would usually be a teenager.

Chapter 21:

Self-Defense

"The right of self-defense never ceases. It is among the most sacred, and alike necessary to nations and to individuals."
-President James Monroe

I t was a nice, unusually cool September day in Carrollton, Mississippi, back in 1885. Men, women, and children were going in and out of the stores shopping and milling around. Three little boys, feet dangling from red leather barstools, were slurping milk shakes at soda fountain while their big sisters flirted with the young proprietor, in his ruffle-sleeved white shirt and black vest. Two old men sitting on cane back chairs were hunched over an old whiskey barrel in front of the hardware store arguing over a checker game.

Main Street in Carrollton was much like the main streets all across the South – half a century old brick buildings with large glass fronts and massive wooden double doors. Most had the name of a family business etched into the glass. Many were run by third and even fourth generations of the same family.

Dapper businessmen standing on the brick walkway could barely hear each other talk over old man Lott's mule that was baying loudly, tied to the wood railing in front of the barber shop. Buggies were passing by with the sounds of horse shoes clip-clopping along, kicking up dirt that was by now covering up the kids' ice cream cones as they walked barefooted along the walkway.

Will saw Miss Esther Broadway, a pretty "high-falutin" white lady climbing up a rickety old ladder in front of Mr. W. H. Johnston's Hardware Store. Miss Esther was putting fall decorations over the door and that old ladder was shaking like the leaves on a tree. Always the gentleman, Will ran up to hold the ladder for her.

In a flash, Charlie Broadway, Miss Esther's nineteen-year-old brother, came barreling out of the store with threats to kill Will. "Ain't no niggah gonna look at my sister," he yelled.

He kept on hollering, "Get off this porch, Will McKinney! You ain't nothing but a damned ole skinny, dried up, worthless, no count niggah. Don't you touch my sister!"

Afraid of letting go of the ladder for fear the lady would fall off, Will was also scared not to do what Miss Esther's brother was telling him. That boy was acting plum crazy.

Oh Lawd, this fella is fittin to be tied, Will thought. He did not want any trouble.

Charlie Broadway grabbed Will from behind as his sister climbed down; trying to explain to her brother that Will was just trying to help. Charlie pushed his sister aside and pulled a knife from his pocket, pushing it up to Will's throat. The two boys began to wrestle and both of them fell off the steps onto the street, dust clouds flying. A crowd of people started gathering around to see the fight.

Suddenly, Will turned toward the sound of a scream coming from Miss Esther. When he turned back around, he saw Charlie Broadway falling face first onto the knife. The white pearl handle was sticking out of his chest, blood running out all around it. Charlie's eyes rolled back, and his head rose up from where he was lying as he looked down at the knife. He reached for it and started to gasp for his breath. It was too late. He gurgled a few times before his head fell to the side. His limp hand let go of the knife as it fell to the ground.

People standing around said the blade went straight through his heart. It must have cut into his lungs, too, because a steady stream of blood was running out of the corner of his mouth. Charlie's eyes remained wide open as he lay dead. Will had not seen that much blood since they slaughtered a big old hog late fall the year before.

"No sawbones kin help him now," Will mumbled as he shooed a bunch of old starving, mangy hounds away.

Terrified of what might happen next, Will just stood there with no plan to run. Everybody else started running out of the store when they heard Miss Esther and the other ladies screaming. All eyes were cast upon Will as word of a lynching spread through the crowd.

The sheriff showed up quickly, grabbed Will by the collar, and took him on to jail so old man Oury, the coroner, wouldn't have two bodies to deal with.

****

Will couldn't afford a lawyer, so when he faced the judge and jury, he did what he thought best. He told the truth.

As he stared out into the courtroom, he saw Miss Esther Broadway crying softly into a pale pink hanky. She knew he did not mean to hurt her brother. She asked the judge not to hang Will; he was just trying to help her. Because of the circumstances, and how Will had proven himself a "good Negro," the district attorney asked the judge to give him only one year to serve.

Since he had already served a month before the trial, they would let him do his time in the county jail. The state penitentiary would not take any prisoners anyway if they had less than a full year left on their sentence. The law allowed farmers and other local citizens to get prisoners out for contract labor to do work for them so they could work off their sentence. However, nobody at the time would take contract prisoners.

"Thank God above fur me jus gettin one ye-ah, even though I know in my heart I ain't did nothing wrong. I knowed it coulda been a whole lots worse," Will said when the judge asked him if he had anything to say.

Although about as intelligent as the judge, Will was afraid to talk like a well-read white boy to any white man, especially the judge, who might accuse him of mockery.

"Sho do hate I won't be able ta help Mrs. Emma with chores. She got too much to do by herself. She too busy keepin house, makin clothes and soap, not ta mention choppin her own rows ta grow um sumpin ta eat. She got all dat cannin ta do in da fall by herself too. My brothers got too much to do by they selves too. Least ways, wit me up heah, they's one less mouth ta feed at home," Will said quietly as the sheriff escorted him to the jailhouse.

Will would have rather been out working doing something instead of sitting in the jail cell but he just minded his own business, waiting for the day he could go to college and get out of Carrollton for good.

Busy with two jobs, Ed and Charley came to visit him whenever they could. The fact that they put his little blood brother in jail was taking its toll on Ed's ability to keep his cool. It was hard enough to be a black boy in a small Mississippi town, but the three brothers had suffered more than most. Feelings of bottled-up depression and outrage started flooding Ed's mind.

He remembered his father, Adam, telling them one time that even a coward backed into a corner with no place to go would kill you given the opportunity. Though he wasn't a coward, Ed knew his father was trying to tell him that anybody is capable of defending himself after having been pushed so far. Will could see the Indian coming out in Ed. He knew Ed was thinking about revenge but convinced him that he would be out in less than a

year and it would be best if things were just left
alone. Ed backed down at the request of his baby
brother.

Will was disheartened to be in jail rather than
getting ready for his first year of college, but he was
glad to be in the county jail instead of state prison.
He would bide his time, be a model prisoner and stay
a "good niggah" until he was free. Will was born and
raised in the South – he knew how to get along. Mrs.
Emma would be proud of him for being such a good
Christian boy, even when others persecuted him.

Will did not want any other incidents to come
up that might make his brother Ed any more angry
than he already was. He knew his brother was a good
young man but that he also had that Indian temper.
He knew Ed and Charley wanted him out of jail and
that they knew he shouldn't have been there in the
first place. However, he knew the reality of the whole
thing too. He had grown to love them very much
and prayed for them each night.

****

Sheriff Hamilton was just an old farmer who
needed the extra money and did not mind riding his
old hack to work every day to enforce the law. He
didn't have too much to do in town anyway. He had
taken a liking to Will. One morning before coming
to the office, Sheriff Hamilton stopped at the café for
coffee. He overheard some ladies discussing Emma
McKinney and the plans they had to take food to her
since she was so sick with consumption.

"I know Will McKinney would brighten her day, though," the sheriff said. "I need to take him around to see her."

He went immediately and did just that.

"Will, is that you, son?" called Mrs. Emma from her bed.

"Yes, ma'm, it is me. Sheriff Hamilton told me you was real sick and he brought me over .to see you, thought it might make you feel better," Will said. "He a real good man."

"Yes, he is, and I surely appreciate him, too," Emma said weakly. "I'm only fifty-six years old but I am very sick, may not live much longer."

"You gone live longer than you even know, Mrs. Emma," Will said. "Are Gracie and Pinckney coming home from college this week?"

"Yes, they should be here anytime. I hope you get to see them" she sighed. "Will, come close. I need to tell you something. Your father had something he kept in this little lock box he wanted me to give you when you turned twenty-one. I wouldn't trust anybody else with it because he asked me to promise not to ever open it. He said it was for your eyes only. I don't know if I will be around when you are twenty-one so I want you to have it now," she said as he handed the box and a small key to Will.

Curiously, Will opened the box that contained nothing but a wrinkled, folded up, yellowing piece of paper with a lengthy letter written on it in his dad's handwriting. He sat in a chair next to the window as he read the letter quietly to himself.

"*Back in 1867*," the note started, "*my wife was murdered in our house. At first we thought it was done by Indians. The Pinkerton Detectives thought it was done by somebody traveling on the train. They did her real bad, made it look like Indians, but it wadn't no Indians that did it. Back when Masser Bud was on his death bed, Mrs. Emma said he wanted to see me cause he was real sick. I went over dere and he made evabody else leave and close the doe. Den he started talking to me with tears running out his eyes. He told me he wanted to confess to me befoe he went on to meet his maker. He said he had jined-up with the Ku Klux Clan the year after the war, but that he would protect my family from the Klan. Somewhere along the line after that, Klan members got to where dey didn't trust them old Massers dat still had Darkies on dey place. He said he got a visit from the Klan one night and dey made him dress up in his white suit and hood like the others and pay me a visit to threaten us to leave. Dey was doing that to all the slaves dat stayed on dey plantations. Dat wadn't good enough though. He said dey told him later on that he would be jined by another Klucker name Paul Wilkins who would help him do the real job. He didn't know what that was, but early one morning a mean, vicious white man, a Klucker, showed up at his house, got him out of the bed and told hem to come on. Dey was gonna kill my Lucindy before she 'brought another little Nigger' into the world. Masser Bud said he resisted ever way he could but that mean man threatened to kill Mrs. Emma and dey kids, Pinckney and Gracie, if he didn't jin him. He say yo ma'ama answered the doe cause she knowed it was him and I was gone a huntin. Den the other man run on past Masser Bud and grabbed the fire poker, then he started hitting her. Before dey was done, Paul started to*

*grab stuff outta da cabinets in the kitchen to make it
look like a break-in. When Paul got out on the back
porch he handed a long thin blade funny lookin knife to
Masser Bud and told him to stab her in the stomach to
make sure that little Nigger baby was dead. Paul
wadn't watching too close cause he had stuff from the
cabinets out on the porch he was putting in a flour sack.
Masser Bud said he bent down over her body and
pretended to stab her stomach but was stabbing the
bed. He wiped the blade in her blood; den walked out
on the back porch and gave the knife back to Paul
whilst they ran from the back doorstep. Masser Bud
cried and grabbed my hand...he begged me to forgive
him.*"

Will paused as he looked back at Mrs. Emma
with eyes squinted and brow down. *Masser Bud killed
my ma'ama?* Will thought to himself before
continuing to read. It was almost as if his dad knew
what his reaction would be when he wrote it.

"*He was there. He said the other man did most of
it but he helped. That is why he helped you so much
over the years. He quit the Klan after that because he
couldn't take it no more. I just reached into my pocket
and pulled out a white, funny made cross and gave it to
him. He looked at me, den he looked back at it and
asked me where I got it. He said he had been missing it
for years. I told him the first time I had seen it was just
before the war ended. It was a new cross back then and
he was wearing it around his neck... I told him the
second time I seen it was when that group of Kluckers
came to my house. A man about Masser Bud's size,
who didn't say nothing, but looked at me through them
holes in the mask was wearing it... The last time I had*

seen it was when I found it in my bed, next to my wife's body along with the broken chain. It was covered with her blood on the day she died."

Will broke into tears without looking up. He continued to read.

"I knew Masser Bud had been sick lately and probably wouldn't last too much longer. I got that old funny looking white cross out and had been carrying it my pocket. I was gonna ask Mrs. Emma if I could go to his funeral if he was to pass away before I did I was gonna put that old cross in his casket when he died, cause I didn't want it round here no more. Will, my son, I just hope you can forgive Masser Bud, too. He made peace with his maker. Please don't have hard feelings with Mrs. Emma. I don't believe she ever knowed what happened. I love you, son." The note was signed simply, *"Your Daddy."*

"I love you, too, Dad," Will said out loud with a forced, sad smile on his face.

"Everything okay, Will?" asked Mrs. Emma. "Do you want to talk to me about it?" she asked earnestly.

"No ma'am," Will said softly as he bent down and kissed her forehead, then turned to the sheriff, ready to go.

Will McKinney, a docile and meek soul, returned to jail with Sheriff Hamilton so he could once again be locked up and caged like a wild animal. However, the sheriff received word a few days later that Mrs. Emma was back to her old self, feeling fine after seeing Will.

Chapter 22:

Down at the Saloon

"The most common and durable source of faction has been the various and unequal distribution of property."
- James Madison

W hile Will continued to serve out his time, everything else went on as usual around Carrollton. The saloon on the corner certainly had its share of business. Across the street a few young boys sat on an old wooden bench made from two stumps and a couple of boards. They watched intently to sneak a peek at the barelegged dance hall girls through the two-foot gap between the two ribbed swinging saloon doors. They also liked hearing the music from the bartender's piano and an occasional fiddle.

One day a fancy-dressed, out-of-town fellow with a black felt derby perched on his head and stiffly starched ruffles on the cuffs of his white shirtsleeves strolled into the saloon for an afternoon refreshment. Johnny, the bar keeper, noticed that every now and then the man removed his gold pocket watch, extended the chain to look at the time, and put it back while staggering around the bar.

Johnny thought the man spoke a little too
refined for his taste and he thought it strange that he
kept telling the ladies of the saloon that he was a fine
Southern gentleman, much too refined to pay for
their services. The truth of the matter was he had too
much to drink and was unable to entertain the ladies.
He soon staggered out the swinging doors, leaving
them open just long enough to treat the boys across
the street with a glimpse of the naked thighs of the
dancers.

Just about the time the city slicker went through
the saloon doors, the Brown brothers were going in
the swinging doors to deliver molasses. One of the
boys stumbled and almost fell, steadying himself
against the white man.

"Boy, just what do you think you are doing,
bumping into me with that old jug of sorghum?
Don't you know you two Negroes, half-breeds, or
whatever you call yourselves should yield to a white
man of my stature exiting this facility?" Robert
Moore, the well-respected businessman from
Greenwood, slurred, obviously under the influence
of alcohol.

For years, Ed Brown had kept his pain and
anger bottled up. On this day, he could take no
more.

"White man, we got business in this saloon. The
door swings both ways. We don't stand aside for no
white man. We're proud of our Choctaw blood," said
Ed as he and Charley continued into the saloon.

The piano player stopped and a hush came over
the crowd. All eyes were cast upon the door as the
frail, almost lady-like gentleman confronted the

Brown brothers, who some said were just itching for a fight that day.

"Niggah, Geronimo, or whatever you choose to be called, you come back here right this instant to face your accuser. Just look at the molasses you have spilled on my fine Italian trousers and custom-made shoes. You have soiled my fine apparel beyond repair and I demand payment. Go sell your molasses to the keeper of this saloon and return forthwith to pay your debt with honor," said Moore indignantly.

"I don't know who you think you are, Mr. Fancy Man, but I only spilled molasses on you when you bumped into me with your old drunk wobbling ass while I was trying to make a delivery. The bartender charges an extra three cents a shot for any glass of whiskey that has a cut of this fine molasses. The last thing I want to do is waste it on a hi-fa-luten bastard like you," Ed said in a loud and angry tone as he walked closer and closer to Moore.

"Why you no-good, irreverent, copper-colored son of..." Moore roared. He continued to raise his right hand upwards as if to strike Ed.

"Take this, Fancy Pants," Brown said as he raised the molasses jug up slightly as if to strike the left side of Moore's head. Losing his balance, Moore fell without being struck by either of the Brown brothers.

"Good thing you fell backwards before I hit you with my jug on that pretty head of yours," Ed said sarcastically.

He turned toward the large, overbearing bartender as creaks of loose pine boards shifting under his feet overrode the silence.

"What have you got there, red man?" asked the bartender in a loud gruff voice as he rolled his handlebar mustache between his thumb and forefinger.

"Four jugs of our finest molasses," Charley said with a smile. He was just ready to get their business done and go visit Will.

"I thought you boys were going to bring us some unscheduled entertainment. You know you probably ain't heard the last of that little encounter. Y'all just may have to be put in your place before it's over with," the bartender said, as he placed the four-gallon jugs of molasses under the bar.

"Here's your four dollars…now y'all get on out of here before that white man comes back with a posse and shoots up the place," he said as he rolled up the sleeves on his long-sleeved white shirt and unbuttoned his black vest, giving it some relief from his bulging beer belly.

"You know that sorghum is worth a dollar fifty a jug. Anybody else would probably pay that for it," Ed said.

"Want it back? Hell, you done spilled part of it. The other two saloons have done closed in this town. I am the only one left cutting whiskey with it. If you want to go sell it to the hotel café to put on biscuits, go ahead. Give me my money back," the bartender said with a smirk as he rubbed the bar with his rag, leaning forward on one elbow.

"We'll take it," Ed scoffed as he grabbed his brother Charley by the arm and escorted him out.

"Think we'll see that white man again, Ed?" Charley asked in a concerned tone.

"I doubt he'll even remember the whole thing when he wakes up. I saw him staggering over towards the hotel, so he's probably just sleeping it off. But, know this, brother. We ain't got to worry about that white man. I'll kill that son-of-a-bitch the next time he messes with us," Ed said.

"Yeah, guess you're right. Our daddy sure wouldn't have taken kindly to us getting no treatment from a white man like that," Charley said.

"Nope, can't start taking nothing off these white men. If you do, you will have it do from now on. I see that now. If you stand up to them, they ain't going to mess with you. I ain't taking nothing off none of them with their fancy talk and fancy clothes. They ought to have to work for a living as we always did. Look what they did to Will for just defending himself. They just want to treat us like an old stray dog and kick us out of their way. Don't want us soiling their clothes or having our smell clogging up their noses. Just think, this used to be our fathers' and their fathers' land as far as you could see," Ed said angrily.

Sure was a good thing I grabbed Ed when that drunk white man fell out the door, thought Charley. *If he had not gotten up and dusted himself off, there might have been a killing. Ed and I could have gotten ourselves lynched.*

"Ed and Charles Brown," a voice yelled out. "I need to talk to you boys," their landlady said as she saw them walking down the street, stuffing money in their pockets. "Ya'll are behind on your rent a whole month and I need the money now."

"We ain't got no money right now," Ed lied.

"Well, I may have to move you lying boys out. I'm going to have the sheriff come around to collect my rent or send ya'll on your way," she said.

"Let me tell you something, lady. We got four shotguns, not to mention pistols in that house, and the first damn man that steps foot on our porch to try to get money out of us or throw us out is going to meet the wrong end of them guns," Ed said, as his brother Charley remained quiet.

"Why, how dare you to threaten me, you savages? I will not accept such treatment from you," she scoffed as she stomped away in disgust, mumbling in anger with every step, bottom lip poked out.

"C'mon, Ed," said Charley, "We have had enough trouble for one day. I need to stop by the blacksmith shop on the way back, but let us get on home. I just hope that sheriff ain't poking around when we get back. You should not have told that white lady we had guns and would use them if anybody came. They might be laying and waiting for us to come home and shoot us on the spot. Even worse, they might string us up to that old pecan tree in the front yard."

Maybe the lady had not told anybody or maybe they just hadn't gotten there yet, but when they returned home, all was quiet—for the time being, anyway.

Chapter 23:

Distinguished Southern Gentlemen

"To free men, threats are impotent."
-Marcus Tulluis Cicero

It was early morning, February 12, 1886, and Editor James M. Liddell, Jr. was changing the date on his calendar at the *Yazoo Valley Flag* newspaper office in Greenwood. Robert Moore went in to see his longtime friend, who happened to be not only a newspaper editor but also a lawyer and a refined Southern gentleman as well.

"Well, well, well....Mr. Robert Moore, my friend. I have not seen you in a coon's age. How have you been sir?" Liddell asked his old friend.

"Why, I am obviously not as well as you, my distinguished colleague. I see you have found pleasure in the finer things in life...I am judging from this elegantly decorated office appropriate for a millionaire, if I dare say so," Moore said with a big smile, sounding very much like a wealthy plantation owner or maybe a riverboat gambler.

"Why, thank you, sir, for such kind words. Of course, this is no more than I would expect from such a fine Southern gentlemen as you," Liddell said as he opened a box of expensive imported cigars, offering one to his distinguished visitor.

"God has given us a beautiful day in which to be most thankful. Why, I witnessed an orange-breasted robin perched above your door belching a beautiful song as I entered your establishment today. The weather is unseasonably warm and it may be a sign of early spring, my dear sir," Moore said as he puffed on his cigar with the lighted match burning closer to his fingers.

"I agree, sir," Liddell said as he blew smoke across the room. "Now tell me, Robert, to what does a paltry newspaper editor like yours truly owe the honor of your presence this lovely day?" asked Liddell.

"I am not sure if your services as a newspaper editor would be more appropriate, or your expertise as a counselor at law in my current situation," Moore said with a sideways grin.

"Do tell, my friend… Although much time has passed since our last visit, would I be too presumptuous in referring to you once again as Bob?" asked Liddell.

"Not at all, my dear friend, and if I, too, may dispense with the formality and call you simply James, I would like to enlighten you as to the reason for my visit," Moore said.

"Please, Bob, continue with the reason for your visit," Liddell said.

"The story that I plan to reveal goes like this… While on a business trip in your fair town of Carrollton on January 15, in the year of our Lord

1886, I made my home for the night at the Peteet Hotel.

"Anyway, my parched, dry throat called for a drink of the bartender's finest bourbon. I believe I had consumed not more than one or two when I heard these two copper-colored young bucks using foul language that I found most offensive to even the saloon lady in my company. As I left the company of the beautiful lady and made my way to the door, one of these half-breed Negroes commenced to pour molasses about my trousers and shoes. He made statements directed at me that were dishonorable, causing me grief and distress in the presence of other honorable Southern gentlemen. As I commenced to explain to this scoundrel and his next-of-kin, he attempted to assault me using a large earthenware whiskey jug or something of the sort. He and his brother, whom I learned to be Ed and Charley Brown, together made advances towards me as my back was to the door. They placed their filthy hands on me, causing a stench that very nearly resulted in my regurgitation. The hotel was surely my next stop, at which I would draw a hot bath. However, I backed away, stumbling onto the equally filthy street, where these savages had previously walked with no telling what substance clinging to the bottom of their raggedy old boots. You know I am not a fighting man, James. I can only assume that these Negroes have not yet learned their place in our honorable society," Moore said, taking a breath as he ended his story.

Liddell sat straight up in his chair when he heard Robert Moore reveal the names of two he had confronted. He remembered a confrontation between the Carrollton newspaper editor and the Browns' father some years back. His eyes were squinted and his lower jaw protruded outwards.

"That is a most deplorable story, my friend," Liddell said with his legs crossed, as he angrily pressed the lit end of his cigar against the sole of his shoe.

"You say this terrible tragedy occurred near one month ago now, today being the twelfth day of February? Is that a precise statement, sir?" asked Liddell as he made a note using his quill dipped into a bottle of ink at the corner of his desk.

"Most assuredly, counselor. I remember it well, for it was the day before my dearly departed father's date of birth which occurred on January sixteenth," Moore said.

"Why, we cannot stand for such disrespect perpetrated against our valued citizens from anyone of the Negro race. These savages must be taught a lesson they will never forget!" Liddell barked out, eyebrows raised, as he rose to his feet, leaning towards Moore with both hands still on his desk.

"How do you propose we handle this infraction, counselor? Should you tell this story from your ink well, so as to incite the white citizens, including regulators, into frenzy, or is this a matter for the bench?" asked Moore.

"A story told from a well of ink, you ask? I think not, my dear colleague. Nor would I waste the justices' time on such a trivial matter that best be handled using a smite across the face of these arrogant, disrespectful, lowbred desperados. I am thoroughly embarrassed by the conduct of the third-rate citizenry of my town. I will take this matter on your behalf, my dear friend. Further, I will personally see to it that these villains of our ghetto section learn respect for the affluent white citizens of this entire territory. I assure you, it will not happen again," Liddell said with his voice constantly rising as he slammed his fist down on the top of his custom-made, hand-carved rosewood desk.

"Need I accompany you in your travel home today if for no other reason than the purpose of identifying this bandit, sir?" asked Moore.

"That won't be necessary, sir. I have another editor friend whom I believe once had an altercation with this family. I plan to meet with him. I have also once been acquainted, although from a distance, with the rogues you have so fluently described with skin the color of my own kitchen utensils. Misfits of their caliber will soon cease their despicable acts toward our superior race as we continue to diminish the Republican Party and seat nothing but our own respectable Democrats once more. My most educated and gallant brothers from the war are now commanding the most powerful positions in the state that will continue to destroy the Negro. You may be on your way, sir, and enjoy the rest of this God-given pleasant day. I plan to attend to my final business hereto, before retiring to my home in Carrollton. Time permitting; I will, not later than tomorrow evening, approach your opponent. You may call on me before one week has passed for a full report of my encounter with these Negroes," Liddell said, assuring his friend.

"What price shall I pay for your services, if I may ask, Mr. Liddell?" Moore asked inquisitively.

"Payment for my services this day shall not be necessary. My payment will arrive in the satisfaction that a couple of brash and boastful heathens of inferior race have for once been put in their place by a man of extreme prominence," Liddell said with the utmost confidence as he escorted Robert Moore out the door, patting him on the back and wishing him a pleasant evening.

There was no doubt there was going to be trouble. Liddell did not waste any time cleaning his side arm and jumping on his black stallion. Before long, he was leaving the city limits of Greenwood and heading back to Carrollton.

James Liddell was looking for a fight.

Town of Carrollton circa 1890

Much like the home described as the homeplace of Will McKinney
Library of Congress Photographic Collection

Allan Pinkerton on left with Lincoln   Pinkerton at Antietam Battlefield
Photos from Library of Congress Photo Collection

Civil War Era Hot Hair Surveillance Balloon
Library of Congress

William A. and Robert A. Pinkerton Circa 1855
Library of Congress

Busy Rail yard circa 1865
Library of Congress Photographic Collection

Passenger Train Circa 1885
Library of Congress Photographic Collection

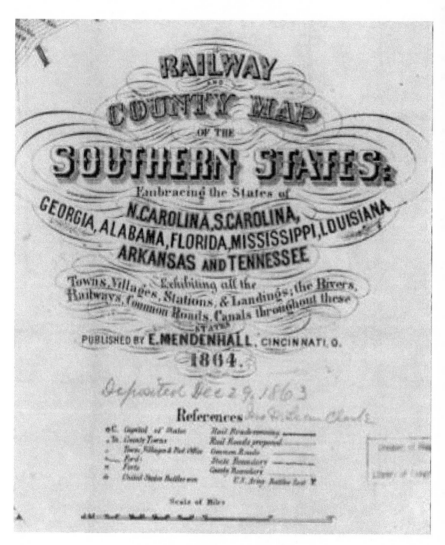

Mississippi Department of Archives and History

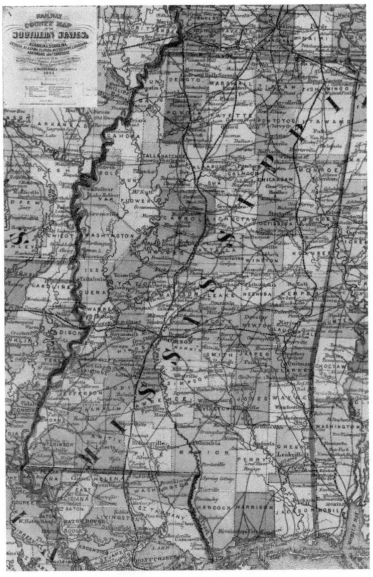

Mississippi Department of Archives and History

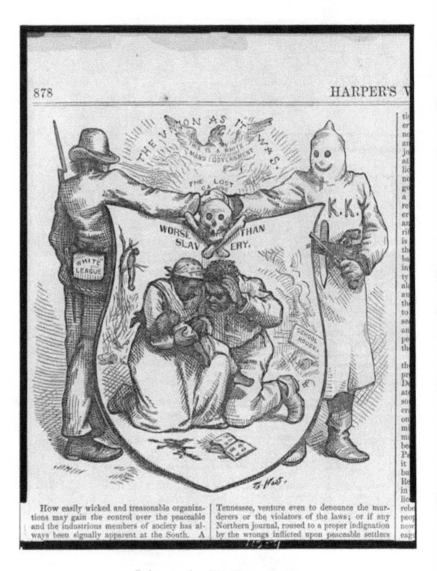

Early poster about Klan, Harpers Weekly

Library of Congress Photographic Collection

Mississippi Historical Society.

On October 29, 1875, there was a big torchlight procession at Carrollton. The whites of Carrollton got the Winona club over to help them. After the parade and the usual speaking the courthouse was discovered in flames. It is said that the Republican postmaster set fire to it in order to charge it to the Democrats. In fact, he was discovered running from the burning building, was chased and, in getting over a fence, broke his leg. He died a few days later from the injury.

Died of a broken leg???

A Mississippi delegate cast the single deciding vote to give the 1876, tied presidential election to Rutherford B. Hayes (R). The deal was made in the back room of the all black Wormely Hotel in Washington, DC with the agreement that the all federal troops would be removed from Mississippi and that the North would never again interfere in Mississippi affairs. Tilden was defeated but it was worth it to the South. Now the blacks had no protection at the polls or anywhere else. Hayes took office in 1877 and removed all troops. This act was termed The Compromise of 1877. The deal held true until the Kennedy Administration.

Photo of the Carrollton Conservative Office today taken by Rick Ward

THE YELLOW FEVER SCOURGE.

THE DISEASE AT GRENADA, MISS.—THE PEOPLE FLYING IN A PANIC—DEATHS IN NEW-ORLEANS.

Special Dispatch to the New-York Times.

MEMPHIS, Tenn., Aug. 11.—Telegrams received from Grenada, Miss,, confirm the sudden appearance of yellow fever, or some equally fearful malady in epidemic form, at that place. The Mayor of Grenada has telegraphed to the Memphis health authorities for disinfectants, yellow fever nurses, and other aid. The Howard Association is organizing a corps of nurses, disinfectants have been sent, and Dr. Brown, of the Memphis Board of Health, has gone down to examine the character of the disease. Grenada is about 80 miles south of Memphis, and is now said to be crowded with refugees from New-Orleans, by whom it is thought the disease was brought to that place.

Later.—News has just been received that seven deaths occurred at Grenada to-day, and that 15 or 20 new cases were reported. A special train has just left Memphis for Grenada with a corps of nurses, in charge of Gen. W. J. Smith and Col. Butler P. Anderson, of our Howard Association. Reports come in from various sources that the citizens of Grenada are in a state of great panic, leaving the town and taking up their abode in the woods and anywhere they can find shelter.

Superintendent Burke, of the Mississippi and Tennessee Railway, has issued orders stopping all trains coming into Memphis, and the sanitary officials are taking every precaution against any one coming into the city clandestinely. The people here are almost on the eve of a panic.

Dr. Brown, who was sent to Grenada by the Board of Health to-day, telegraphs to Dr. Saunders, President of the Memphis Board of Health, at 9:45 to-night, as follows: "Yellow fever and no mistake. Fifty cases down, with five deaths to-day."

NEW-ORLEANS, Aug. 11.—Twenty-two new cases of yellow fever and 14 deaths were reported by the Health Board to-day. At Port Eads, to date, 25 cases and five deaths are reported.

ST. LOUIS, Aug. 11.—In view of the fact of no abatement of the yellow fever in New-Orleans, the Health Officers of this city have decided to put the quarantine hospital, situated on the river 14 miles below the city, in condition for occupation, and keep a certain degree of surveillance on the up-coming steamers and trains arriving from the infected ports below.

Rev. Father Tamey, President of the Lazarist Order and late Professor of Cape Girardeau,

The New York Times

Published: August 12, 1878
Copyright © The New York Times

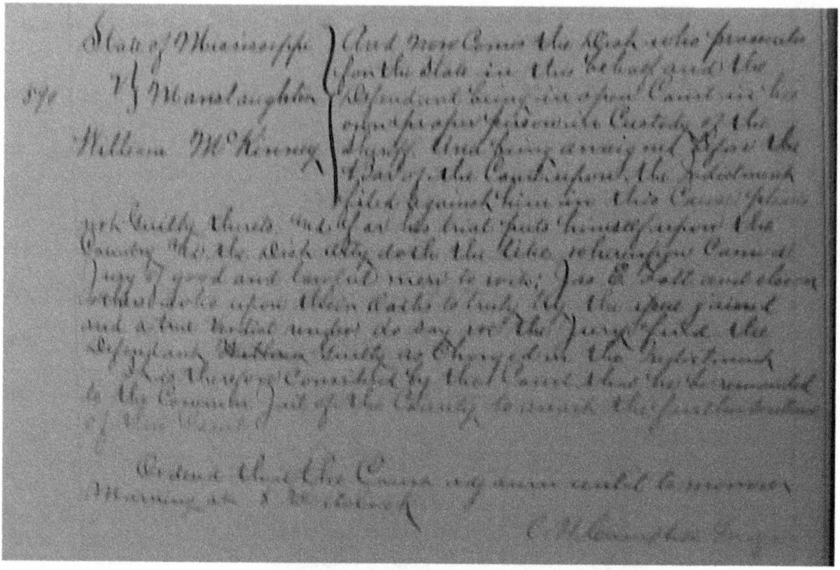

870

State of Mississippi
V } Manslaughter
William McKinney

And now comes the [illegible] who prosecutes for the State in this behalf and the Defendant being in open Court in his own proper person in the Custody of the Sheriff, And being arraigned before the Bar of the Court upon the Indictment filed against him in this Cause pleads not Guilty thereto, and [illegible] puts himself upon the Country and the [illegible] doth the like, whereupon came a Jury of good and lawful men to wit; Jas E. Fall and eleven others who upon their oaths to truly try the issue joined and a true verdict render do say we the Jury find the Defendant William Guilty as charged in the Indictment.

It is therefore Considered by the Court that he be remanded to the County Jail of the County to await the further orders of this Court.

Ordered that the Court adjourn until tomorrow Morning at 8 o'clock.

[illegible]

Copy of Will McKinney's indictment record from Carroll County Records, by Rick Ward

Lynching at a courthouse

To the Hon C. H. Campbell Judge &c

The undersigned Grand Jurors for March Term 1886 of the Circuit Court for the first Circuit and Chancery Court District of Carroll County respectfully submit the special Report of their action and deliberations. In Compliance with Your honors Charge directing special investigation of the recent tragedies in our County town We have as best we Could performed the duty required and having failed to find an Indictment against a single person participating in the deeds of violence and common we deem it but just to the Court, to ourselves, and to the Community in which we live in so far as we Can, without infringement upon our obligation of secrecy— to inform the Court of our action and to give the general result of our deliberations in this matter. We find first and acknowledge with the deepest regret the fact to be that on the night of the 18th day of February A.D. 1886 a body of armed men masked Came to the town of Carrollton took Charge of J. T. Hamilton the Sheriff forced from him the keys to the Jail and took therefrom one Will McKinney a Colored boy about 19 years old, Carried him to the Court Yard and hung and shot him to death. This boy Will was was he who at the last October term of this Court was indicted for Manslaughter in the killing of One Charlie Broadaway a white boy about the same age, was Convicted at the same term for the full offense Charged and there being no Contractor for the County, was serving out the term of twelve months imprisonment in the County Jail, the punishment fixed by the Court for his Offense. By such Conduct the Officers of the law who work faithfully for its enforcement and execution are made to feel that through its forms they Contribute more or less to the Cruel and heartless destruction of

Carroll County Grand Jury Report on Will McKinney's lynching, photo by Rick Ward

AN EPIDEMIC OF LYNCHING.

THE RESULT OF EXECUTIVE CLEMENCY TO MURDERERS.

NEW-ORLEANS, Feb. 20.—From a gentleman just arrived from Central Mississippi it is learned that some days ago an attempt was made at Carrollton, Miss., to assassinate a man named William Liddell by shooting at him. Mr. Liddell was dangerously wounded, and subsequently a negro was arrested charged with the crime. The indignation of the citizens was very great, and last Thursday night a lynching party was organized to proceed to the jail and mete out summary punishment to the assassin. The Sheriff of the parish in which Carrollton is situated received information of what was going on, and secretly removed the prisoner to a place of safety. The party arrived at the jail, and when they found that the object of their vengeance had escaped they seized a negro boy who had been committed to jail for having killed a white boy, but who had made out a good case of self-defense, and took him out of prison. They placed the rope intended for the negro man around the boy's neck, and without further ado hanged him to the limb of a tree.

The greatest indignation prevailed among the law-abiding citizens of Carrollton at the outrage, as the boy was not considered to have deserved such punishment. It is said that Judge Campbell, who committed the negro boy, remarked that the prisoner had made out a good case of self-defense, and had the victim been a negro and the accused a white boy he would have been instantly acquitted by a jury without leaving their seats. This is the fourth lynching heard from in Mississppi this week, and there was one across the line in Louisiana. A dozen have taken place since New Year's. This epidemic of lawlessness is chargeable to the action of Gov. Lowry in respiting all the convicted white murderers in the State that have come into his hands. The well disposed people say they are compelled to do their own hanging for the good of society, while the irrepressible gangs of rough riders hang at random for practice.

The New York Times

Published: February 21, 1886
Copyright © The New York Times

James Monroe Liddell Jr. Circa 1890

Liddell Home in Carrollton today (photo by Rick Ward)

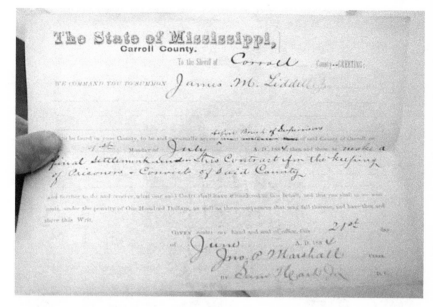

Photo provided by Susie James

"The Reason why the colored American is not in the World's Columbian Exposition,"

1893

The Convict Lease System and Lynch Law are twin infamies which flourish hand in hand in many of the United States. They are the two great outgrowths and results of the class legislation under which our people suffer to-day. Alabama, Arkansas, Florida, Georgia, Kentucky, Louisiana, Mississippi, Nebraska, North Carolina, South Carolina, Tennessee and Washington claim to be too poor to maintain state convicts within prison walls. Hence the convicts are leased out to work for railway contractors, mining companies and those who farm large plantations. These companies assume charge of the convicts, work them as cheap labor and pay the states a handsome revenue for their labor. Nine tenths of these convicts are Negroes.

http://www.historyisaweapon.com/defcon1/fredouconlea.htmlhttp://www.historyisaweapon.com/defcon1/fredouconlea.html

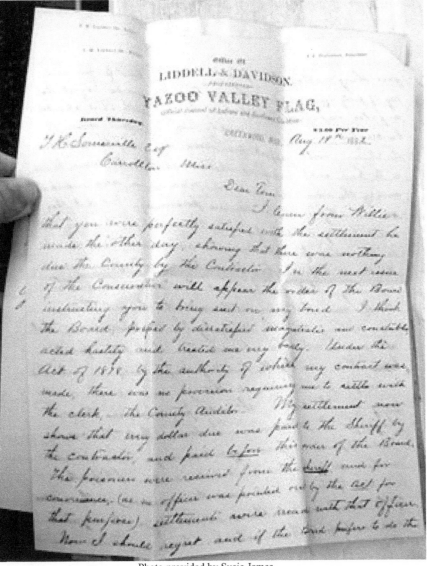

Photo provided by Susie James

Mayor's Office today photo taken 2009 by Rick Ward

Merrill's Store (coffin/furniture store) now John S. McCain Museum
Photo taken by Rick Ward 2009

Carrollton Episcopal Church

Carrollton Presbyterian Church

Carrollton Methodist Church

Carrollton Baptist Church

Pythagoras Masonic Lodge

Courthouse photo taken 2009 by Rick Ward

Courthouse Entrance   First level of stairs   Top level of stairs

What it must have looked like
Library of Congress Photograph Collection

1880 Census Record, Leflore County (Greenwood), family of Houston Whitworth

Inside the courtroom facing west

Notice the front row was added since then and the rest pushed back against the wall. At the time of the shooting there was space behind the back row to walk behind (and take cover). Also, note the elevation.

Inside the courtroom facing northeast

Inside the courtroom facing northwest

Inside the courtroom facing southwest

Inside the courtroom facing south

TERRIBLE TRAGEDY.

Ten Negroes Shot to Death and Three Fatally Wounded,

In the Courthouse at Carrollton, Miss

The Meagre Details Gathered from Different Points.

JACKSON.

JACKSON, Miss., March 17.—[Special.]—About a month ago James M. Liddell, Jr., a prominent young lawyer of Carroll county, was shot and wounded by three negroes. The trial was set for to-day. Representative Davis, of Holmes county, received a telegram yesterday stating that the trial was set for to-day, and to come at once. A riot to-day is supposed to have grown out of this trial. Nothing further is known here at this hour.

GRENADA.

GRENADA, Miss., March 17.—[Special.]—News of a terrible tragedy enacted at Carrollton, an interior town twenty-four miles southwest of Grenada, was received here this evening. Fifty men rode into the town, repaired to the courthouse, where thirteen negroes were awaiting for a trial to commence, when the white men walked in and shot ten of them dead and mortally wounded the other three. It grew out of an attempted assassination of Jas. Liddell, a prominent citizen, who was shot and seriously wounded by three negroes several weeks since.

WINONA.

WINONA, Miss., March 17.—[Special.]—At Carrollton to-day a fearful tragedy occurred, in which ten negroes were killed and three wounded.

Some weeks ago two negroes attempted to assassinate J. M. Liddell, Jr., inflicting some painful but not serious wounds. The negroes engaged in this dastardly effort are known to be the most defiant and lawless in the county, and since their attempt on Liddell's life have been more open and defiant than ever.

For some reasons not known they swore out a warrant a few days ago for Liddell's arrest. It was at this trial to-day that the killing occurred.

The negroes present were mostly armed. About 1 o'clock a party of armed men numbering forty or fifty rode up to the courthouse, dismounted and went in and at once commenced firing on the negroes with the above result. They then left by the same route they came. They do not live near Carrollton.

First Report

No 113 George Jackson } Ordered that George Jackson be allowed the sum of ($6.00) Six Dollars for digging graves for 6 Paupers. and that a warrant issued all the members of the Board voting for same. See Code of 1880 Section 626 & 627

No 114 Tandy H.C. Oury. Coroner } Ordered that Tandy H.C. Oury Coroner be allowed the sum of ($10.00) Ten Dollars for attending to burial of 10 Colored men (Paupers). 2 days and 1 night services. and that a warrant issued to him for said amount all the members of the Board voting for same See Code of 1880 Section 626 & 627

A Negro burial from the Library of Congress

Crime scene sketch the appeared on the front page of the New Orleans Times Picayune
March 19, 1886

Location of Peteet Hotel   Captain Ray's Store

Approximate Location of Shooting based on newspaper accounts

Photo of Town of Carrollton 2009 taken by Rick Ward

Governor Robert Lowry
Mississippi Department of Archives and History

Mississippi Governor's Mansion
Photo from Library of Congress Photographic Collection

It affords food for reflection at this day to look over the names of those engaged in the business of constitution making, and the counties they claimed to represent twenty-two years ago. Happily for the State and its people, nine-tenths of the vultures are gone, never again to return to the people they plundered and oppressed in the hour of their direst misery. Many have gone down to dishonored graves, others have sought new fields of plunder, and it is safe to say not half a dozen of the gang of white free-booters who were engaged in the business of statesman-ship in 1868, are to be found within the borders of Missis-sippi to-day. The few negro members of the "Black and Tan Convention," who still survive, have returned to their original vocations, and are to-day competing with the bar-bers, boot-blacks, hack-drivers, blacksmiths, waiters and fiddlers, who never abandoned their business to play the role of statesmen. Such an upheaval of society, such a disturbance of governmental affairs, as could again bring back to power such a brood of ignorance and villiany would bankrupt the most fertile imagination ever vouch-safed to man to conceive.

A History of Mississippi by former Governor Robert Lowry

OLD CAPITOL BUILDING JACKSON, MISSISSIPPI

Mississippi Department of Archives and History

TEN NEGROES MURDERED

SHOT DOWN IN COLD BLOOD IN A COURT OF JUSTICE.

A TRAGEDY WHICH GREW OUT OF A SHOOT-ING AFFRAY—WHITE MEN FULLY ARMED INVADE THE COURT HOUSE.

NEW-ORLEANS, March 17.—Information is received to-night of a tragedy in the Court House at Carrollton, Miss. It is impossible, owing to the isolated position of the town, to give full particulars, but the following facts are gleaned from different points within telegraphic reach: About a month ago James M. Liddell, Jr., a young lawyer of Carroll County, was shot and wounded by three negroes in ambush. The wounds were painful but not serious. Liddell suffered only temporary inconvenience. The negroes were arrested but made counter charges against Liddell, and both cases had been fixed for trial to-day. At the opening of the court this morning the negroes were on hand with their witnesses. About 1 o'clock a party of 40 or 50 white men, armed with carbines and revolvers, rode up to the Court House, dismounted leisurely, hitched their horses and entered the court room. Few words were spoken before the party opened fire on the negroes, riddling them with bullets and shooting them down as they attempted to escape. Ten negroes were killed and three others mortally wounded. None of the negroes in the court room escaped injury. Having finished their work, the party withdrew, remounted their horses, and left the town by the same road they came in on. Those at the Court House who witnessed the affair say they do not know the attacking party, and all allege that none of the men live near Carrollton. Carrollton, where this tragedy occurred is the capital town of Carroll County, and is in the interior far from any railroad or telegraph line, but on the line of the proposed road from Greenville to connect with the Georgia Pacific. It is 24 miles south of Grensda and about 8 miles west of Winona. The Illinois Central runs across the southeastern portion of the county about 20 miles away. The population of the county is about evenly divided between white and colored people. The county takes good care of her schools and churches and the people have been regarded as exceptionally law-abiding. In fact, it is in these portions of the State that have heretofore borne good repute, where the informal taking of human life has been most noticeable in the past few months. The people there charge it to the immeasurable leniency of Gov. Lowry in commuting death sentences. Some very important convictions of both white and black murderers have taken place in the past few years, but in nearly all, if not every instance, the Executive power has been interposed to save the murderer from the gallows. The people have grown tired of this action, and have in half a dozen cases lately done their own lynching to save the costs of court. This may not be a case in point, but doubtless is an outgrowth of this sentiment.

The New York Times

Published: March 18, 1886

Copyright © The New York Times

Manitoba Daily Free Press.

WINNIPEG, FRIDAY, MARCH 19, 1886.   NO. 221.

| | SITUATIONS VACANT. | BUSINESS CHANGES. | CANADIAN. | Lord the Hamilton, the First Lord of the Admiralty, to Salisbury's Cabinet. | RAILWAY LANDS. | publishing the resolution behind anti- and the burdens being it are towards the |

MISSISSIPPI TRAGEDY.

Further Details of the Shooting Pic-Nic at Carrolton.

The Causes which Led to the Fray and the Terrible Consequences.

ELEVEN MEN SLAUGHTERED

BLOODY WORK OF A MOB IN A SOUTHERN COURT ROOM.

NEGROES SHOT DOWN LIKE DOGS AND JUMPING FROM WINDOWS IN VAIN EFFORTS TO ESCAPE.

NEW-ORLEANS, March 18.—The horrible details of the massacre of 11 negroes at Carrollton Court House, in Mississippi, were received at midnight, and indicate a terrible and inexcusable massacre, brought about by the vindictiveness of two colored men, in whose veins flowed more Indian than negro blood, and a merciless retribution visited upon them by a hundred armed and mounted men, from the neighboring county of La Flore. where lived the young man who had been shot and wounded by the half breeds a few weeks ago.

From statements of white and colored alike, it is shown that the immediate cause of the affair was, that a short time since, a gentleman from La Flore County, while visiting Carrollton, being decidedly under the influence of drink, was hit over the head by Ed Brown, one of the deceased, with a jug of molasses, inflicting a dangerous blow on a man not able to take care of himself. At a meeting just after this between Lawyer Liddle and Edward Brown some harsh words passed. Subsequently Liddle was ambushed by the Brown party, shot and slightly wounded. The two Brown brothers and John Johnson were arrested and gave bond to appear for trial. On last Friday, the 12th inst., Edward and Charles Brown made affidavit before the Mayor, against Mr. Liddle and six others for assault with intent to kill and murder them on the 13th day of February, as stated above. The accused in the affidavit included some of the best citizens, who were not present at the time of the shooting and knew nothing whatever of the difficulty. All the parties were arrested and the case came up for trial yesterday.

On the morning of the trial, and before the court convened, Ed Brown boasted on the streets that he would carry his body guard with him in court, and, true to his word, when the case was called the Court House was filled with negroes. The case being called at 12 o'clock Messrs. Somerville and Askew, and Capt. D. N. Esten appeared as attorneys for the defendants, and were proceeding to investigate the charges against Liddle. Just at 1 o'clock about 100 well armed men rushed into town on horseback, heavily armed with Winchester rifles. At this time Ed, seeing the crowd from the window, arose from his seat, drew his pistol, and began firing on Mr. Liddle. That caused great consternation and excitement and the firing became promiscuous.

The room was at once completely enveloped in smoke. The crowd, consisting of 100 armed men, with every conceivable kind of firearms, double-barrel breech-loading shot guns, Winchester rifles, pistols of all calibres, including the long horse pistols, with their immense balls, had ridden into town at the same moment from different directions. Dismounting, they proceeded to surround the Court House, placing themselves in between the fence and the Court House to prevent any escape, and as the Browns tried to escape a portion of the crowd which had been stationed in the hall opposite the Court House rushed up the steps and filed down the right aisle, which is on the east side, and then fired on the southwest corner where the negroes were.

The negroes nearest this army were innocent men who fell a prey, falling four or five on top of each other. The Browns were reached and went down in the twinkling of an eye before the volley of musketry in the hands of the determined men. There was a general stampede of those who would escape the missiles of the crowd, thinking to reach the window, 30 feet high, and jump to the ground; but the crowd around the Court House all being strangers, supposed each man trying to escape one of the Browns. One man, Amos Mathews, who plunged through the eastern window nearest the jury room, when an equal distance in and out, had the whole left side of his head blown off by one or more loads of buckshot or a Winchester rifle. He fell with his breast on the window sill, dead, and his brains streaming to the ground 30 or 40 feet below, where it remained to-day. His wound was found to be as long as an ordinary man's arm, and the weight of blood striking the ground was heard across the street. It fell with such force, and in such quantity, quite two gallons, that it spattered two or three feet upon the Court House wall.

Peyton Hemingway, a confederate in the plot and one of the leading backers of the Browns, jumped from the second story of the Court House, and running toward Mrs. Aldure, had 25 or 40 shots fired at him, but only received one slight wound and escaped. One young negro jumped from the second story jury room, striking the ground without injury and ran away with several guns turned on him, only one shot striking him anywhere, and that in half of his shoe sole. Balls were lodged in the walls, ceiling, doors, and windowsash, piercing the glass and mutilating the benches.

The armed forces retreated down stairs, heard two remaining shots, and hurried back to find that Capt. D. N. Estes, who was addressing the court when the firing began was trying to assist several old, faithful negro friends in their last hours, and that Ed Brown, who was supposed to have been killed, was resting on his elbows, not having strength to rise further, and had aimed two deadly shots at Capt. Estes, who was unhurt, no doubt owing to the feeble and dying condition of the half breed leader, who in his last extremity had this bitterness in his heart. These shots brought back those who were slipping away, but they found their work incomplete, and turned a whole volley into the body of Ed. Brown, riddling him from head to foot. One of these balls, evidently from a Winchester rifle, passed through three seats of heart pine, 1½ inches in thickness. The Browns received not less than 10 shots each.

A number of negroes jumped from the second story of the Court House and escaped without a bruise from jumping, and were unhurt from the flying missiles.

In ten minutes all this occurred, and those who rode by the city limits into town returned by the same route in twenty minutes. They were not citizens of Carroll County, for there were three good old negroes killed whom all the white people of that county respected and would have protected. But these strangers, friends of the parties on trial, coming from a distance and supposed to be swampers, knew not who the man was who attempted to jump from the window, unless it was one of the Browns, or a friend who had gone there armed to shield and protect them, and hence they became a prey to the indiscriminating shots.

The following is a list of the killed:

Andrew Robertson, Charles Brown, E. Brown, Joe Lang, John Money, Simon Kane, Jim Harris, Amos Matthews, Scott Moore, French Hughes, Coley Little, Jim Johnson. The following is a list of the wounded: Will Dodd, Jim Keys, Christian Preacher, Jim Rows, Jake Kane, very seriously; Bill Ewing, Charles Price, Henry Cole, Coley Thompson, badly shot and reported dead.

No inquest was held, as the Coroner recently held one in a case of a violent death, and the county would not pay for it on the ground that the manner of death was known to everybody. Carrollton is a small interior town, with a dozen or more merchants and about 800 people, and the old home of United States Senator George and State Treasurer Hemingway, of Mississippi.

The New York Times
Published: March 19, 1886
Copyright © The New York Times

Times=Democrat.

THE WEEKLY TIMES-DEMOCRAT has more than four times the circulation of any weekly issue of any secular newspaper published in New Orleans. The postoffice statistics show that the Daily and Weekly TIMES-DEMOCRAT pay 47 per cent of all the postage paid by newspapers and periodicals of every description at the New Orleans Postoffice.

Democrat and New Orleans Times: Consolidated December 4, 1881.

W ORLEANS, THURSDAY, MARCH 18, 1886   PRICE, FIVE CENTS.

WASHINGTON.

CHANCES FOR THE MEXICAN AND HAWAIIAN TREATIES.

Report on the Alleged Calcasieu Timber Depredations—the Tehuantepec Ship Railway Bill—The Telephone Investigation.

The Mexican and Hawaiian Treaties.

WASHINGTON, March 17.—The Mexican treaty and the Hawaiian treaty were both referred at the beginning of the session to the same sub-committee of the House ways and means committee, composed of Messrs. Mills, Hiscock and Mayberry. In the one case resolution is asked in order that the treaty may be made operative. In the other the demand is that the treaty be repealed...

A FRIGHTFUL TRAGEDY.

THIRTEEN NEGROES SHOT DOWN AT CARROLLTON, MISS.

A Mob Gallop Into Town, Surround the Courthouse and Shoot the Occupants—Only a Few Escape Uninjured.

WINONA, March 17.—At a magistrate's trial in the Courthouse at Carrollton, held to-day before Mayor Elam, in connection with the trouble recently between a few negroes and J. M. Liddell, Jr., there were about twenty colored men present...

WEATHER PROBABILITIES.

For the Gulf States (Shreveport, La., Fort Smith, Ark., Little Rock, Ark., Galveston, Tex., and Indianola, Tex.): Southerly winds, warmer, fair weather, except light rains on the coast.

Times-Democrat.

THE WEEKLY TIMES-DEMOCRAT…

A Democrat and New Orleans Times; Consolidated December 4, 1881.

NEW ORLEANS, FRIDAY, MARCH 19, 1886.   **PRICE, FIVE CENTS.**

ew Prices

SIDER THEM

WITH CARE AND

the Goods

ULAR RESORT

CONICAL PURCHASERS,

ES' BUTTON BOOTS

At $1 75 Per Pair

INFANTS'

HEEL BUTTON SHOES

FROM $1 75 TO 40 CENTS.

ITS' NEAT GAITERS,

LACE BOOTS,

AND BUTTON SHOES,

$1 to 1 75 Per Pair.

LED BUTTON BOOTS

New, hand side, $1. $1 25.

Ges' Fine Kid Boots

$3 TO $4 50 PER PAIR.

ADIES' SHOES, FINE

Hand Button Boots

$5.00 PER PAIR.

AT THE GREAT

"ED STAR"

CARROLLTON TRAGEDY.

CONNECTED WITH AN AWFUL END OF THE AFFAIR

[column text largely illegible]

WASHINGTON.

[column text largely illegible]

To the Honl C. H. Campbell Judge &c

The undersigned Grand Jurors for March Term 1886 of the Circuit Court for the first Circuit and Chancery Court District of Corrall County respectfully submit the special Report of their action and deliberations. In Compliance with your honors Charge directing special investigation of the recent tragedies in our County town We have as best we Could performed the duty required and having failed to find an Indictment against a single person participating in the deeds of violence and terror we deem it but just to the Court, to ourselves, and to the Community in which we live in so far as we Can without infringement upon our obligation of secrecy- to inform the Court of our action and to give the general result of our deliberations in this matter. We find first and acknowledge with the deepest regret the fact to be that on the night of the 18th day of February A D 1886 a body of armed men masked came to the Town of Carrollton took Charge of J.J Hamilton the Sheriff forced from him the Keys to the Jail and took therefrom one Will McKinney a Colored boy about 19 years old, Carried him to the Court Yard and hung and shot him to death. This boy Will was was he who at the last October term of this Court was indicted for Manslaughter in the killing of One Charlie Broadaway a white boy about the same age, was Convicted at the same term for the full Offense Charged and there being no Contractor for the County, was serving out the term of twelve months imprisonment in the County Jail, the punishment fixed by the Court for his Offense. By such Conduct the Officers of the law who work faithfully for its enforcement and execution are made to feel that through its forms they Contribute more or less to the Cruel and heartless destruction of humanity. And as officers of the Court charged with the duty of diligently examining into the Commission of crime, not failing to discover any of the perpetrators of the deed we feel it our duty to condemn without reservation the act of barbarous cruelty and turning vengeance upon a helpless Corpse.

We desire to report specially in reference to the most largely circulated in this Court House, that we found some evidence to get at the facts of the sad occurrence that we have examined one hundred & sixty five witnesses, and make this public report of our investigation for reasons that are not only that they are slaves but also the view of the fact that the neighborhood has assumed a national character and that the investigation has been pressed by us with all the rigor in our power, thus the result should be made known through us to the world. The jury desire to say in this connection that the facts and statements of witnesses used in this report were developed in the course of this investigation and are submitted here with a consciousness of truth, and without any regard to the views of the press or anxious world.

The evidence shows that on the evening of the 12th day of the ___ of J__ Liddell Jr. had some hot words with Ed Robson which leads Caled him a son of a bitch. Soon after the ___ of ___ and Liddell went to supper. On coming out from the Hotel, Liddell was told that several Negroes including the said Ed & Charley Brown were on the street between ___ & Mrs. ___ Crews' ___ and abusing him. And as he was passing there the street by these party of Negroes he stopped near Charley Brown and took hold of his shirt and raised it and asked what does all this mean. He then asked Ed Brown what are you doing here. Brown replied it is none of your God damn business. Whereupon Liddell slapped him in the face and was immediately fired on by the two Browns and others wounding him in the ___ thigh.

It is the ___ of this body that the Browns after the first hot word were off and armed themselves and came back to this place for the purpose of assassination. Liddell after being wounded by ___ of his assailants Liddell returned the fire slightly wounding Ed & Charley Brown. Two days after this difficulty Ed & Charles Brown ___ away and before the jury ___ of Carrollton John Johnson having fled the country and none of the others who first ___ being ___ and ___ examination entered into bond for their appearance at this ___ of the Court. ___ stood ___ until he ___ ill through ___ sufficiently from his wounds returned to his home in ___ and on the 10th of March. On the 15th Ed & Charles Brown made affidavit against Liddell and six others charging them with assault with intent to kill and murder them. The investigation shows that none of these parties were present with Liddell at the time, but being near some of them ___ up to the difficulty. Most of these were armed

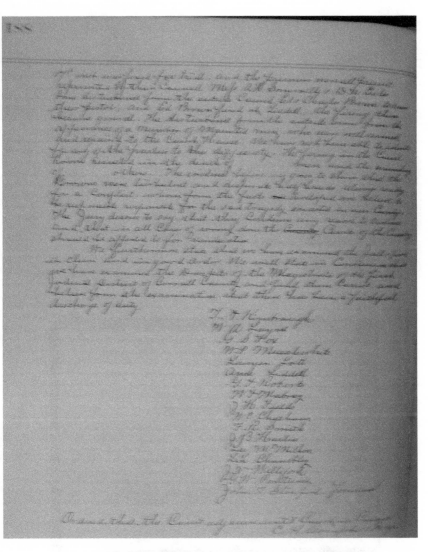

Copy of Grand Jury report taken from book in Carroll County Courthouse
Photo taken by Rick Ward

Senator James Z. George law office today (photo by Rick Ward)

Malmaison Mansion owned by Greenwood Leflore (Library of Congress Photo)

Hiram Rhodes Revels
First Black US Senator
Chaplain in the Union Army

Blanche Kelso Bruce
Former Slave
First Black US Senator to
serve a full term in the senate.

Chose not to seek office at the end
of his term due to the state of the
white supremacy state of affairs.

Adelbert Ames
Union Civil War General
Appointed Mississippi Governor
Elected Mississippi Governor

Was said to have been brought up
on trumped up charges by the
Mississippi Legislature and
resigned.

James Z. George
United States Senator

Credited as primary author of the
1890 Constitution
It totally disenfranchised blacks.
When Governor Ames begged the
President for help when blacks
were being killed at the polls, he told
the US Attorney General there were
no problems in Mississippi.

John Henninger Reagan
US Senator from Texas

Refused to allow any bills or
resolutions related to the Carrollton
tragedy on the floor of congress.

SUBJECT FILE

49TH CONGRESS,	HOUSE OF REPRESENTATIVES.	MIS. DOC.
1st Session.		No. 203.

ALLEGED HOMICIDES, CARROLLTON, MISS.

APRIL 5, 1886.—Referred to the Committee on Rules and ordered to be printed.

Mr. O'HARA submitted the following

RESOLUTION:

Whereas it is a matter of public information that on the 18th of March, 1886, in the town of Carrollton, the county seat of Carroll County, Mississippi, a lawless band of persons rode to the court-house and then and there indiscriminately murdered, by shooting, a number of peaceful citizens of the United States; and

Whereas it is alleged that the governor of said State of Mississippi has absolutely refused to take effective measures to bring to justice said murderers; and

Whereas it is alleged that the grand jury in and for said county of Carroll has neglected to act in such manner as would bring said murderers before the courts to answer for their crimes; and

Whereas the Constitution of the United States guarantees to each and every one of its citizens full and adequate protection of his life and the enjoyment of his property: Therefore be it

Resolved, That a committee of five members be appointed by the Speaker to investigate the facts connected with said alleged murders, and to report, by bill or otherwise, such measure as will check or prevent in future the wanton and barbarous destruction of human life.

Resolved, That said committee, when appointed, shall have power to subpœna witnesses, administer oaths, and do all other acts necessary to a full investigation of the subject-matter; that said committee may appoint a subcommittee to visit the State of Mississippi to take testimony and do such other acts as may be necessary in the premises; and that the expenses of the committee shall be paid from the contingent fund of the House, not to exceed —— dollars.

O

THE CARROLLTON MASSACRE.

COLORED CITIZENS OF PHILADELPHIA DE-NOUNCE THE OUTRAGE.

PHILADELPHIA, May 17.—Jenny Lind never packed Musical Fund Hall 30 years ago with a more enthusiastic audience than was gathered within its walls to-night. On the stage where the magnificent songstress stood a generation ago, when most of the black men of the country were slaves, were seated some of the best representatives of that race now freemen. Among them were Robert Purvis, Congressman Robert Smalls, of South Carolina; Editor Fortune, of the New-York *Freeman*; William Still, James E. Masten, the Rev. Theodore Gould, Josiah C. Wear, and Dr. B. T. Tanner. State Senator Bertie Adams, and Representative Boies Penrose were also present. A thousand men and women of all shades of color, from the intensely black man to the handsome-faced octoroon, with a plentiful sprinkling of white men and women, were seated. It was a meeting called by the citizens of Philadelphia under the auspices of the Africo-American League to express their indignation at the Carrollton, Miss., massacre, in March last, and other outrages against the colored people of the South. Resolutions were adopted amid great enthusiasm, denouncing the massacre in the Court House at Carrollton, Miss., of 13 colored men in March last, and the promiscuous lynching of colored men in the South and charging the Southern State Governments with being parties to the crimes.

When Robert Purvis stepped to the desk on the platform he was received with wild cheers, and it was some minutes before he could calm the applause and proceed. He pleaded that his friend Robert Still should be made Chairman, as he was physically unable to attend to the duties of Chairman, but the audience cheered for Purvis. In a full, rich, round voice, and with an impressive and passionate manner he said: "No matter who is selected to preside there is but one mind on this subject. The only wonder to me is that we have not risen up spontaneously at this damnable outrage. My blood boils when I see the gingerly, mealy-mouthed manner in which the press of my country has handled the subject. I am almost compelled to believe that we are looked upon as aliens. We are native Americans. I read an article recently relative to the colonization society headed "Africa for the Africans." There is not a single African in the United States. Simultaneously with the landing of the Pilgrim Fathers in 1620 came a slave ship from Africa into the Virginia colonies. Congress stopped the miserable traffic in 1808. The Rev. Byron Sunderland, of Washington, recently delivered an address on colonization in a church in this city. He says the colored men are waiting and watching to be wafted to Liberia. This clerical wolf who has stolen the livery of heaven to serve the devil in tells a lie. I wonder at the man's audacity and impudence. He would not even dare attempt to send the slime of Europe, the men who are making the mobs and disturbing the peace, back to their country, and yet he thinks the colored man should be sent back to Africa. They do not want to go. This is the land of our birth. Here we will live and here we will die.

Why does he wish to banish the men who are at all times for the best interests of our country? He declares that 500,000 of our people are looking to be sent to Liberia. That is simply lying by the wholesale. Welsh Dulles, the Treasurer of this Colonization Society, catches the epidemic of lies and repeats the assertion. We are fixtures here, and, while we do not object, in the light of individual enterprise, to allow a man to go anywhere he pleases, why is it that these superannuated fossils and men without pulpits go roaming around the country, getting funds for 'Africa for the Africans?' It is a stupendous fraud and an outrage. It is hatred of our race. None have been more loyal and peaceable than the colored race. The Colonization Society has no desire to do good for the African's descendants. The first clause in its charter says, 'To Liberia or anywhere else.' Yes. We may go to ——, but we are not going. The fathers of the white race drove the red man out and forced the black man in. Our claim to remain here comes from the blood and sweat which has enriched the soil. Let any set of men get up an association to send back the Irish, the German, or the Italian. Don't you think there would be indignation meetings from all classes of foreigners?"

Speeches were also made by Congressman Smalls, of South Carolina; T. Thomas Fortune, of New-York, and others, and letters of regret and sympathy from Gov. Pattison and other prominent men were read. The resolutions were adopted with great enthusiasm.

The New York Times
Published: May 18, 1886
Copyright © The New York Times

NEW-YORK, FRIDAY, MARCH 26, 1886.

employment for the 800 boys than the making and washing of shirts.

A BLIGHT TO CIVILIZATION.

COLORED PEOPLE IN MISSISSIPPI PARALYZED WITH FEAR—EFFECT OF THE CARROLLTON MASSACRE.

WASHINGTON, March 25 (*Special*). –Letters continue to be received here, giving further details of the recent slaughter of colored men while attending court in Carrollton, Miss. The latest report places the number of killed and those who have died from wounds at seventeen. The attention of the President has been directed to the matter by ex-Senator Bruce and ex-Congressman Lynch. They have received many letters from the scene of the slaughter which represent that many colored people, paralyzed by fear at the outrage, fled to the woods and that among these were a number who were wounded. These letters state that it is not known how many had died of their wounds, but the number is much larger than was at first reported. The slaughter was committed near the home of Senator George, and his son is said to have been one of the "Regulators."

Mr. Bruce and Mr. Lynch in their interview with the

STRIKERS ATTACK

A RIOT ON THE MISSOU

FIVE HUNDRED YARDMEN STRIKE.

ST. LOUIS ISOLATED AT LAST—MA .KNIGHTS OF LABOR—TROUBLE EX

[BY TELEGRAPH TO THE TR

ST. LOUIS, March 25.—The M succeeded in sending out another frei ing. It was manned by 125 policeme sistance of 100 more in the yards the men and boys anxious to interfere. T lowed two miles by the mob, the cha until it had almost reached The police had to threate with revolvers to keep it off. ceeded without interruption to Pacific

THE LATE MASSACRE.

President Cleveland Says It Is a Blight Upon Our Civilization.

WASHINGTON, March 25.—Ex-Senator B. K. Bruce and ex-Congressman John R. Lynch, of Mississippi, called on the president and directed his attention to the massacre of thirteen negroes at Carrollton, Miss., on the 7th inst. They represented that they had received numbers of letters from colored people in that section requesting that the matter be laid before the president for such action as he may deem proper to take. Messrs. Bruce and Lynch stated that the colored people were almost paralyzed with fear by the outrage and that a number who had been wounded had fled to the woods, and it was unknown how many were killed and had died of their wounds. The attention of the president was directed to the fact that the governor of Mississippi had taken no official action in the premises and was represented as having intimated that no action could be taken, as it would trench upon the authority of the county in the premises.

The president listened with attention to the recitals of Messrs. Bruce and Lynch and expressed himself in decided terms against such affairs as a blight to our civilization. He expressed himself as surprised that the state authorities had taken no steps to have the outrage investigated and the guilty parties brought to justice. He intimated that the matter had been called to his attention by the attorney general. The interview lasted upwards of an hour, and Messrs. Lynch and Bruce expressed themselves as much pleased at the cordial manner of their reception, the earnestness of the president, and the interest he took in having the matter rightly investigated.

TWO WOMEN LYNCHED BY MISSISSIPPI MOB

Mother, Son, and Daughter Put to Death.

The Three Victims, Negroes, Were Accused of the Murder of a White Man and His Wife—One Confessed.

CARROLLTON, Miss., Aug. 1.—The murder of Mr. and Mrs. Taliferro, at their home here on the night of July 30, culminated to-night in the lynching of Betsie McCray, her son Belford McCray, and her daughter Ida McCray, all negroes.

The lynching mob was composed of about 500 white citizens of Carroll County, who marched to the jail in order, demanded the keys from Jailer Duke, proceeded to the cells of the unfortunate negroes, bound them by the necks and hands, and carried them to the corporate limits of the town, where they hanged them to a tree by the road and riddled their bodies with bullets,

Ida McCray confessed to the knowledge of the murder, and stated that her mother Betsie, and brother, Belford, helped commit the murder. She further implicated three other negroes, who will probably meet a like fate. Betsie McCray refused to make any statement. The McCrays had been remanded to jail by the Coroner's jury.

Early this morning the streets were crowded with citizens of the county, who were in town to hear the investigation of the Taliaferro killing. The Sheriff of Leflore County had come on the morning train and brought with him Bill Davis and Belford McCray, who were suspected of having murdered Mr. and Mrs. Taliaferro. They were lodged in jail with the other suspects.

At the suggestion of Judge W. F. Stevens, a committee, consisting of District Attorney W. S. Hill, Dr. Samuel L. Hart, Watt Turner, L. E. Southworth, and A. H. George, went to the jail to examine witnesses and investigate the killing and report to the citizens in the Court House, before the jury of inquest should proceed with its work. This they were doing in a quiet and successful manner, when it was learned that about seventy-five men, growing impatient at the delay, were ready to come to the jail and take the suspects and hang them.

The committee immediately went to the Court House and called the people together. They seemed satisfied when assured that the negroes would not be spirited away and that the final investigations would be held in public in the Court House. They added to the committee four of Carrollton's best citizens, who were neighbors of Mr. and Mrs. Taliaferro. . . . .

The committee immediately went to the Court House and called the people together. They seemed satisfied when assured that the negroes would not be spirited away and that the final investigations would be held in public in the Court House. They added to the committee four of Carrollton's best citizens, who were neighbors of Mr. and Mrs. Taliaferro.

The committee then proceeded to the jail to complete its work. The mob continued impatient and restless. In the meantime Gov. Longino had telephoned Judge Stevens that he would leave Jackson for Carrollton on the 2 o'clock train and come over from Winona on a special. The committee being apprised of this, did their best to kill time so that the Governor might arrive and use his influence. However, they deemed it necessary at about 4 o'clock to make another report to the people.

Mr. Hill reported that the committee had concluded after a faithful and thorough examination that while Belford and Betsie McCray knew that the Taliaferros were to be killed and had absented themselves from home so that they might prove an alibi, the ones who had actually committed the crime had not yet been caught, but that they believed that these would finally divulge the whole plot. Mr. Hill left it to the crowd as to whether the committee should proceed with the investigation or drop it, and have the jury of inquest proceed. The crowd was unanimous in instructing the committee to proceed with the investigation at the jail. However, as the crowd was dispersing from the Court House they met about fifty men, armed with shotguns and rifles, who had not been in the Court House to hear the last report.

These men proceeded to the jail, where the Deputy Sheriff promptly opened the door. Three men went up stairs, and brought out Belford, Betsie and Ida Mc-Cray. Judge Stevens, Messrs. Hill and George and other citizens begged and pleaded with them, as did Lynn Taliferro, the son of the murdered couple, not to kill these negroes, as they would thereby thwart the efforts of justice. It was to no purpose; the mob was determined to hang the prisoners. They took the three negroes under the hill, about a quarter of a mile from town, and hanged them. They then fired at least 500 shots into their bodies.

The Governor arrived just as the mob was returning. At the Court House he addressed a large crowd. No doubt if he could have reached there in time he would have prevented the lynching. The Governor returned on the evening train.

Jim Lane was brought in just as the mob was dispersing. It is not known what further work the mob will do, but there are many rumors afloat. Some say that three or four more negroes, living in the Taliaferro neighborhood will be lynched tonight, and it is feared by some that one white man in that neighborhood may meet the same fate.

The New York Times

Published: August 2, 1901
Copyright © The New York Times

FINDS ANOTHER VICTIM.

Will Price, a Negro, Is Hanged and Shot by the Mob at Carrollton, Miss,

New Orleans, Aug. 5. — The Picayune's Carrollton (Miss.) special says: Your correspondent has just learned that the armed mob which has been in the Taliaferro neighborhood for two days looking for Sallie Layton and others some time during Saturday night killed Will Price, the negro who worked for Mr. Taliaferro and lived within 200 yards of his residence. He was found dead in the road on Mr. Duke's place Sunday morning some distance from any trees or anything to which to hang anyone, with a rope around his neck and mutilated by gunshots. Esquire John Irving held an inquest over the body. The verdict was: "Came to his death by the hands of unknown persons." It is said that he went to the Taliaferro residence on Saturday night and told Jack Taliaferro all about the murder, and said that the plan was to kill both the old people and Jack, the youngest boy, while Lynn was away and shoot him when he returned. Your correspondent cannot learn the particulars of the killing of Price or whether the mob has killed anyone else.

NO MORE NEGROES LYNCHED.

Posses, However, Searching for Accomplices in Taliaferro Murder.

Carrollton. Miss., August 3.—The air has been rife with rumors of additional lynchings all day, but in each case these reports have been without foundation. A posse of men are scouring the country in an effort to apprehend several negroes suspected of complicity in the murder of Mr. and Mrs. Taliaferro on Tuesday night last, but up to 9 o'clock tonight no arrests have been made.

The only persons lynched in connection with the murder were the three McCray negroes, full details of which were sent in these dispatches last night. Sheriff Woodall stated tonight that he had released all negro witnesses, and that no further trouble was anticipated. The town is quiet tonight.

Jackson. Miss., August 2.—Governor Longino has returned from Carrollton, where the three negroes were lynched last night. The governor says the state has again been disgraced by this affair, which is all the more horrible because the lynched negroes were accused not of the assassination of Taliaferro and his wife, but simply of complicity in the crime or of guilty knowledge of the fact.

No more hangings took place in Carrollton until the legal hanging of Bob Myers 13 years later.

Old jail where McCray family was abducted
Photos taken April 2010 by Rick Ward

Inside the old jail showing cell blocks

Last Legal Hanging in Carroll County, Mississippi.
Bob Myers – 1914. Photo Courtesy of E.W. "Pete" Moore of Carrollton, MS.

Abraham Lincoln
As president, he secured money from congress to send blacks back to Africa and Haiti. Told black leaders their race suffered greatly, many of them by living among us, while others suffered from their presence. Although his plan for "colonization" was supposedly voluntary, he had General Butler count the ships in our navy and merchant ships and their capacities to see if he could send them all back at one time.

Ulysses S. Grant
He refused Governor Ames' request for troops when blacks were being killed at the polls. But the next year he said this:

"Mississippi is governed today by officials chosen through fraud and violence such as would scarcely be accredited to savages, much less to a civilized and Christian people."

Andrew Jackson

is actions against the Indians by today's
andards would probably constitute charges
r Terrorism, Genocide and Ethnic
leansing. His use of Indians to help fight
ars and then turn his back on them to take
eir land was unforgiveable.
e gave Indians an ultimatum to take the
eal or suffer the death of their entire
ations. Talked with the Indians though his
ecretary of War instead of diplomat when
egotiating the Treaty of Dancing Rabbit
reek in 1830.

Greenwood Leflore

Took land, money and other assets as pay for
selling his people out to move them to Oklahoma
while he stayed home and built a mansion on the
land. Refused to side with the south in the Civil War
and stayed in his mansion while supplying Union
Soldiers with goods to use against Mississippi
Confederate soldiers. He kept slaves after the
Emancipation Proclamation and willed them to
his family members who petitioned Congress for
reimbursement of 27 slaves given to Union Army.

Hernando Desoto Money

US House of Representatives 1875-1885
US Senator 1897-1911
James Z. George's law partner and James
K. Vardaman's first cousin. Made this
statement on floor of senate: *"If every
colored man in the south twenty-one
years of age had been graduated from the
finest university of Europe or America he
would not be fit for the obligation of
duties of American citizenship.*

James Kimble Vardaman

Mississippi Governor 1904-1908
US Senator 1913-1919
sin of Senator Hernando Desoto
ney. Made some of the most
rageous comments against blacks
de in the 20th century publically. He
 quoted in the Macon Beacon
vspaper at a July 4th celebration
ech as saying the Declaration of
ependence did not apply to *"niggers
 dogs."*

Theodore Bilbo

Mississippi Governor 1916-1920 and 1928-
1932, US Senator 1935-1947
The second most outspoken racial white
supremacist of the century from
Mississippi. Was against the Anti-lynching
bill. Revealed publically on Meet the Press
that he was a member of the Ku Klux Klan.
Didn't believe blacks should ever be
allowed to vote anywhere.

James M. Liddell with wife Mary L. Brantley Circa 1890

HISTORY OF MISSISSIPPI.   453

1877 M. H. Tuttle.   H. H. Southworth, Jas. M. Liddell.
1878 W. D. Peery.   Jas. M. Liddell, Jr., Benjamin T. Marshall.
1880 W. D. Peery.   T. H. Somerville, H. Talbert.
1882 Jas. M. Liddell.   H. C. Williamson, C. B. Turnipseed.
1884 Jas. M. Liddell.   H. C. Williamson, J. S. Johnson.
1886 Jas. R. Binford.   H. C. Williamson, L. M. Southworth.
1888 Jas. R. Binford.   T. W. Sullivan, L. M. Southworth.
1890 L. M. Southworth.   T. W. Sullivan, E. L. Conger.

Above is a listing of State Senators on the left and Representatives on the right

The "Souvenir" was a US Army, Fort McPherson, Georgia base newspaper.

The Philippine American War began on February 4, 1899. The 29th U.S. Volunteers were formed in March of 1899, and served in the Philippine American War. The Philippine American War lasted until 1902, though some fighting occurred as late as 1906. It was fought only in the Philippines, and was a much more brutal and bloody conflict than was the Spanish American War.

"SOUVENIR" 29TH Regiment United States Volunteers.
ILLUSTRATED AND PUBLISHED BY EDWARDS & SONS,
ATLANTA, GEORGIA, SEPTEMBER - 1899.

29THE REGIMENT U. S. VOLUNTEERS
The 29th Regiment was organized under the act of Congress March 2, 1899, by General Order 122, authorizing the organization July 5, 1899, at Fort McPherson, Atlanta, Ga. The original plan was to form the regiment from the following five states; Georgia, Florida, Alabama, Louisiana, and Mississippi, but such slow progress was made that it was decided to include other States, in consequence of which there were enlisting stations opened in Tennessee, the Carolinas, and as far north as Indiana and Illinois. The 2d and 3d Georgia Regiments which were mustered out last summer furnished most of the men. Two hundred and twenty-three were enlisted at Fort McPherson.

This Regiment was organized for service in the Philippine Islands. The Regiment was completed about the middle of September, and was ordered to proceed to San Francisco, Cal., where they would embark on transports for the Philippine Islands. The 29th Regiment was organized under personal directions of Colonel Edward E. Hardin. The success which awarded Colonel Hardin's efforts is an excellent proof of his skill as a soldier and a man.

OFFICERS' SCHOOL
Major David B. Case, Captain Holman G. Purinton, Captain Jas. M. Liddell, Captain Wm. F. Faulkner, 1st Lieutenant Edward H. Almand, 1st Lieutenant Robt. J. Arnold, 1st Lieutenant Lawrence L. Carson, 1st Lieutenant Jas. R. Rash, 2d Lieutenant Robt. O. Patterson, 2d Lieutenant Geo. M. Holley, 2d Lieutenant John M. Miller.

AFTER GRADUATION

COMPANY D. 29TH REG. U. S. V.
Edward H. Almand, 1st Lieut., James M. Liddell, Capt. Sergeants. Boss Reese, 1st Sergt., Algie Algie A. Brown, Wade L. Shields, Jos. B. Cooley, Q.M. Sergt., Jack Turner, Louis Kellermeyer.

A MIXED GOVERNMENT

Civil Rule Inaugurated at Manilla Today.

Manila, Aug. 7—The new municipality, which replaces the military government, will comprise thirty-eight officials, twenty being natives and eighteen Americans. The latter are at the head of a majority of departments.

Some of these departments are as follows:

Municipal board — Senor Merrera, president; Harry Baldwin, formerly United States marshal at San Francisco, and Captain Tutherly, formerly of the Twenty-sixth volunteer infantry. Eleven natives are members of the advisory board.

City attorney—Ex-Lieutenant Hausserman with three native and two American assistants.

Judges of the municipal courts—Captains MacManus, formerly of the Thirty-ninth volunteer infantry, and Liddell, formerly of the Twenty-ninth. There are also five native justices of the peace.

The Cedar Rapids Evening Gazette August 7, 1901

THE POST-STANDARD, SYRACUSE, N.Y., SATURDAY MORNING, APRIL 13, 1901.

Famous American Veterans and Soldiers Indorse Pe-ru-na

NOTHING HELPS IN SPRING LIKE PE-RU-NA

No Other Catarrh Remedy Has Ever Received Such Great Popular Indorsements.

Major Liddell Uses Peruna at Home.

Major J. M. Liddell, Major of the Fifth Immunes, recently ordered to the Philippines, and well known in Mississippi, has used Peruna in his family for years. He gives his opinion of this great catarrh remedy from several years' constant observation and personal use. He says:

"I have used Peruna for years and I know of no better medicine on the market. It is a grand tonic and should be used in every household. As a cure for catarrh I know of nothing better."—J. M. Liddell.

Game in the Philippines

"A paradise for hunters," is the way Judge Liddell descibes the country in the vicinity of his home and plantation on the southeast coast of Mindoro. One game Mindoro excels in is the tomarao, rarest of animals, and one which is found only in Mindero. This fierce animal, much like an American buffalo, is held in universal dread by every native on the island, who look on him as a far more formidable creature than the maddest of wild carabaos.

Mrs. Liddell, wife of Judge Liddell, is perhaps the only white woman who has ever seen a tamoroa. A few weeks ago one came within fifteen feet of the window of the Liddell kitchen, where she was instructing the cook, and peered in. The natives in the neighborhood took to their heels and then the tamarao walked off.

But if the tamaroa is the piece de resistance among the game of Mindoro it is not the only game to be found on the island. There are myriads of deer, wild chickens, and game birds of all sorts. There are also plenty of wild boars on the island, some of them of extraordinary size and none of them noted for their docility. Judge Liddell has one tusk fully eighteen icnhes long. This came from a monster boar, which charged the hunters repeatedly before he was shot down.

Wild carabao hunting is another pastime of the Mindoro planters and one that is not destined to sooth the nerves of weak-hearted men. These big animals are at all times dangerous, and when once wounded or angered will charge their hunters with all the ferocity of an African buffalo.

James Liddell, a son of the judge, had an experience with one of them recently that will not be forgotten in a hurry. He was hunting and shot the big fellow, knocking him off his feet. As the carabao lay still he approached him and when not a foot away the carabao leaped to his feet and charged.

There was no time for a shot, so young Liddell did the only thing open to him—grappled with the infuriated beast. Three times the animal gored him, and finally the boy made his escape. What the Filipinos in his party regarded as the miraculous feature of the incident was the fact that the carabao had permitted him to escape.
—Manila Times.

Top of page 1

PERSONAL AND CONFIDENTIAL.

Manila, February 14, 1913.

Dear Mr. President:

I am addressing this letter to you as President although
you will have left the White House by the time it reaches
you. I feel as though you would like to know some thing about

Bottom of page 14

I wish you would give my most cordial regards to Mrs. Taft
and to Miss Taft, and believe me yours always -

Most respectfully.

Governor-General.

Honorable William H. Taft.
C/o J.M. Forbes and Company,
Sears Building,
Boston, Mass -

Bottom of page 6

Judge Southworth, who between you and me is a scalawag,

Continues to page 7

He really brought no message but said that the Democrats
would maintain all their pledges and that we could expect
a clean sweep of the officials out here and that good
Democrats would be rewarded. I believe he considers himself prominently for some important position. His record
here is a little doubtful. When Judge Liddell was judge
of the Court in Manila Southworth was loaning him money
and defending nearly 3 percent of the cases which came
before him. He had an organization to obtain early information of all arrests and Filipino runners who made
people believe that they stood a better show if they got
him as their counsel than if they trusted their cases to
others. He certainly got a remarkable proportion of
acquittals, getting 44 dismissals out of 56 cases tried.
Governor Smith was so displeased with these revelations
when they were investigated in 1907 that he got Judge Liddell
to resign but later for some reason that I can't understand

J.Z. George Statute
In congress

James Z. George tomb at Evergreen Cemetery in North Carrollton

Photographs taken by Rick Ward in mid-2009

 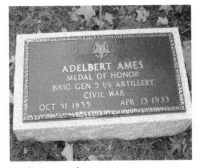

Adelbert Ames monument and grave marker

Confederate memorial/monument
Taken by Rick Ward in the summer of 2009

Marker at the birthplace of Elvis Presley

Marker for birthplace of Kermit the Frog

County memorial to their restoration of the courthouse

This is the plaque, the memorial that does not exist
for those men who lost their lives on March 17, 1886
inside the Carrollton Courtroom.

Hangman's Noose used as bell-pull in the Courthouse
at Carrollton, Mississippi.

August 25, 2000. Photo by Susie James.

Chapter 24:

The Conservative

"Freedom has its life in the hearts, the actions,
the spirit of men and so it must be daily earned
and refreshed - else like a flower cut from its life-
giving roots, it will wither and die."
-Dwight D. Eisenhower

L iddell left his father's house the next morning
on February 13, 1886, and walked over to the
Carrollton newspaper office, home of the
Carrollton Conservative, so he could see Tandy Oury.

"This old press must have come across with
your father from the old country, sir," Liddell said as
he turned the wheel on the press with his hands,
waiting on Oury to finish business with a customer.

Even a thin man could barely move between the
equipment and stacks of paper on the floor of this
small print shop just down from a similarly cluttered
hardware store. Shelves on the walls were lined with
cans of thick, dark ink almost in a paste form,
dripping on the sides of some of the canisters. A
strong chemical smell filled the air.

"My dear man, what brings you to the finest
newspaper office in this town, looking for a job aren't

you?" asked Oury as he wiped ink off his hand onto his apron before shaking hands.

Dispensing with small talk, Liddell got right to the point as he noticed Oury's office worker attempting to eavesdrop.

"Could you have your young lad assistant stand in and keep shop while you join me for a cup of fresh brew across the street in the hotel lobby...my treat?" Liddell asked, as the only customer left the shop.

"This must be of dire importance for a lawyer to pay. I guess your only saving grace is that you too are an editor, a much more notable profession, I might say," Oury said. He laughed, removed his visor, placed his spectacles in his shirt pocket then walked across the street with Liddell for a hot cup of coffee.

"Sir, if my memory serves me correctly, I believe you engaged in some sort of disagreement and hostile action some years ago with one Adam Brown, a half-breed Negro and Indian," said Liddell.

"Sir, your information is quite correct. I did indeed accost that scoundrel, who was most displeased when I once wrote of his failure to maintain a business. Back in 1872, he pulled a Colt revolver on me. I did not think such a fine weapon would fail, but his did – twice. It must have been old powder. I was able to draw and fire to defend myself. He limped away, gut shot, but was still alive," said Oury. "He was born a free man in Tennessee and moved here before the war. Although he once had pockets full of money, he used very poor judgment on many a business dealings and became a pauper. Worst thing he did was get friendly with all the blacks and low-class whites, talking them into boycotting other fine, upstanding business establishments. He was a rich man with funds earned in a blacksmith shop. His wife was an Indian but had been a slave, too. He bought his wife's and her brother's freedom from their masser. He owned and operated two plantations and had a rather profitable store at one time. That is until the other Negros began to listen to his foolish boycott ideas. You know, something had to be done about that."

"I find that most fascinating, Mr. Oury, that a man of his extraction would obtain such large sums of money in a blacksmith shop," said Liddell.

"Thinking of suing him, are you?" asked Oury with a smile. "Don't waste your time; he is dead now. The physician was none other than your dearly departed father, Dr. William W. Liddell. He believed the bullet I put in Brown later caused gangrene, killing him of infection. Brown had two able-bodied sons that worked for him. Ed, I believe, would be close to thirty years of age by now and Charley might be all of about twenty-four or twenty-five, if I recall. I don't want you to hold me to those numbers, though. Old Adam had three beautiful Indian maiden daughters with long black hair and piercing eyes that would look into yours with the vengeance of their father and the sincerity of the Choctaw."

"On the contrary, sir, I am more interested in his son, one Ed Brown, especially, and maybe his brother that hangs around with him. So, you do know of their whereabouts?" Liddell asked.

"I am very familiar with him and the entire family, sir. Ed's mother, Juliet, a full-blood Choctaw, blamed me for killing her husband, Adam Brown.

Her father, Edmond Richardson, and she had been slaves for Masser Alfred Jackson, another dear friend of mine here in Carroll County," Oury said.

"Do tell, sir, could you please inform me of any such disturbances caused by the younger Browns, Ed or Charley?" Liddell asked.

"Juliet married old William McKinney, that Negro postmaster that burned down the courthouse. He was killed that night, election night 1875, and she died a few years later in the yellow fever epidemic. His son, Will, lived with Ed and Charley before a white man took him in. He then died mysteriously, too. Will McKinney took back up with his stepbrothers and killed a white boy a few months ago. He is in jail now. I have been looking for the Browns to try to break him out. People in town felt sorry for him and he only got a year to serve. Guess they will let it be," Oury explained.

"So, what about this Ed Brown?" Liddell asked.

"Ed Brown is said to be a barroom brawler about town, although I have not myself witnessed such behavior. I received information on one occasion a few years ago that he had insulted Mr. Levi Bagley, who pulled a shotgun on him, pulling the trigger with intent to kill. Just like Adam Brown's gun aimed at me, Mr. Bagley's shotgun snapped, resulting in a tussle, but I never heard of the event again," Oury said. "I know of no arrest record on either of them though."

"That is exactly as I suspected, Mr. Oury. Your information has been most informative and necessary to my cause," said Liddell as he placed his coffee cup on a small table to the side of the elegant sofa where he sat.

"I have not yet heard of the offense this brute must have caused against your favor, Mr. Liddell. Certainly, you would not be interested otherwise, am I correct, sir?" Oury asked.

"Not against me personally, Mr. Oury, but against a dear, defenseless colleague of mine, which in itself boasts an attack on the honor of all of us in the white race. Now, one month ago, this Ed Brown humiliated my friend in a public place just down the street here by pouring sorghum molasses on his fine Italian trousers and shoes. Brown then assaulted him with most profane words in the earshot of a fine lady...of the saloon profession, mind you. Lastly, Brown struck him with a jug of molasses, causing him to further soil his fine clothing and risk injury as he fell outside the saloon. I am not sure of the culpability of his brother. However, he too must receive harsh treatment. My friend is small and weak in stature, not capable of protecting himself so I intend to take it upon myself to avenge his honor," Liddell boasted.

"I think I see the subject of your interest walking down the street now. Mr. Liddell, do you intend to confront him?" asked Oury, excitedly.

"I most certainly do, sir, and maybe I will give you something to write about if this action proves newsworthy for a one-horse town like ours. Probably wouldn't make such papers as mine in the big town of Greenwood," Liddell said.

He walked back across the street, with Oury keeping his eyes on Ed Brown.

Chapter 25:

The Ruckus

"It is the duty of the officials to prevent or
suppress the threatened disorder with a firm hand
instead of timidly yielding to threats... Surely, a
speaker ought not to be suppressed because his
opponents propose to use violence. It is they who
should suffer from their lawlessness, not he."
-The American Bar Association

L ater that day, on February 13, 1886, James M.
Liddell Jr. confronted Ed Brown, who stood
alone with his brother. Pointing as he walked
straight towards Ed in a threatening manner, Liddell
confronted Brown with both hands now on his hips.

"Hey, boy, are you Ed Brown?" Liddell asked in
a condescending manner.

"Who wants to know?" Brown barked out
quickly, angered by Liddell's attitude.

"Approximately one month ago, did you smear
molasses on a gentleman departing the saloon and
unnecessarily rough house him, using despicable
language in the presence of a lady?" asked Liddell, as
if he were the sheriff interrogating a suspect.

"I don't know what despicable language means, pretty boy, but I've got some language for you…you son-of-a-bitch," Brown barked out as he moved his foot aggressively away from the wall he was leaning against and quickly threw a chewed-up stick of straw from his mouth.

"Why, you…" Liddell began as he raised his hand to strike at Brown.

Concerned bystanders held him back while several men stepped in to quell any further violence. The crowd soon broke up and the street on the west side of the courthouse was back to normal.

Liddell went back to the hotel, where he had coffee and enjoyed dinner. As he started to leave, a couple of local men approached him and told him the two he had trouble with earlier were now a part of a much larger group hanging out near the saloon. Witnesses said they had heard them talking bad about Liddell, using foul language and threats. Liddell, accompanied by half a dozen white men who strayed along behind him, walked out onto the main street and stopped in front of Captain Ray's store, where the group was loitering. He came face to face with Ed Brown again.

"Just what do you mean by this gathering?" asked Liddell, as he raised his derby slightly from his head, almost appearing to be offering a formal greeting.

"None of your goddamned business," Ed said smartly.

At that time, with the derby still in his hand, Liddell struck at Brown, maybe hitting him with it, or maybe dropping it and slapping Brown with his open hand. Witness accounts vary. Ed Brown and his brother reportedly drew their weapons and fired upon Liddell as he drew a Colt double action revolver and fired back. Guns were blazing in all directions, lighting up the early night sky. Other blacks were behind trees and buildings. Altogether approximately twenty shots erupted in the streets of the small town, according to witnesses.

When the shooting stopped, Liddell had a bullet wound in the right elbow and a second bullet in the fleshy part of his left leg. Liddell shot Ed Brown in the abdomen and Charley Brown had a nasty gunshot wound to his shoulder. Neither person was seriously injured. Another man, a friend of the Browns, was also injured while fleeing.

The Browns had felt threatened by the party of six that joined along behind Liddell. Nobody ever found any of the men that were supposedly behind the trees or buildings, if they were ever there at all. Nobody really knew who drew or fired first.

The town marshal took Liddell and the Browns before Mayor Elam, who was the acting town justice. Liddell went home to attend to his wounds. The sheriff put the Browns in the county jail, in a cell next to Will McKinney, on that night of February 13.

Word got out around town that a large gang of armed men would be coming to town in a few days and would take the Browns from their cell and lynch them. Sheriff Hamilton was worried and planned to move them to a safe location that following Monday. However, Mayor Elam had them brought to his office that Monday morning, February 18, and arraigned them. He then allowed them to post a

$200-bond each with a promise to appear in circuit court the following month.

Chapter 26:

Wrong Place, Wrong Time

*"While one person hesitates because he feels
inferior, the other is busy making mistakes and
becoming superior."*
-Henry C. Link

The sheriff was getting ready to go home to get something to eat, as he did most days during the lunch hour. He always brought back leftovers for his prisoner, Will McKinney.

"Your wife is surely a good cook," Will told the sheriff. "These vittles taste about as good as Mrs. Emma's," he said, wolfing down thick, creamy chicken and dumplings.

"I was lookin over yo papers. Ain't you got a birthday coming up, boy?" asked Sheriff Hamilton, peering over his glasses and wondering for the fifth time how such a skinny black boy could consume so much food.

"Ta tell ya da truf, boss, I ain't right sho when my birthday is, but my daddy told me I was born in da fust week of Febuary. I mus have jus tunned nineteen-year-old a few days ago, dat bein da case," Will said.

"Tell you what, boy, I'm gonna brang you some bread puddin back, made from all them ole bread scraps that didn't get eat around our house last week," the sheriff promised. "Maybe that will fill you up."

Will never got any cakes before, but Mrs. Emma used to fix him some fried apple pies. He knew how busy and old she was, and unable to labor over the stove too much now. He sure was looking forward to something sweet, though. He never made a fuss either way.

The sheriff left about lunchtime but was late getting back. Will was beginning to wonder what had happened to him. He didn't like being in the old jail alone. Although he was happy that his brothers had been able to pay their bails and get out of jail that morning, he had to admit that he missed having them in the next cell. Will did not have a lot more time to spend in his jail cell. He looked forward to getting out and rejoining Ed and Charley. Anyway, he had that bread pudding on his mind and he couldn't think of much else.

****

The gang of angry white men gathered on a dirt road just south of town at twelve noon that day. They dismounted and passed around jerky for their own lunch while they waited. They drank water from canteens attached to their saddles and gave the horses shoots of sugar cane to chew on.

The area, cluttered with trees, was a perfect hideout for them to see the sheriff as he came up the main street from his home following his lunch. They knew what time the sheriff went home for lunch every day, but they did not know if he had the key to the jail cell with him. They planned to catch him off-guard and take the key from him.

At 1:10 p.m., the sheriff came riding by. A scout from the gang reported the sighting and the group mounted their horses following along behind. They forced their horses into full gallop to catch up with the sheriff going down the last hill as the town came into view.

As the sheriff entered the dark, cool jailhouse building, he placed a portion of food that he was going to deliver to his only remaining prisoner, Will McKinney, on his desk. He heard a loud roar of horse hooves coming to a stop from a fast gallop. He glanced out the window and saw nothing but a cloud of dust. As he placed his belongings down on his desk, hung his key ring on the wall and turned around, a group of masked outlaws with guns pointed was facing him.

"We don't want no trouble with you, Sheriff," The leader said in a muffled tone under a bandana. "We heard you been talking about hiding these niggers. You cooperate with us and there won't be no trouble for you. We just want them half-breed niggers you got back there," the masked man said as he pointed at the cell.

"What? Oh, no, you've got this all wrong," the sheriff cried out.

Before he could explain, the outlaw interrupted.

"Sheriff, don't be taking up for no filthy nigger ag'in ya own!" a man yelled out as he struck the sheriff across the face with his pistol, knocking him unconscious across the desk, blood streaming from his face.

"Grab his cell key off the wall!" the leader yelled out.

As part of the group made their way back to the cell doors, they found Will by himself.

"Where's your brothers, boy?" the leader yelled out.

"Don't know, sir," Will said quickly.

"Go check all the rooms, see if the sheriff has got the other ones doing something," the leader instructed members of the gang. "Least we got one of em."

The group returned to the front of Will's cell, where the leader was standing with the cell keys in his hand.

From down the hall, one of the gang members yelled out, "Nobody else here but us, boss."

Will could see them through the bars but could not tell what they were saying. Will did not know what to think. By then he had forgotten about his bread pudding. He wondered if something had happened and maybe this was the sheriff's posse gotten together to go out to look for some desperado outlaws.

"Say, boss, you know, it is kind of dark in here and all, but that nigger don't look like no half-breed to me," one of the outlaws said.

"Naw, he's their stepbrother, the one that killed that white boy awhile back. What's yo name, boy?" asked the leader in a loud, demanding voice.

"Will McKinney, sir," Will said with confusion.

"Oh, yeah, boss…McKinney; he's right, that is the name of that boy who killed the Broadway kid," one of the gang members said.

Will was suddenly scared speechless, eyes wide open and hands glued to the bars.

He squeezed his fingers together, dropped his head and began praying.

One of the men had a long rope with a hangman's noose on one end. While two of the men dragged Will out of the jail and out to the big oak tree in front of the courthouse, the others threw a rope over a big, old, low-hanging limb. The leader of the pack put the noose around Will's neck. The other end was tied to one of the men's saddle horns. In his usual state of mind and demeanor, Will did not resist or speak out against them.

One outlaw shouted out, "Niggah, you was just at the wrong place at the wrong time." Then he started yelling at Will about killing a white boy and not getting any more sentence than he did. They said they would sentence him now.

Will had begun to pray to Jesus because he knew what they were about to do. This was no game to scare him.

The man on the horse slapped that animal so loudly it sounded like a rifle going off. Will heard the horse galloping while it jerked him up into the tree. His neck got broken while he was praying aloud, asking the good Lord to save him. The good Lord did not save him from death that day but did take away his pain quickly and saved his soul.

The rider returned, dropping Will's body to the ground and took ahold of the rope as if to take Will down. Instead, he cut the rope from the horse then he and others hoisted Will's body up into the tree again, tying the cut end to the tree trunk. The men wanted to make sure he was dead. They shot young Will so full of holes he could not have held down a dipper full of water.

They were using his body for shooting practice while others in town were looking out all the windows of the stores and courthouse. They all had them a good laugh. Everybody in town came by and looked at him. The men left when they had enough fun, bragging about what they had done. Will hung there by the neck, with his head tilted to one side, swinging ever so slightly every now and then when the wind would blow. Blood dripped from his fingertips and spilled from his mouth. Smoke even lingered around the square.

Word spread around town quickly as to what happened. Nobody bothered to cut Will's body down and it just hung there as an example to any other Negro showing what might happen to them if they wronged a white man.

A few hours later, the sheriff arrived out front in a mule-drawn wagon empty of any contents, a Bible held tightly in one hand as he wept. A knife was ready in the other hand as he approached the limp body. He cut the rope from the tree trunk.

As the body made a loud *thump* while hitting the ground, a black lady near the tree yelled out, "Help him, Jesus, help him, Lord. We gone pray for them white men's souls."

The sheriff covered Will's body with a blanket he had thrown over his shoulder. Two bystanders walked over to help lift the body.

Without looking to see who approached him, Sheriff Hamilton yelled out, "Don't touch him."

He bent over, lifting Will's body as his arms dangled, holding him chest to chest. The sheriff then stood upright, carrying Will like a mother burping a baby. He began the short walk past the wrought iron gate of the courthouse and gently sat Will down on the bed of the wagon. He softly placed a cushion from the wagon seat under his head, lying him down as if to rest. He pulled Will's limp, bloody body to one side of the wagon to make room for a wooden coffin he would pay for himself at the coffin store next door. He knew Will should not even have been in jail in the first place.

The sheriff buried Will in the ground next to his mother and father, wearing the bullet-ridden clothes he had on when he died. The sheriff dug the grave out back of the McKinney's old home place in the McKinney Cemetery, high atop a hill with a towering oak surrounded by dogwood trees. Nobody else came when he lowered Will into the earth except Mrs. Emma, barely alive herself, bringing a bucket full of water and a dipper. The sheriff felt as though Will would have wanted his privacy.

Mrs. Emma placed flowers she had picked onto his grave, weeping as if she had lost her own child.

Chapter 27:

The Doctor Visit

"Single acts of tyranny may be ascribed to the accidental opinion of the day; but a series of oppressions, begun at a distinguished period, and pursued unalterably through every change of ministers too plainly proves a deliberate, systematic plan of reducing us to slavery."
-Thomas Jefferson

At the end of the day, his forehead throbbing in pain on the outside, secondary only to his heart torn in two on the inside, the sheriff set out to receive treatment for his injury. He made his way up the long street on foot, head down, feet dragging, and unaware of his surroundings; he cared little about the pain he felt.

The sheriff's heart was wrought with pain far greater than the open wound with flesh distended on each side of his upper brow. No matter what, he was unable to rid his mind of the last shovel of dirt he cast on Will's grave. Knowing the history of Will losing his mother at birth, and listening to his father describe from his deathbed the story of how she passed, he thought what a tragic life the young man had lived. For a moment, vengeance ran through his mind and he stopped abruptly in his tracks. However, postponing this treatment further could lead to infection and it was time to go inside. Dealing with the outlaws could wait.

It was as if his steps grew shorter and shorter as he walked slowly up the long pathway to the mansion known as the Oaks, the last resting place of "old man" Doc Liddell. He spoke little of the happenings of that day, but knew the eighteenth day of February would be a day that would last in his memory.

The cool, late winter air had helped clog the blood flow from his injury. Reluctantly, he raised his right arm, fist closed tightly, and knocked three times on the large wooden door.

"Who's there?" yelled a voice from inside.

"It's Sheriff Hamilton. Mind if I come in?" he asked loudly.

"Please do," a short black woman, clad in a headscarf and apron over her dress, said with a smile. She all but curtsied as she greeted the sheriff while opening the door with her right hand and her left palm upward, pointing to the parlor inside.

Upon entering the stately old white home, he called out for Doctor Liddell, his voice bouncing off the high ceilings. James Liddell was resting in a bed with a bottle of whisky, over half-empty, sitting on the table next to him. He was suffering from the minor gunshot wounds sustained from the fight with the Browns five days before, though he acted as if he was hurt much worse than he really was. In walked his brother, a doctor in study, who had taken over his father's practice after his premature death several years before.

Forgetting for a moment that the doctor was even there, the sheriff began to have flashbacks about Will as he found himself in the presence of the man vicariously responsible for the whole mess. He saw in his mind young Will out working happily in a field instead of behind the bars in a dark, cold cell.

"James, I understood you were once a county prisoner contractor. According to the clerk, there was none available. Young William McKinney would have been a good person for you to get out as a contract worker," the sheriff said.

"No, Sheriff, I quit doing that last year. The northern newspapers were just making too big of a deal about us just using it is a substitute for slavery. As proprietor in the *Yazoo Valley Flag Newspaper* and amidst accusations of nonpayment, I just did not need anything hounding me like that anymore. I got served papers in a dispute for payment over one I had gotten out of jail to work a few years ago. I just wrote a letter to Mr. Somerville and they worked it out."

"Too bad you couldn't have gotten that kid out to work," the sheriff said.

James Liddell made no other response about prisoner contracts or Will McKinney and the sheriff was not even sure if they knew about McKinney's death. He made no mention of it to either of them. It made him forget the reason he was even there, and in the dimly lit room his injury was not apparent.

"Doc, I need you to check me out," the sheriff said as he walked into the light where William Liddell stood. "I found the wrong end of a Colt .45 above my nose about midday."

Dr. Liddell had the sheriff lie flat on his back on an examining table in one of his rooms.

"I'd say you found the right end of that Colt .45. The butt does far less damage than that of the muzzle, Sheriff Hamilton. That is a nasty gash you have, sir. It's going to require several cat gut sutures," he said.

Doctor Liddell immediately went to work on the sheriff.

"Gonna leave a bad scar but may not be so bad if we leave the stitches in a little longer than normal. Nose is broken, too, but not much we can do about that. It will heal on its own. Why don't you come back in three weeks and let me remove the sutures for you? Go on by the drug store and get you some camphor to help you breathe 'til that swelling goes down. Drink some whiskey for the pain," said Dr. Liddell as his brother James looked on.

"What happened to you, Sheriff, those darkies jump you? Surprised the cowards didn't hit you from behind instead of in the face," James said, waiting for the sheriff to respond.

"Naw, it wasn't them, just a bunch of old run-of-the-mill outlaws," the sheriff said, as he walked away, playing down the significance of the attack and not mentioning McKinney's death.

The people who lived around Carroll County seemed to be oblivious as to what was going on. Obviously, the courthouse and the jail sitting square in the middle of the small town of Carrollton were county buildings. They just occupied small spaces on the forty-acre section of the town limits. It was as if what happened did not matter to the citizens – even if it happened in their own backyards.

****

The grand jury met and conducted their investigation as to the circumstances surrounding Will McKinney's death. They issued their final report, which read:

"We find first and acknowledge with the deepest regret, the fact to be that on the night of the 18th of February AD 1886 a body of armed men masked, came to the Town of Carrollton, took charge of T.T. Hamilton, the Sheriff, forced from him the keys to the jail and took therefrom one Will McKinney, a colored boy about 19 years old, carried him to the court yard and hung and shot him to death. This boy Will was he who at the last October term of Court was indicted for Manslaughter for the killing of one Charlie Broadway, a white boy about the same age, was convicted at the same term for the full offense charged and there being no Contractor for the county, was serving out the term of 12 months imprisonment in the County Jail, the punishment fixed by the Court for his offense. By such conduct the Officers of the law who work faithfully for its enforcement, execution are made to feel that though its of arms they attribute more or less to the Cruel and heartless destruction of humanity, and as officers of the Court charged with the diligent inquiring into the commission of crimes and failing to discover any of the perpetrators of the deeds, we feel it our duty to

condemn without reservations the act of barbarism visiting such terrible vengeance of a helpless convict."

****

Days passed and tensions seemed to loosen up based on everything that had happened. Will McKinney was just another Negro who met his demise at the hands of outlaws in the small town of Carrollton, Mississippi.

The Browns, furious about the loss of their baby brother, kept their distance from town after the incident, knowing they had their own problems.

On the morning of March 10, the sheriff arrived early at Dr. Liddell's house for his suture removal. As he was going in, James M. Liddell was going out.

"Feeling mighty spiffy, sir," Liddell said as he tipped his hat to the sheriff. "On the way to my newspaper office in Greenwood. I haven't been around there in three weeks."

The sheriff exchanged greetings but did not say much. He was concerned about the trouble that he was confident James Liddell had started. He did not think they had heard the end of it, regardless of the mood about town.

"Well, good morning, Sheriff. Looks like a couple of those sutures have fallen out by themselves. I guess you have been frowning quite a lot. Let's get the rest of them out," Dr. Liddell said as the sheriff sat upright on an examining table.

"Doctor, I am a little worried about your brother," said the sheriff

"Oh, you mean James? Don't worry about him. He can be the finest, most polished gentleman when he needs to be, but he has got a temper like our uncle, Senator James Monroe Liddell, the man he was named after. Guess Daddy naming him after his brother did that to him. You see they call him Junior because when he was in the legislature at only twenty-four years of age, our uncle with the same name was still in the legislature, too. That was the only way they could keep them apart when they were addressing or talking about them. I am the junior with the same name as my late father, Dr. William Walker Liddell, but I never used that suffix. James really is a fine man, Sheriff. You look after him around town now, you hear?" asked William Liddell.

"Yes, I sure will, Doc. I know yo daddy would have wanted that," the sheriff said as he began to leave. "What about my bill, Doc?"

"Don't worry about it, sir. I will bill the county for this injury in the line of duty," Liddell said.

Chapter 28:

The Charges

"Laws are like cobwebs, where the small flies are caught and the great break through."
-Sir Francis Bacon

O n Thursday, March 11, the Browns went to see Colonel W. B. Helm, an attorney, in an attempt to get him to represent them in court. He told them that their case was "too reprehensible for him to take hold of it" and advised them "to peaceably and quietly leave the community." They refused and became outraged.

The next day on Friday, March 12, the Browns felt they'd had enough. They were facing an indictment and the person who started the fight with them, James M. Liddell, Jr., was free of any charges, riding back to Greenwood two days earlier as if nothing had ever happened. Their stepbrother had been murdered by a gang who came after them. They got together and decided that no matter what, they would see to it that James M. Liddell, Jr. faced charges. They went to the mayor's office and spoke to him in his role of police justice.

"We want to sign charges against James M. Liddell, Jr. and his friends for assault and attempt to kill and murder," Ed said as he looked at his brother nervously sitting beside him.

Ed hit Charley on the leg and Charley then shook his head up and down as if he were in total agreement with his brother, but was very reluctant to do so.

"You want to do what?" said Judge Elam as he scurried quickly around his desk, looking Ed in the eye. "Do you have any idea the trouble you are about to start, young man?" shouted the judge.

"We didn't start no trouble, Judge. James Liddell started the trouble. We bumped into his friend accidentally going into the saloon and spilled molasses on his pants. We had a disagreement and then the man went away. Then a few weeks later, Liddell came to us smarting off about the incident and tried to slap me until some other people pulled him off. He was wearing a gun. We went back and put on our guns for protection. He returned with his six friends and they accosted us again in the street. He hit me with his hat and hand because he didn't like what I said to him when he confronted me. They started shooting. I know he's gonna tell ya'll that we pulled a gun first. We had witnesses too and it will all come out in the court," Ed said.

"Son, if you do this, you will be lucky to ever make it to court," Judge Elam said with equal parts disgust and genuine concern.

"Let us worry about that, Mr. Mayor," Ed said.

Charley Brown just gazed at the floor without speaking a word.

"Okay, you asked for it. Here are the affidavits. Raise your right hands and swear that the information you are about to give is true and correct to the best of your knowledge so help you God and I mean, so help you God," Elam said worriedly as he shook his head back and forth while filling in the blanks on the affidavits.

The tone was somber in the mayor's office as he stared at the affidavits before issuing a warrant for the arrest of James M. Liddell, Jr. and his six friends. The Browns left as if they were handling any day-to-day business and did not look back.

The mayor walked nervously across the square to the sheriff's office and jail. "Sheriff, I have a warrant for the arrest of James M. Liddell Jr. and six others. The Brown brothers swore them out for assault and attempt to kill and commit murder. I need you to serve them. Don't be in a hurry about the other six. They were probably just bystanders," the mayor said quietly, as he appeared to be in shock, moving slowly towards the door.

The sheriff never said a word. It was almost as if he were expecting it. That was beside the point, though. What he expected to follow would be far more shocking than the words on a warrant commanding a law enforcement officer of the county to "take the body of one James M. Liddell Jr. if found to be in his county and arrest him."

He knew Liddell was at the next county over, working daily at his newspaper office in Greenwood but returning home nightly. That night, Friday March 12, the sheriff walked over to the Liddells' house and served the warrant on James M. Liddell,

Jr. He released him on his own recognizance to appear before the court five days later. The preliminary hearing would be upstairs in the courthouse before Mayor Elam at noon on Wednesday, March 17. The other hearings were expected to follow, depending on the outcome of this.

The Liddell brothers were not only shocked at the audacity the Browns had, but also James Liddell's anger was far greater than it had ever been or at least the sheriff had ever seen. Liddell began throwing things and knocking bottles off shelves, screaming "Nigger" at the top of his voice.

"Don't they know we are a superior race and they were intended to be subservient to us?"

Chapter 29:

Rumblings Around Town

*"It is bad to be oppressed by a minority, but it is
worse to be oppressed by a majority."*
-Lord Acton

Word travels fast in a small town like Carrollton. In less than twenty-four hours, the news was all over town what the Browns had done. How dare they accuse fine, upstanding citizens of any wrongdoing. Who did they think they were?

Everyone had a tale to tell about the brothers – some true, most untrue. W.H. Johnston's store on the west side of the square was the hub of discussions about the situation. Ed Brown had been in their store around Christmas time, recalled one employee. "He was drunk and spouting off about killing white men if they approached him, cussing every other word," she recalled. "I'm pretty sure that was Ed Brown."

A group of women gathered in Merrill's store on the southwest side of the square. They were gossiping about how they had not been able to walk the main street anymore for fear of the Negroes. They said the Negroes regularly bumped into them, elbowed them, and made them move over to make room for them. Something had to be done because they no longer felt safe enough to walk around town anymore without at least one strong able-bodied white man by their sides. In their minds, the Negroes of the community were out of control.

Business owners feared customers would not feel safe doing business in downtown Carrollton. The hotel owner feared customers would be unwilling to stay amongst the unsettled atmosphere caused by the Negro community. The saloon owner feared a major fight could cause death and destruction on his property. Most stores had become meeting places for discussions. What were they to do? The people of Carrollton were demanding a solution.

Groups of men started meeting in secret on a regular basis. Husbands were leaving their wives alone at home to attend secret meetings, instilling more fear and confusion. They were as secretive about their actions as the Masons in the Pythagoras Lodge were about their discussions. A group called the Red Shirts, chartered a few years before to intimidate the Negro Republicans and White Scalawags, was becoming more threatening. This was the group that had become quite successful in starting fights with Negroes at the polls. White Democrats would stop at nothing to try to eliminate blacks from gaining any kind of power or position, even resorting to stealing poll boxes at the recent election in order to assure their political victories. Although the Ku Klux Klan was phasing out by then, there were a few unorganized vigilante groups still actively lynching Negroes and burning them at the stakes.

The whites had re-taken the government, most of the good people of Carrollton believed, and these two blacks were not about to mess things back up. Not everyone in the small town was as radical as some of the politicians were; many were God-loving, church going, family-loving Southerners who were raised to believe that the color of their skin determined their lot in life. Therefore, they were justified in making sure the black man stayed in his place. Whatever their belief, they all came together under the leadership of Houston Whitworth, a farmer from Leflore County near Greenwood, who had been known to have plenty of guns and scores of horses. He had both the assets and desire, not to mention leadership, to attack the Negroes in great numbers.

Meetings transpired in stores, churches and lodges, even private homes. The town of Carrollton preferred to lay low and not take any part in possible riots or lynchings that would likely come. Carrollton was a small town with many affluent and influential people, including doctors, lawyers, and politicians. US senator and former chief justice of the State Supreme Court, James Zachariah George, was a well-known Carrollton resident. One of George's sons was said to have been involved in the anti-Negro movement and was possibly a gang member himself.

As the scheduled day for court came closer, white families who had long-time Negro workers warned them not to go to the courtroom to watch the hearing on March 17. They warned their farm workers and house cleaners to stay home for fear of their safety. Many of those Negroes made that information known to other Negroes in the community.

For days, leading up to the court hearing, people – both black and white – around Carrollton speculated as to what could happen in the courtroom that day. Some of the townspeople thought a vigilante group might be there. Some thought this would be a good opportunity for black people to show their support for the Brown brothers, who, they thought, just wanted to be treated like human beings. White citizens figured this hearing would surely teach the blacks their place in the world. If the Brown brothers had to suffer to be an example, then that was just how it had to be.

Most of the Negroes around town felt just as strongly about their rights as the Browns felt about theirs. Nothing could keep them away. Reportedly, Ed Brown bragged in the street before going into the courtroom that day that he had his bodyguards with him and he was not worried about the white men. Like so many Indians before him, he just might underestimate the strength of armed white men, which could lead to tragedy.

"Hey, Brown," another colored man yelled out to Ed as he saw him coming out of the blacksmith shop the morning of the hearing. "I understand you gotta go to court in a little while. They gone put you in jail?"

"Hell, naw, and I ain't *gotta* go to court, either. I am going to court because I want to. They done bound me over to the grand jury. Me and my brother, Charley, signed the charges against the white men ourselves. We ain't facing our trial yet. This ain't no trial anyway. It's just a hearing to see if Lawyer Liddell is going to be bound over to the grand jury. Me and my brother didn't have no hearing," Ed said. "The other men will go to court later."

"You mean the white man is on trial today and you is the witness?" asked the man incredulously.

"That's right and I got other witnesses, too," Ed said.

"Oh Lord, brother, them folks gonna string you up in front of that courthouse if you ain't one lucky buck," the man said as he walked away.

The morning of the hearing, Ed and Charley were feeling unnerved as they walked with friends and family members toward the courthouse. They felt if harm were going to come to them, it would be before the hearing started. The hearing was scheduled for twelve noon.

The Browns wanted to be right on time, not a minute early or a minute late. There was an eerie feeling on the deserted streets as they made their way slowly toward the center of town, watching people peer from the shop windows. White men sat on their horses with Winchester rifles in the scabbards attached to their saddles. An early-morning light rain had settled the dust, as Ed and Charley walked up the brick pathway to the door of the Carroll County Courthouse, constantly glancing over their shoulders.

As Ed led the group through the front door, he looked around the dog-trot hallway of the courthouse until his eyes found the massive cherry stairway that dominated the bottom floor of the courthouse. The courtroom was above. The group mounted the stairway, quietly taking each step to the second floor landing before making a ninety-degree turn the rest of the way up. When the Browns and their entourage came to the door to the courtroom, the overwhelming confidence they had felt was beginning to ebb. Charley felt a magnetic force pulling him away, telling him not to enter the courtroom, as his heart pounded visibly against his chest. Thoughts ran through Ed Brown's head that no disrespected black man or Choctaw had ever sworn affidavits against a respectable member of the white community. He let it pass and opened the door slowly, as it creaked a bone-chilling sound.

Without yet looking inside, Ed Brown turned to look at his friends just as a nearby church bell rang out. It was high noon. The time had come; there was no turning back.

Chapter 30:

The Ride

"The soul that has conceived one wickedness can
nurse no good thereafter."
-SOPHOCLES, *Philoctetes*

Late morning, March 17, 1886

A gang of outlaws on horseback, a hundred, maybe more, rode hard from Greenwood to Carrollton. They approached the steep bluff that separated hill country from the flat delta soil. This was the halfway point on their journey.

Leaving the delta behind in their wake of dust, the horses struggled to climb the steep hill, oblivious to the cool temperatures. The fast ride was taking its toll on the horses, who were huffing and puffing, nostrils wide open, sweat pouring down the sides of their necks, coats now darkened and saturated as they continued their ascent. The air was filled with the sight and sound of heavy breaths from the huge, muscular animals. Thirteen miles had passed and there were twelve more to go.

The leader, Houston S. Whitworth, checked his pocket watch with one hand and held the reins in the other as he spit tobacco juice to the side of the dusty road and adjusted his hat. A self-made racist killer before the war, who tasted even more blood as a soldier and liked it, he was determined to lead the gang of outlaws on this mission. In many ways, still a rogue rebel warrior unable to accept the South's defeat, a bloodthirsty animal of a man, chosen above all others for this job.

Nearing the top of the bluff, a rider coming up from the rear had slapped his horse's butt; dust flew with each slap as he gained on the others. He had broken ranks and Whitworth heard him coming.

"Slow the pace," Whitworth said as he raised his left arm, signaling to slow down.

The gang slowed to a trot as the rider form the rear caught up with leadership out front.

"We got deserters, boss...men turning around at the back of the group. I was worried about those two. Want us to go after them?" the rider asked as the group slowed to a stop.

Without a word, Whitworth pulled his long, brass cylindrical telescope from the saddle. Turning his horse half around, he extended the scope to three times its original length and placed it up to his right eye while closing his left.

"Want us to chase 'em down? I got the fastest horse in the herd," the rider impatiently barked out, waiting for the cue to go.

The deserters heading back towards Greenwood were still visible from the crest of the high bluff they had now reached.

"Where's my sniper?" Whitworth asked in a low, unconcerned tone without even taking the scope from his eye.

"Here I am, sir!" Deadeye Jenkins exclaimed as he hurried up from only two rows back.

Still looking through the scope expressionless, his tongue moving about inside his bottom lip, Whitworth posed his question without even looking at the sniper. "Think you can take 'em out, boy?"

"They didn't call me Deadeye Jenkins when I served in Lowry's Rifles for nothing," he said eagerly.

"Do it... Nobody deserts my group," Whitworth said calmly as he turned his horse back around, confident the job would be finished.

The sniper began the long pull from its holster of his specially designed Northern sniper rifle he had taken off a dead Yankee at the base of a big oak tree near the end of the war. It seemed the end of the barrel would never come as there was, by then, more gun than there was shooter. Highly polished blue steel, walnut grained wood stock—this was truly a professional weapon designed for one thing.

It was a modified design of the 1859 Sharps breech loading rifle, stretched from a thirty to a full forty-two-inch barrel, one of a kind, none another like it in the country and still none better, his prize possession. A one-thousand-yard shot would be as easy as getting a hound dog to eat a piece of red meat.

"Still, Nellie," the sniper said to his horse as he stood on the ground and laid this monstrosity of a weapon across the saddle, pointing the front sight down the bluff at the unsuspecting riders. He lifted the long blade rear site and moved a sliding scale into place, counting out yardage with his aim. He set the rear hair trigger inside the trigger guard, anticipating his first shot. The mood was quiet except for horses neighing and moving about, lifting their heads and turning in circles. It was as if they too were anticipating the deafening blast about to take place. Then suddenly a scream cried out.

"No, no, wait!" a rider screamed as he approached the sniper. "That's my cousin and his baby brother. They ain't gone tell nobody. They jus sceered. Don't shoot."

The sniper paused but held the rifle in place, the deserters moving farther and farther away. As Deadeye looked up, seeking a response from Whitworth, he saw movement out the corner of his eye and heard the sound of clearing leather.

Whitworth drew his Colt revolver and fired one shot into the gut of the concerned cousin.

"Oh, my God," the man screamed as he hit the ground bleeding profusely, holding his hands over the wound with blood spurting from between his fingers. He rolled over and over screaming in pain. Whitworth still had his pistol aimed at the wounded man.

"Shoot the riders," Whitworth said out the corner of his mouth, without showing any expression.

Boommmmmmmm! The sound of the sniper rifle resonated as a cloud of smoke rose from the barrel. The smaller of the riders fell as his head exploded like a watermelon blasted with a shotgun. Blood dispersing in the air in a circle around the body settled as the kid fell dead.

As the sniper continued to focus on the next rider, by then riding hard and fast, as if to be attempting to escape the wrath of a man proficient at his trade, the sniper adjusted his sight.

Boommmmmmm! Again a deadly shot rang out as another cloud of blood burst into the cool air. Almost as if in slow motion, the man's horse skidded to its knees, head dropping as if it had caught the exiting bullet before tumbling end over end.

Still not yet moving his revolver away from the dying man on the ground, Whitworth looked up at the gang, as they were looking at him. With his head as still as a statute, spitting tobacco juice from one side of his mouth, his squinted eyes scanned the crowd, looking each one directly in the eyes. It was as if he had the ability to detect other would-be traitors or scare them into following his lead. Nobody would abandon him and if anybody had any doubts before, they surely would not now.

By then the man on the ground laid in a puddle of blood the size of a washtub and was still bleeding.

"Kill me, too, you bastard!" he yelled out, looking Whitworth in the eye as the rest of the gang remained quiet. "Kill me, I said. Put me out of my misery. I ain't gone survive this gut shot. Put me out of my misery. Kill me, dammit!"

Whitworth, still pointing the gun in his direction, cocked the hammer and aimed at his head.

"Be still, you son-of-a-bitch," Whitworth said with a cold face as he continued to aim.

Then, suddenly, Whitworth reached up with his thumb, grabbed the back of the hammer, his finger still inside the trigger guard; he lowered the hammer and slowly placed his pistol back in the holster.

"Kill me, you ruthless bastard," the wounded man yelled. "Give me the same benefit you would a lame horse."

At first, it appeared Whitworth would speak and address his last request. Instead, the cold-blooded Civil War sergeant-turned outlaw moved his lips around in a circular motion, and spit a large wad of tobacco into the man's face.

"You ain't as good as no horse. You got your own gun. Take it out and use it," Whitworth said in disgust as he dropped the reins and dug his heels into his horse's side.

"Let's ride. Court just started, according to my pocket watch," is all he said as he and the rest of the gang uncaringly left the dying man taking his last breathe from the dust of the hooves of their mighty horses.

Chapter 31:

The Vigilantes

"We hold these truths to be self-evident, that all men are created equal, that they are endowed by their Creator with certain unalienable Rights that among these are Life, Liberty, and the pursuit of Happiness."
-Declaration of Independence

The gang of outlaws road hard into Carrollton. Houston Whitworth once again checked his pocket watch then untied the bandana from his neck to wipe his brow. The stubby hairs on his face from a three-day-old growth bristled as he wiped his cheeks. His black boots, covered with dust from the trip, were barely recognizable.

The horses dropped to a gallop a few miles outside town. Glancing over at his most hopeful regulator, Senator James Z. George's son, Whitworth paused, looking the young man straight in the eye to assess if the boy was sure he wanted to go through with the plan.

Whitworth extended his hand and offered George a chew while still galloping. Not a word was said, but both men knew what the other was thinking.

George was a young wannabe whose dad was a decorated Civil War general. He hated Northerners. They had incarcerated his dad in a Northern, bone-chillingly cold military prison for two years after capturing him. The rest of the gang, mostly a bunch of assorted criminals, just wanted to be involved with killing Negroes.

"Slow the pace," Whitworth said as he raised his left arm, signaling to slow down. "We need to give the horses a break. We are okay with the time."

Only the top trusted men knew the entire plan. Many of the riders knew little about their mission. They treated it as if it were a mission of war. Nobody could back out. That was clear at the top of the bluff a few miles back. They had no chance anyway until arriving on the scene. If they betrayed the gang during a shootout, they too would die.

A quick stop off to the side at a branching road off to the left just before reaching town would be the venue for assignments. Most of the men were Civil War veterans and were familiar with formations, leaders, and missions. They could all shoot and most felt far superior to the black race.

"Whoa, boy," sounded over the trampling hoofs as they pulled the reins back tightly, bringing the group of horses to a halt near a field that was bordered by a tree line on the left side of the road. Whitworth gave the order to "dismount" followed by "gather round" as they moved into the field.

"Listen up, boys. We have a job to do. I appreciate all of you coming along and apologize for no more information than you have. That little incident back on the bluff should tell you why the details were secret. If known, things could have been worse.

"I want to name four squad leaders: Johnson, Williams, Moore and Lott. You men work for Mr. George. We are going to the Carrollton Courthouse only about a mile from here. Your jobs will be to cover the four openings in the courthouse to make sure nobody goes in or out after we arrive. Check your weapons and get prepared. You squad leaders pick out fifteen men each, remount, and get back in formation on the road. Mr. George will address you shortly. I want ten of the meanest and most able, Nigger hating, experienced soldiers as volunteers to line up in front of me. You men will join me in the initial assault. The rest of you will hold the perimeter of the courthouse grounds; nobody arrives and nobody leaves. All Niggers and deserters are fair game. Y'all got any questions?"

"Okay, squad leaders," George said. "Johnson, you have the north entrance, Williams the south, Moore on the east and Lott on the west side. Gather inside the breezeways, forming human shields as soon as we arrive. After the boss makes his move and the first shot rings out, if you see 'em, shoot 'em. I know most of you men have far more experience than I do since I was too young for the war, so help me make my daddy proud."

Chapter 32:

The Courtroom

"Time will bring to light whatever is hidden; it will
cover up and conceal what is now shining in splendor."
-Horace (Ancient Roman Poet, 65 BC)

E d opened the courtroom door slowly,
peering cautiously into the vast room. His
fragile confidence was boosted when he
realized that the room was almost empty.

Large wooden church-style pews with high
backs ran down the center of the room and on either
side, creating two narrow aisles. The pews were
elevated at an angle to be higher in the back for
spectators to see over the heads in front of them.
There was a hallway-type opening behind the last
pew. It allowed people to move from one side of the
room to another without crossing through the pews
or walking up front in the sight of the judge. The top
of the back pew was so high the judge up front could
only see the heads and shoulders of most people
passing behind it to take their seats.

"All rise, the Honorable Judge Elam presiding."
the bailiff barked out as he saw the judge enter the
back of the courtroom.

The Negroes had all moved to the left side of the courtroom and sat together. The Browns and their witnesses sat in the front row. They were almost directly behind the table occupied by the defendant, James M. Liddell, Jr., who was winking at the judge as he walked by. His two lawyers were on both sides of him facing the judge.

At precisely 12:02 p.m., the judge took his seat in the center of the north wall, facing the crowd. There was a chair positioned to his left, reserved for witnesses. The judge and the lawyers were separated from the rest of the spectators in the room by a black wrought iron fence less than waist high.

The only whites in the room were Mayor Elam, who was presiding over the hearing as police justice; Mr. Oury, town marshal, was there serving as bailiff. James M. Liddell, Jr. had his two lawyers, Mr. Alfred Somerville and Captain D.M. Estes, a well-known Civil War Confederate captain, on either side of him.

"Be seated." the bailiff shouted after the judge took his seat and looked around the room.

The hearing began without incident. With only six or seven white men in the room, the Browns seemed to calm down. No prosecutors were assigned to assist the Browns, who were, in all actuality, witnesses for the state. However, Liddell had good representation. Besides being a lawyer himself, he was represented by not one but two of the finest counselors that money could buy.

Ed Brown was the first witness. Immediately after receiving instructions from the judge on when to speak, the defense attorneys began badgering him relentlessly. They insisted on showing that he initiated the contact, provoked their client, and shot first, causing Liddell to return fire in self-defense. There was no jury to convince, as this was only a preliminary hearing. All the lawyers intended to do was show Mayor Elam (who was only a layman, intimidated by the law and highly respected lawyers) that their client had acted in self-defense. They would argue that Liddell acted in self-defense against a known hothead with a history of engagements with other citizens in the town.

There would be no guilt or innocence proven in this hearing. It would establish whether there was probable cause to charge Liddell with a felonious crime. Liddell's lawyers declared that Liddell acted in self-defense against a crazy half-breed. Therefore, their client should go free, without prejudice and not considered for further action by the grand jury.

Ed Brown's demeanor showed signs of hostility on the stand. His defensive stance showed through. Charley Brown, a quiet, peaceful follower of his brother, had little to say.

All prosecutorial witnesses had spoken before an hour had passed. Liddell took the stand and refuted everything the Browns had to say. Who started it was an issue. Who drew first, who fired first, was the common argument. However, one thing was for sure—everything Ed Brown said, James Liddell would say just the opposite. This was visibly upsetting the Browns. Their spectators made loud sighs from time to time, as they heard the lies told. The judge reprimanded them by striking his gavel.

James Liddell's brother, William, was on the stand, seated just to the judge's left. He gave lengthy testimony in favor of his brother and his brother's actions. Much testimony was given about the credibility of his family and the lack of credibility of the Browns. Additional blacks could have been there as witnesses. However, none offered to speak on the Browns' behalf. They had come only as spectators. Desire for justice and fairness brought them to the courtroom that day, but fear of retribution kept them from testifying.

When the defense had no other questions or reason to examine their witness, William Liddell remained seated next to the judge while the defense lawyers argued their case, which had barely lasted an hour. William Liddell sat in the center of the courtroom, watching the black members of the congregation. The Browns were to his right. The center pews and the pews on the other side of the courtroom were empty.

At a few minutes past 1 p.m., activity in the courtroom ceased as the group heard a loud roar outside. All ears and eyes went directly to the courtroom door as the group heard what sounded like an entire herd of horses stampeding in the town streets. Upon hearing the noise, the Browns looked out the window at the dust and saw men with guns dismounting. Not knowing what else to do, Ed and Charley ran for the door.

When they were within a few inches of the door, a large group of men armed with Winchester rifles, double barrel shotguns, breechloaders and various types of pistols, including the long horse pistols with immense lead balls, rushed into the room. Gunfire erupted. Smoke began to fill the room.

When the smoke cleared, strong, productive, living, loving men and teenagers who breathed the same air as those filled with hatred were now only helpless, lifeless bodies, their blood spilling onto the knotty pine floors. It was total chaos.

Ed and Charley Brown were the first to fall. Shocked, hysterical Negro men began to run for their lives. A small group tried to get past those in the doorway to make it down the stairs when suddenly a volley of shots rang out. There was a mad dash in a small confined space. Bodies began to pile up on top of each other four or five deep. The outlaws fired fifteen to twenty shots in the stairwell, dropping Negroes like flies.

The only other way out of the room was the many windows now behind them. Men ran back as quickly as they could in the crowded room to jump for their lives into the hands of outlaws waiting outside to finish the job.

Amos Matthews, who plunged through the east window, shot in the left side of the head with buckshot, fell suspended across the windowsill. His brains dripped down the outer wall. Walter McCloud and Peyton Hemingway jumped out a window together, carrying the sash with them. McCloud disappeared, shot in the heel. Hemingway hit the ground without a scratch and as many as twenty-five to forty shots barely missed him as he ran toward Mrs. Aldure's house. He suffered only minor injuries. Jake Cain hit the ground safely, only to be shot in the back as he started to run. He lived to tell his story.

More and more jumped for their lives in the midst of rapid gunfire, some wounded slightly, and others more seriously, but there was no way out. It was massive chaos. There was screaming, begging, shooting, pushing, shoving, smoke, and bleeding all over the courtroom. The number of Negroes left standing was small.

When the shooting stopped, not one of the white men in the courtroom had even a scratch. As the outlaws had done their damage, they started back down the stairs as if to pursue others who were still running. These men were all spectators and/or potential witnesses. There was nobody charged with a crime in that room, other than James M. Liddell, Jr., that anybody should have worried about escaping.

After the shooting stopped, one of the defense lawyers saw the mortally injured Ed Brown raise up on his elbow and fire his gun at Captain Estes in a last-ditch effort to defend himself before he died. His efforts were futile, but the men downstairs heard the shots. Houston Whitworth, leader of the group, rushed back up the stairs with followers and riddled Ed's body with multiple gunshots from his head to his feet to ensure his death.

In less than fifteen minutes, ten Negroes, including Ed and Charley Brown, lay dead. Two others, severely wounded, died before the day was gone and one more unexpectedly that evening, bringing the known death toll at the time to thirteen men.

Bullet holes riddled the pews; most of the bullet holes in the walls were waist-high or higher. The north wall where the white men either sat or stood erect prior to the shooting now had an untold number of bullet holes. All of the bullets somehow evaded each of the whites. Outlaws shot out some of the windows; people trying to get away knocked the others out. Bullet holes pierced the windowsills and the stairway walls. God only knows how many bullets ended up in the bodies of the dead.

Just as quickly as the 100-plus man contingency of outlaws rode in and accomplished their mission, they rode back out unseen by anyone. Witnesses who gave vivid details about the events of the day somehow could not even remember when questioned later as to whether or not the men wore masks.

The men initially described the incident as a riot. Their justification for labeling it as such was that they insisted that, once again, the Negroes had provoked the firefight. They say Ed Brown fired the first shot in the direction of James Liddell when the men rushed into the courtroom. When he started firing, according to them, they returned fire in self-defense. The other Negroes continued to draw and fire, sealing their own fate with shots of self-defense in return.

Shortly after the incident, Sheriff Hamilton anxiously, but sadly, entered the room. As he started to ask questions, the defense lawyers began to answer questions on everyone's behalf. Most of the white men were wearing dark suits, covered in the front with dust.

"Why was this blood bath necessary?" the sheriff shouted, with a mixture of both sorrow and anger.

"Let me tell you something, Sheriff," the marshal said. "It was high time these niggers learned their lessons. They have pushed our women off the streets, refused to pay their rent, picked fights, cursed citizens in businesses, and threatened to kill them. I know it was mostly the Browns, but these other niggers were their followers.

We have cut off the snake's head and destroyed the rest of his body. I should have realized that little snakes become big snakes and killed the whole damn family when I killed their old worthless Daddy back in '72 or '74, can't remember which. Now that it is done, though, we won't have to deal with that kind of disrespectful conduct anymore. Our ancestors will not have to worry about them taking over the polls again. Giving up a few innocent niggers is a small price to pay for what we accomplished here today. Don't you forget it!" said Tandy Oury, one of the town's most prejudiced men.

With a sad shake of his head, Sheriff Hamilton looked around the room at all the other men. Although none of them spoke up to agree, he could read it in their faces that they all agreed with Oury. Even though he was about as prejudiced as anyone else because of the way he was raised, he was not a killer.

He watched as William Liddell, a man practicing to be a doctor like his dad, walked over bodies, turning his head, not wanting to look at them or to see if they could survive. An injured man ignored by Liddell began to crawl away from the bottom of the steps. Many bled to death.

The sheriff was saddened. He knew this incident would never go away. Too many people saw it. Too many people knew of possible trouble. Too many people died. At times, he was glad he was not there that day. At other times, he wished he had been. If so, he would have probably been the only person on the Negroes' side and may have died. However, he would have avenged some of their deaths.

That was the last day he would ever leave his post to go home for lunch. He remained in the jail from the time he got to work in the morning until time to leave. If he had a prisoner in the cell, he would send the deputy to calls for service. He soon, quietly, and without fanfare, resigned his office as sheriff.

****

The Police Court (now known as the board of supervisors) authorized the payments for burial, coffin-making, grave digging, cemetery attendance, and cleanup of the courthouse.

Tandy Oury, coroner, was paid ten dollars to attend to burying ten of the men.

The record also said that "George Jackson, et. al." was paid six dollars for digging six graves at nearby Oak Grove Cemetery for paupers who died. Jeff Johnson was paid five dollars each for the coffins for Amos Mathews, John Money, Ed Brown, Charley Brown, Simon Cain, and Andrew Roberson. Alex Stansbury was paid ten dollars for cleaning the bloody, bullet-riddled courtroom.

Chapter 33:

The Eyewitness

"All things are subject to interpretation;
whichever interpretation prevails at a given time
is a function of power and not truth."
-Friedrich Nietzsche

T he first news accounts on the evening of the incident from the Greenwood/Winona area were very biased, blaming the Negroes for starting a riot. As the New Orleans correspondents arrived and started putting together the pieces, the stories changed significantly, shifting the blame to whites, even in Jackson and other Mississippi towns.

The New Orleans Times-Democrat was a very aggressive newspaper with huge circulation. Two papers, the *New Orleans Democrat* and the *New Orleans Times,* had merged only five years before into the *Times Picayune,* maintaining the best of the day in investigative reporters. Their office learned that while they were sending correspondents to the scene of what was now being called a massacre, at least one important Carrollton resident and witness was passing them going south on the Excursion Train of the Illinois Central Railroad.

On the morning of March 18, the editor obtained some limited passenger information from a Winona wire and dispatched correspondents to the meet passengers from Carrollton due to arrive at 11 a.m. at the New Orleans train station.

While questioning passengers, one reporter learned that none other than James Liddell Jr.'s brother, William W. Liddell, had arrived on the train. The reporter could not locate him in the crowd. It was determined that he had already taken a buggy to a boarding house at number 7 Carondalet Street in New Orleans. The reporter quickly obtained transportation to that location and called on William W. Liddell.

Liddell told the reporter he would cooperate with the understanding that he and his brother's real place of residence remained confidential. Further, that he would write nothing about his affluent father, the late Dr. William W. Liddell, his namesake, who had been a member of the state legislature during the Civil War. Liddell told the reporter his uncle, James Monroe Liddell, had served numerous terms as both a state representative and senator, retiring just three months before. He even mentioned his own brother, James, as having served in the legislature in 1878 and 1879 at only twenty-four years old. He insisted that this family's name not be tarnished.

"A well-known Confederate colonel, James R. Binford, from Duck Hill, has taken my uncle's place. He is currently serving with two well-respected state representatives, Mr. H.C. Williamson and L.M. Southworth. You must protect their honor as well. Sir, I would also place caution on the town's reputation. It should not suffer, having taken no part in this so-called massacre. Above all, the reputation of US Senator James Zachariah George has to remain untarnished, as he also served impeccably as chief justice of the Supreme Court. Why, even State Treasurer W.L. Hemingway was an old-time resident of Carrollton. Our ancestors named our fair town after one of the signers of the Declaration of Independence, Mr. Charles Carroll, who once lived in Carrollton.

"You see, sir, the image of Carrollton is of utmost importance if not just for all the political reasons, but the fact we are currently negotiating for the railroad to pass through our town. Governor Lowry is working very hard for that in negotiations with the railroad, as is Senator George in Congress. You know we will have both the Illinois Central and Georgia Pacific. Fear created by an incident such as this could cause the railroad to circumvent our town altogether, hindering growth and progress for many generations to come, my dear man. Our little town is more powerful politically than you can even imagine," Liddell said.

The reporter was ready to agree to anything after listening to this speech. He did not care about all those outside issues and influences. He only wanted to find the underlying cause of the massacre. As far as he knew, nobody else had gotten the opportunity to address an eyewitness from the courtroom shooting. He had an award-winning exclusive interview. Although he saw Liddell was not the type to jump right into the story at hand, he was a voracious talker.

The correspondent was shocked, and taken back by Liddell's charm. He would later describe Liddell in his article as "a gentleman of pleasing address and good conversational powers." Liddell told him of the gorgeous Greek-Revival style home he resided in, designed and built by none other than Mr. James C. Harris, the same architect that designed Greenwood Leflore's mansion, Malmaison, and the very courthouse where the massacre occurred.

"Sir, your stories are fascinating but I am approaching a deadline and really need to remain with the facts of the Carrollton tragedy if I am going to finish my story," the reporter said, as he had by then lost his patience.

"Very well, but for the sake of the newspaper stories, make sure that it appears in print that I live fifteen miles (as the crow flies) northwest of Carrollton in a community inhabited primarily by another prominent family known as the McCains. Old man William McCain had a sizeable plantation and over fifty slaves before the war. Most of them stayed with the family after their release. My older brother, James, was friends with John Sidney McCain. They would cover for him if anyone asked of his residence. It is of equal importance that my brother James be listed as residing in Greenwood even though he only worked there as editor of the *Yazoo Valley Flag* newspaper," Liddell said. "He did, by the way, have a bunk in the back of his place of business."

"Yes, sir, I will make sure we represent your residences accordingly and not mention the fact that the two of you really reside in your father's old home in the town of Carrollton. No, I will not mention your father or any of the politicians that concern you. This information is safe with just the two of us," the reporter said.

"I cannot overemphasize that the pressure must be taken off the Carrollton community, its finer residents and its well respected politicians. This must appear as a Negro uprising quelled by the white Democrats tired of the Negro gaining power through the Northern armies, carpetbaggers, scalawags, and previous occupation by federal forces. Our poll results will show in the years to come who owns the power in this state and it will not be the Negro. We have a little saying in our party, just between you and me, before we further discuss this incident, sir, and that is: 'Win fairly if you can, but win.' Hell, if we did not take measures into our own hands Negroes would still over-run our party.

"The plantations before the war took more slaves than it did plantation family members to run. When those darkies got the right to vote they took over not only the state but also the political power in Congress. I do not know how it works here in your fine state of Louisiana, but the legislature in Mississippi elects our US senators and congressional representatives, instead of the people. We have over ten thousand Negroes in Carroll County and only eight thousand whites. A few of the carpetbaggers and scalawags remain and, of course, are voting republican. In the past, we could not win an election without winning forcibly, but I thought the tides were changing. However, you just look at the last poll results. There were less than twenty black

Republican votes cast for governor. They were scared to come to the polls," Liddell laughed.

He sat back, pouring himself a glass of bourbon from a flask inside his coat, while offering one to his newfound friend, who declined.

"Mr. Liddell, can we please move forward with the subject at hand?" asked the reporter, now practically begging. "I absolutely must insist due to the time it will take me to prepare my report and get it through the editing process for press time."

Chapter 34:

Just the Facts

"Facts are stubborn things; and whatever may be our wishes, our inclinations, or the dictates of our passion, they cannot alter the state of facts and evidence."
-John Adams

Finally, Liddell started the real interview off by saying, "While I do not seek newspaper notoriety, I have nothing to conceal and will willingly give you all the information I have, relative to the occurrence you are in search of."

He went on to again make sure the correspondent erroneously noted that he lived fifteen miles northwest of Carrollton and his brother, James, lived in Leflore County, even though that had no bearing on the matter at hand. He also said he was not present during the altercation between his brother and the Browns, and only knew what his brother and friends had told him about that incident. He was able to testify to hearsay since it was only a preliminary hearing.

"As far as the hearing goes, I was seated on the judge's left side after providing a bit of my own impromptu testimony on behalf of my brother.

Looking out at the courtroom there were only a few white adults on my left and a few young boys. Nobody was in the center. There were some twenty-five Negroes to my far right in the center. The Brown brothers sat on the front row diagonally behind my brother, who sat between his two lawyers slightly to the judge's right and facing the judge. Ed Brown was sitting on the far end of the front row closest to the window on that side. I remained seated where I was as the last witness while the defense argued my brother's case to quash the warrant sworn out on him. I was looking over at my brother and just over his head at Ed Brown. A loud disturbance started and the sound of galloping horses could be heard outside," Liddell said.

"My brother turned to say something to one of his lawyers and I noticed Ed Brown starting to get very excited, looking back and forth, obviously in fear. He began to make a rush for the door. He turned around trying to beckon the other Negroes to come on out. They all got up and started. By then a group of armed men met them at the door and prohibited them from going down the steps. The armed men immediately opened fire, but I could not tell if it was in response to a shot fired by the Browns or some other Negro. Just then, people started jumping from the windows. I did not see whom the men were, doing the shooting and I cannot tell you if they were wearing masks or not. After I saw that my brother had not been hurt, I left Carrollton within the hour, headed to Winona to catch the Excursion Train down here to New Orleans."

"Mr. Liddell, much has been said about who did what and when. You seemed to have had a bird's eye view of everything without moving. Was the first shot fired by Ed Brown in the direction of your brother?" asked the correspondent.

"As I alleged, I cannot say that. In fact, I did not see any of those who did the firing. The benches in the back of the room were too high for me to see over. When the firing was over, I walked down the stairs past the wounded Negroes, turning my head away as I did not care to see them. I had to step over dead Negroes on the landing and I noticed that some of the wounded were crawling away from the dead. I made sure of my brother's safety, then left," William Liddell said.

"Mr. Liddell, you say you did not see any of those who did the firing. I would like to read you a quote from a special in the Winona paper on the day of the incident. They are talking about the men who rode in and did the shooting. Their paper says, 'They do not live near Carrollton.' How do you suppose if you as an eyewitness in the room didn't see the assailants, that anyone else can rule out that they came from Carrollton?" the correspondent asked.

"Not having provided that information to the Winona press, I am not sure why you would ask that question of me," Liddell said with a confused look.

"Sir, I ask you that question because you insist that I conceal the fact that you live in Carrollton and that your brother, James, lives in Greenwood when you and I both know both of you live in your father's old house in Carrollton. Finally, the Winona paper protects the citizens of Carrollton by indicating the assailants do not live in Carrollton. Why is everybody so protective of Carrollton?" asked the correspondent.

"As I explained to you before, we have a very affluent town with several very prominent families. We are mostly white with only a small group of Negroes living on the outskirts of town. Our buildings date back to the early 1830s, as do our beautiful churches. Most of our homes are well built, stately and reflect Greek revival, Victorian and other fine architecture, many designed by famous architects. We do not wish to have the riff-raff often found in so many of the Southern towns. The discussion of the railroad coming through town is on the table as we speak and we cannot allow the press to continue with its propaganda that reflects negatively on the town. This incident occurred in the Carroll County Courthouse, which does not belong to the Town of Carrollton even though it sits in the center of town on the square. It is most unfortunate that Carrollton must withstand the worst of this devastating tragedy. The people of Carrollton have heard their names smeared across this country in the last few days. They do not know anything and do not want to be involved. Most would concur it was wrong but many fear for their own safety. There could be implications far beyond what you or I can currently see," Liddell said.

"I have one final question to ask you, Mr. Liddell, before I have to go to press so I really must hurry. Do you see any reason or justification for the slaughter of the Negroes on Wednesday?" asked the correspondent.

"I do not, and I condemn it in the strongest terms," Liddell said with the utmost insistence.

Chapter 35:

The Governor

"For a people who are free, and who mean to remain so, a well-organized and armed militia is their best security."
-Thomas Jefferson

Governor Robert Lowry had just finished his lunch by himself at the long wooden table. On this spring afternoon, he sat in the stately Governor's Mansion, spared by Grant and Sherman's fires of the Civil War.

The town was destroyed to the extent that it was called Chimneyville for many years. However, the Union used the Governor's Mansion as both a headquarters and hospital. The state legislature was in session in the old Capitol building. It was also spared during the war.

By then everybody was screaming from the state capitol to the US capital over the incident at the Carroll County Courthouse in Carrollton, Mississippi.

As the governor started to eat his bread pudding coated with thick brown bourbon sauce, one of his aids handed him a telegram.

To: The Honorable Robert Lowry, Governor of the State of Mississippi.

A Times Picayune correspondent from New Orleans will call on you at your office not later than 2 p.m. this afternoon, arriving by train at 1:16 p.m. Respectfully request short interview regarding Carrollton incident.

Thank you, Hargrove/Editor.

"Who the hell do these news people think they are?" Lowry blurted out, as his Negro servant poured more coffee, only to see it spilled when Lowry banged his fist on the table. "Get me my aide Willie!" the governor yelled out to the servant.

"Yes, sir, Mr. Governor," the servant said as he wiped the spilled coffee with a white towel clinging to his waist, then hurried off.

"You need me, sir?" asked the aide, as he hurried to the governor's side.

"Yes, I do, Jonathan. Send a runner over to the capitol and get Senator James R. Binford, the man who took Senator James Monroe Liddell's seat this session. Hell, Liddell should be here himself to handle this since it looks like his nephew and namesake started the whole damn thing in the first place. I want Binford to come see me immediately. Further, I want you to tell the security staff if a news correspondent shows up around 2 p.m. not to send him in until 5 p.m. At that time, I will see him," Lowry said angrily.

"Yes, sir, on my way, Governor," the aide said as the governor started eating his bread pudding again.

"Willie!" the governor yelled out.

"Yes, sir, I am right here beside you, sir."

"Don't startle me like that, Willie! I thought you were in the kitchen. There ain't enough bourbon in this bread pudding sauce. See if you can fix that and bring me a shot on the side, too," Lowry said, as Willie scooted away to the kitchen. "Make that a double shot!"

****

About half an hour later, the governor's aide escorted Senator James R. Binford in to see the governor. By now the governor was sitting in his favorite chair, feet propped up, reading papers back and forth from New Orleans to Natchez and Winona, as he smoked his cigar.

"Sir, you called for me?" Senator Binford asked.

"Senator, I am sick and tired of hearing about the goings-on in your district. This is not a matter for me to have to deal with. I know you just took this district over from Liddell but if you take command of a ship that has a hole in it and you do not fix it, you may go down with it. The papers from here to New York, Washington, and everywhere in between are all over this matter. Now I have a New Orleans correspondent on his way to see me about this. What do you suppose I tell him?" asked Lowry.

"Governor, I would just make sure they know this was a premeditated riot perpetrated by the Negroes and our fine, law-abiding citizens, acted in the best interest of the county to quell the disturbance," Binford said.

"Well, that all sounds good but it might be very difficult to explain why our fine, law-abiding citizens showed up heavily armed to be non-violent spectators an hour after the hearing had begun. Not to mention the fact that they started shooting as they entered, leaving bullet holes in the wall of the stairway before even entering the courtroom," the governor said.

"Governor, it has been stated over and again by people from Carroll County that the Negroes fired first and our people were simply defending themselves," Binford said.

"Don't get me wrong, Senator Binford, I don't want to give in to the papers. I do not care any more about these niggers than you do. I fought in the war just as you did and I saw my friends give up their lives and property because the North did not believe in slavery. I have not forgotten my friends, and I never will. I am simply raising these issues with you as a man most close to the town so I can be prepared to respond to this city slicker reporter from New Orleans. So tell me, as a lawyer myself, looking at a potential provocation claim, how do I address the fact that these men rode into town in large numbers, over a hundred, rushing up the stairs with long guns in hand? Would that not have provoked you, Mr. Binford?" asked the governor as he slammed his fist down on the table.

"Well, I am sure it would have, Governor, but who's going to make that claim with all the Negroes dead? Besides, who is going to authorize a hearing in a public setting to address that?" asked Binford.

"Okay, Senator, we will come back to that thing about the public setting, but one last question. These Negroes were scared out of their wits, unable to get down the stairs past the armed men so they began jumping out of windows to save their lives, knowing the fall might take their lives. What danger or threat could they possibly have posed to shooters who shot them in the back while jumping or running from the building?" asked the governor.

"No problem, sir; they have all been buried and our judges won't be granting an exhumation order to find bullets in their backs. All the Negroes were said to have been armed," Binford said.

"Right. Have you notified Senator James George in Congress?" asked the governor.

"I have not personally, sir. However, his son has dispatched a telegram informing him of the New York news editorial. They are saying that he was one of the assailants led by Houston Whitworth of Greenwood, a former sergeant from Company C, 12th Mississippi Infantry Regiment. The response he got back was to lay low. Northern congressmen were confronting him about proposed legislation to deal with future incidents of this type," Binford said

"Okay, here's my response, short and sweet. The incident happened a few days ago. All is quiet now. The county has not asked for assistance. They believe the law enforcement sources on hand can handle it. If I were to intrude without their request, I would be performing outside my authority. Besides, law enforcement personnel on the scene have concluded that it was an uprising started by the Negroes and the whites acted in self-defense,'" the governor said.

"That sounds good to me, Governor," Binford said. "May I be of further assistance?"

"No, I know you are very busy in the legislature trying to wrap it up. I am sincerely thankful for your assistance. However, back to that other issue about witnesses in open hearings. It is Friday and I need you to return to Carrollton for the weekend and visit your circuit judge. Tell him to make a show by having an investigative grand jury. They do not need to find anything. I want the press off my back. Oh, by the way, while I still have a good memory, I am jotting down notes to one day write a book about Mississippi history. I have just finished the chapter that dealt with the Constitutional Convention of 1868. Take it with you on the train to Carrollton and read it. You will know for sure how much I care about the Negro and what happened to them in Carrollton when you finish my manuscript. Take all these damn newspaper clippings, too," Governor Lowry said.

"I understand, sir, and will do," Binford said.

"Would you please tell my aide to come back on your way out?" Lowry asked.

"I certainly will," Binford replied as he left the governor.

A few minutes later, the aide came back and the governor asked if the reporter had been there yet.

"He came and was told to return at 5 p.m., Governor. He seemed very happy just knowing that you are willing to see him. He expects to get to the bottom of the Carrollton incident by coming directly to you for the real answers," the aide said with a smirk on his face.

"The real answers," the governor barked out, as he laughed. "My daddy's railroad watch says it is almost 3 p.m. I am going to have one more glass of bourbon and take a nap on the sofa. Please wake me by 4:30 so I can freshen up for this inquisitive out-of-towner," Lowry said as he sat down on the sofa and began to remove his shoes.

****

"Governor Lowry, your Excellency, sir, I am Jeff Boudreaux from the *New Orleans Times Picayune*, representing Mr. Hargrove himself."

"So you are, young man. Please, have a seat," Lowry said as he stood towering over the reporter.

"Aren't you going to sit down?" asked Boudreaux.

"Nah, I like standing myself, just woke up from a nap. Need to let the blood flow the other way anyhow."

Boudreaux felt very intimidated with the governor looking down at him as he attempted to start his notes. "Governor, I would like to ask…"

Lowry interrupted immediately, speaking loudly and quickly. "I know what you want to ask, my boy. I have read more newspaper accounts of this mess in the last two days than I want to remember. I am going to tell you what you need to know. This was a Carroll County riot. A gang of Negroes started it. That led to a well-needed armed group of citizens having to act, resulting in the death of some Negroes. It is a matter for them to handle. I have spoken to their representative in the legislature and he says they have not asked for assistance. All is quiet there now and most people feel the sheriff and his people are capable of dealing with this matter. I would overstep my boundaries if I got involved and I do not intend to do that!"

"But, sir, what about calling out the militia?" asked Boudreaux, infuriating the governor.

"The militia, you say!" the governor shouted. "What would they do? Had they been there, they would have been the ones having to shoot down the Negroes. It is all quiet there and we have no reason to believe there would be another uprising, so what the hell would the militia do?" screamed Lowry.

"I don't know, sir, but it seems like they could do something," Boudreaux cried in disgust.

"Son, do you think I don't know what a militia should be used for? Do you know who I am? Do you know my background? Who are you to question my use of a militia? I have you to know I am a decorated Civil War soldier, an officer of the Confederate Army who started out as a private and received a field promotion to major. I was wounded twice at the Battle of Shiloh. I lost 310 of my 425 men. My men of Company B, 6th Mississippi Infantry, was known as the 'Bloody Sixth.' We barely had enough men to complete a burial operation after being slaughtered ourselves. We went on to fight in the second battle of Corinth, Port Hudson, Port Gibson, Bayou Pierre, Champion Hill, and Vicksburg. When Brigadier General Adams fell dead in Franklin, Tennessee, I was a colonel by then. However, I stepped forward to command one of the fiercest battles of the war throughout the Tennessee campaign, leading the brigade before being promoted to Brigadier General myself. Don't you judge me by that piece of paper on my wall merely admitting me to the bar that you continue to stare at, young man! You look me in the eyes! I am more than a lawyer. I *know* what a militia does! They fight to the death and hope death comes upon their opponent before them. That is exactly what they would have done had they been in Carrollton and if so, our white citizens might not have been left standing either! Have you heard enough, Mr. Boudreaux?" asked the governor as he bent down, staring into Boudreaux's face with his teeth gritted, his lips protruding forward and his eyes squinted.

Boudreaux, now speechless and shaking, climbed up from the chair with the governor still bent over him, hurrying to leave and almost soiling his trousers.

Chapter 36:

Senator Binford Returns to Carrollton

*"Thank God for our form of government.
The media won't let there be any cover-up."*
-John McCain

I t was a cold and windy morning on Saturday, March 20, when Senator Binford boarded the train on Capitol Street in downtown Jackson. He welcomed the warm seat on the train to get out of the damp wind but he did not look forward to the trip back. He had a stack of newspaper articles sent by telegraph from newspapers around the country, given to him by the *Jackson Clarion*. It had only been three days since the incident in Carrollton but the news had traveled like wildfire all over the United States. Even foreign countries got it from the wire. A common theme glowed in the Southern papers with the exception of those around Carroll County: There had been a terrible massacre and somebody in an official capacity needed to take action.

After reading the newspaper accounts, Binford removed Governor Lowry's rough manuscript of the

Mississippi history book he was writing. One folder read, "Black and Tan Convention of 1868 by General Robert Lowry." As smart as he was, it was obvious to Binford that Lowry was going to need help as an author. Some of the accounts were just that—no sentence structure, just notes as follow:

Military order issued by fourth district commander Brevet Major-General Ord to hold convention in accordance with the reconstruction act approved March 23rd 1867 to elect delegates to establish new constitution for the state. Many intelligent, respectable whites from around the state prohibited from participation while ignorant, unscrupulous Negroes knowing nothing of the elective process were made docile instruments of equally ignorant but more corrupt and worthless class of white man ever known to be none other than carpetbaggers were. One such imbecile was B.B. 'Buzzard' Eggleston from Lowndes County, a course, illiterate, and vulgar fellow who was chosen to be the president of the convention over the Honorable John Watson a well-known white, lawyer and fine Christian gentleman. These characterless vagabonds, of these bold brigands thus suddenly raised from their native insignificance to a position of prominence, masquerading as statesman and constitution writers were here only because of four newspapers in the state. Happily for the state and its people, nine-tenths of the vultures are gone, never again to return to the people they plundered and oppressed. Many have gone down to dishonored graves. The few Negroes from the Black and Tan Convention, who still survive, have returned to their original vocations of barbers, boot-blacks, hack drivers, blacksmiths, waiters and fiddlers who never abandoned their businesses to play the role of statesman.

The corrupt carpetbaggers, the ignorant Negroes and the baser renegades, who had tried their prentice hands on the work of constitution making, for the few citizen of intelligence and decency had but little part in the construction of that instrument, completed by their labors on May 15, 1868, after having been in session four months and nine days. Each member of this multi-colored aggregation of ignorance, insolence, and imbecility, including Negroes, renegades and carpetbaggers from every quarter of the country, drew $1,290 each along with their Buzzard Eggleston who drew $2,580 for an aggregate sum of $128,710 only to have their constitution rejected and not ratified by the people. This was in spite of the fact that the federal bayonets were gleaming at over 60 voting places throughout the state. In the hour of defeat, a claim was made that several counties including Carroll were carried against adoption through fraud, intimidation and violence.

Well, this pretty much sums it up how Lowry feels about the Negroes. I think it will be a cold day in hell before he ever does anything to avenge them, Binford thought to himself as he leaned his head against the frosty window of the train, trying to get some rest.

****

A few hours later, the train arrived at Winona station. Binford hired a buggy driver to take him some twenty miles to Carrollton.

Upon arrival, he went to the home of Circuit Court Judge C. H. Campbell, where he was welcomed and invited to stay for lunch. The two wasted no time in getting down to the subject at hand.

"Judge, the governor has sent me to talk to you. The massive media accounts around the country of this incident that occurred in the courthouse on March 17 have overwhelmed him. He wants you to recall the grand jury and make it appear they are investigating the cause of this incident while trying to identify the perpetrators. Of course, he wants you to understand that he already knows the perpetrators were the Negroes. Understand?" asked Binford with a smile.

"Senator, as I see it, the governor wants us to empanel the grand jury for investigative purposes and make that fact known to the press. In accordance with law, we are to withhold the material discovered by the grand jury as secret. Is that right?" asked Judge Campbell.

"That's right. Nobody will know what they discover. It will not even be transcribed in the record returned to you by the grand jury foreman. They will offer their condolences and make it known that they have examined witnesses but found nobody to indict for this offense," Binford said.

The conversation was over just in time for a table set with turnip greens, cornbread, ham hocks, banana pudding, and sweet iced tea.

"Okay, I can have each juror notified over the weekend. Don't worry about it," Judge Campbell said as they made their way to the dining table from the study.

Senator Binford spent almost an hour having lunch with Judge Campbell. They talked about the two known suspects, Whitworth and young George. They would get the protection they needed at the state level. However, it was important to make sure the federal government kept its nose out of the case. Empanelling the grand jury would make a show for the media. "It will all go away in a couple of months," the two men assured each other.

"Please give my regards to the governor and tell him we are really looking forward to a railroad coming through our town. I am so tired of having to go to Winona to catch the train to Jackson or New Orleans, even Memphis. Having one here at our doorstep can only be accomplished with the relationship Governor Lowry has with the railroad companies," Campbell said with a smile, as he escorted Binford to the door.

"Wish I could get a meal like that in Jackson," Binford said. "I am going to Duck Hill now and back to Jackson tomorrow. I am putting the finishing touches on a state bill Senator George wanted us to get though. I hope he is having a good time with his own legislative session in Washington right now. Oh, by the way, keep that boy of his out of sight during this grand jury session."

Chapter 37:

Gather the Witnesses

"Meetings are indispensable when you don't want to do anything."
-John Kenneth Galbraith

J udge Campbell went to the clerk's home after lunch on Saturday, March 20. He explained what their job was and apologized for having to notify the jurors on Saturday and Sunday. However, he made sure everybody understood how important it was to get the jurors back in their seats by Monday morning, even if it meant passing the word to them at church the next day.

In addition, he explained to the clerk that upon completing the grand jury's efforts, the record of the proceedings must not name any suspects. They must write it in such a way as to protect the townspeople while at the same time satisfying the media that the county was doing something. The clerk assured him that he would notify a sufficient number of jurors and recall the grand jury for this purpose.

"By the way, who is the foreman of the grand jury?" Judge Campbell asked.

"It is a very fine man that you know well, Mr. John T. Stanford," the clerk said.

"Oh, yes, that's great. You are right, he is a good man, and I know we can count on him. I will go by and see him now. I want him to understand the issues as well," Judge Campbell said.

"Judge, did you know that one of the Negroes who was killed was John Stanford's servant?" asked the clerk.

"Well, no, I didn't know that. What was his name?" Judge Campbell asked.

"It was Scott Moore," the clerk said.

"Okay, well, I will keep that in mind when I talk to him and see how he feels," Judge Campbell said as he made his way to the door.

****

"Judge, come on in. What brings you by today? I haven't seen you in a while," John Stanford said.

"Do you mind if we just sit out here on the porch?" the judge asked, as he heard other people inside.

"No, no, I don't. Just let me grab a sweater. It seems a little chilly out and I know that coat you have on is keeping you plenty warm," Stanford said as he grabbed his coat off the rack by the door and walked out on the porch.

"Have a seat there on the swing, Judge, and I'll sit here in this old chair with deer skin on the seat. That was a twelve-point buck, killed him myself. What's on your mind?" asked Stanford.

"I heard one of your Negroes was killed in the riot. Is that true?" asked the judge.

"Yep, my only Negro, and I hate it. He was a good one and always did good work around here. He had been with me a long time, since he was a young man. He died at age thirty-six mainly because he would not listen. There were a couple of old men down there that were warned not to go down there that day but they went anyway. Their white families are gonna miss 'em. Just one of those things, Judge, you know?" asked Stanford.

"Yes, I do, John, and I am glad you have that attitude about it. Listen, I understand you were the foreman in the last grand jury," the judge said.

"That's right, sure was," Stanford snapped proudly.

"Well, John, I hate to tell you this, but I had a high-level visitor who was sent by an even higher-level visitor. They want us to reconvene the grand jury on Monday to start an investigation on that riot they are now calling a massacre. We are still in the same court term so we will not be selecting new jurors. You will have the same group. I know some of them were drawn from out in the county. Do you know most of them?" asked the judge.

"Sure do, Judge, several of them are in our lodge. The same one you and I belong to," Stanford said, as he grabbed the judge's hand, giving him that coded handshake and a smile.

"Oh, that makes me feel better. Tell me everybody's name you can remember. I hope we can count on them all," the judge said.

"I don't remember all of them but I'll go in the house for a minute. I have a list in there that had all our names on it for jury pay and mileage. Be right back. You ain't gonna visit all of them, are you?" asked Stanford, as he stepped inside the door without waiting for an answer.

Stanford came back out, sat on the swing and put on his spectacles then cleared his throat. Before reading them aloud, the judge stopped him for a moment.

"No, John, I am not going to visit everybody. I am going to count on you as their leader. I have already talked to the clerk who will be transcribing the findings and we are onboard with what must take place. We cannot release information that is secret from a grand jury but we have to at least appear to make an effort and hope the press will go away. Senator George sent his wife a telegram and he is angry with the Yankees bringing this issue up on the floors of Congress. The media keeps trying to get a comment from him up there but he is not talking. Who would have ever thought a town of only four hundred would be in the news around the world? There is no way the Northerners will ever believe we are treating Negroes the way they expect. We have to get all the witnesses we can. Just bring in Houston Whitworth's gang," the judge said.

"Okay, here are the names. There was several from out in the county that I don't know:

T.A. Kimbrough, W.A. Layne, G.S. Fox, W.P. Mussalwhite, Lawyer Lott, Ance Liddell, G.F. Roberts, W.F. Mabry, J.H. Fields, W.C. Chatham, F.R. Smith, J.B. Harlin, Lee McMillon, L.L.

Chambley, J.V. Williford, G.W. Pentecost and, of course, me, John T. Stanford himself, at your service, sir. That's it, I know you recognized some of those names from the lodge, but some are strangers, couple may even be carpetbaggers. You never know how some of them will vote. They may even notify the feds. Good thing we no longer have those military districts and federal forces. The federal grand jury would have indicted the whole town in the federal court system. Do you think the damn Yankees will shut up just knowing we had a grand jury investigation? If we don't indict somebody, how do you think that will go over with them since the thing happened in the middle of the day and everybody saw it?" Stanford asked. "You know I am an honest man, Judge."

"We just have to hope for the best my friend. Just hope for the best. Okay, John, I'll be on my way. If you see any of your jurors, please tell them to be there Monday morning. We do not want to have to issue subpoenas right now. If need be, we can do that later. The clerk is going to be notifying some of them and I guess y'all can catch the rest at church on Sunday. I must go and talk to one other person, the D.A. I just thought I would catch you and the clerk while I was here in town. I'll go out into the county to talk to the D.A. If I miss him, the clerk will inform him on Monday morning before the grand jury is convened," the judge said.

"Yes, sir. Well, you stay buttoned up, Judge. We would not want you to catch cold. Come back anytime. See you at the lodge next week if not before then," said Stanford.

"Oh, you will probably see me Monday morning. I have to give y'all the order with specifics of what to look for. I may do that through the D.A., but may not, either. At any rate, I'm off," the judge said, as he pulled his collar up around his neck and walked away in the brisk air.

The judge began to mumble and talk to himself as he walked down the street. *I hope the DA won't be his usual horse's ass self and cooperate,* he thought. *Never know about that bastard. He wants my job and may try to ambush me. I know damn well he won't like me telling him how to run the grand jury.*

Chapter 38:

The Grand Jury

"Today the grand jury is the total captive of the prosecutor who, if he is candid, will concede that he can indict anybody, at any time, for almost anything, before any grand jury."
-William J. Campbell

All of the jurors received notice and showed up early for the grand jury. The first half of the day on Monday consisted of instructions and rules given by the district attorney while the sheriff's posse was out rounding up witnesses. A few witnesses showed up that afternoon for their interviews, while others were told to come on specific days.

The grand jury lasted a total of six days before examining the last witness and coming to a conclusion. All jurors received compensation for their service and mileage, which was supposed to be the case with witnesses as well. However, no county warrants have been found to show payment to witnesses, which could mean they never examined witnesses as a body at all. The report reads verbatim:

To the Honorable C.H. Campbell, Judge of the Court

The undersigned grand jurors for the March term for the Circuit Court for the first Circuit and Chancery Court District of Carroll County respectfully submit the official report of these actions and deliberations. In compliance with your honor's charge directing special investigation of the recent tragedies in our County, Town, we have as best we could performed the duties required and having failed to find an indictment against a single person participating in the deeds of violence and we deem it but just to the Court, to ourselves and to the community in which we live in so far as we can without infringement on our obligation of secrecy – to inform the court of our actions and to give the general result of our deliberations in this matter.

We desire to report further in reference to the recent tragedy enacted in the Courthouse that we have used every endeavor to get to the facts of the sad occurrence. That we have examined 165 witnesses and make the public report of our investigation for reasons that are not only satisfactory to ourselves but also in vain of the fact that that unfortunate trouble has assumed a National character and that the investigation has been pressed by us with all the vigor in our power that the result should be made known through us to the world the jury desires to say in this Consensus that the facts and statement of facts used in this report were developed in the Course of this investigation and are reiterated with a conscious of truth and so without regard to the views of the press or outside world. Uncontroverted evidence shows that on the evening of the 13th day of February 1886, J.M.

*Liddell, Jr. had some harsh words with Ed Brown in
which Liddell called him a Son-of-a-bitch. Soon after,
they departed and Liddell went to supper. On coming
out from the Hotel, Liddell was told that several
Negroes including the said Ed and Charley Brown were
on the street between Ray's and Poteets cursing and
abusing him. And as he was passing down the street by
the party of Negroes he stopped near Charley Brown
and took hold of his hat and raised it and asked "what
does all this mean?" He then asked Ed Brown "what
are you doing here?" Brown replied, "it is none of your
God damn business" whereupon Liddell slapped him in
the face and was immediately fired on by the two
Browns and others wounding him in the arm and
thigh.*

*It is the sense of this body that the Browns, after
first harsh words went off and armed themselves and
came back to this place for the purpose of Assassinating
Liddell. After being wounded by some of the assailants,
Liddell returned the fire slightly wounding Ed and
Charley Brown. Five days after this difficulty, Ed and
Charley Brown were arraigned before Mayor Elam of
Carrollton. John Johnson having fled the Country and
none of the others who fired being identified and
waiving examination entered into bond for their
appearance at this term of the Court. Matters stood
thus until Liddell having recovered sufficiently from his
wounds returned to his home in Greenwood on the 10th
day of March. On the 12th Ed and Charles Brown made
affidavit against Liddell and six others charging them
with assault with intent to kill and murder them.
Investigation shows that none of the parties were
present with Liddell at the time, but being nearby some*

of them arrived soon after the difficulty. Most of them were unarmed. Wednesday the case was fixed for trial and the prisoners were all present represented by their Counsel who heard some disturbances from the outside Counsel, Ed and Charles Brown to draw their pistols, and Ed Brown fired at Liddell. The firing then became general. The disturbances from the outside noise from the appearance of a number of mounted men who were well armed and headed to the Courthouse. We have not been able to identify any of the parties to the difficulty. The firing in the Court Room resulted in the death of (obliterated text) and the wounding of (obliterated text) others. The evidence before us goes to show that the Browns were turbulent and desperate half-breeds always ready for a conflict whom from the facts developed we believe were responsible for the sad tragedy enacted in our county. The jury desires to say that they condemn any resort to violence and that in every case of wrong doing the Courts of the County should be affected to for vindication.

We furthermore state that we have examined the jail, found it clean and in good order. We will state in conclusion that we have examined the docket of the Magistrate of the First Judicial District of Carroll County and found them correct and believe from the examination that there has been a faithful discharge of duty.

News that the grand jury had failed to identify any of the perpetrators or return an indictment on a single person traveled liked wildfire across the wires. The Northern newspapers, black organizations, and politicians were having a field day with Mississippi. The Congress was in session in Washington, D.C., as was the legislature in the State of Mississippi. The press did not obtain these verbatim details, as they were secret and unavailable for many years to come. They did learn that the grand jury failed to issue an indictment, which was enough for the press to run with. It was what most everybody expected.

Justice was present nowhere in Carroll County.

Chapter 39:

Help from a Former Mississippi Governor

"Every mission constitutes a pledge of duty. Every man is bound to consecrate his every faculty to its fulfillment. He will derive his rule of action from the profound conviction of that duty."
-Giuseppe Mazzini

While discussions continued in Carrollton, the press, not just Northern but around the country and in Canada, insisted on justice prevailing over this terrible massacre. The New Orleans newspapers told the story in depth and telegraphed it to major newspapers around the country. The North was especially outraged. Pressure mounted by daily editorials that used the details and the history of Mississippi to sensationalize an event that needed little dramatization. The act itself was reprehensible and regardless of the two sides of the story, nobody, even the brother of the person in court at the time, condoned the act publicly.

Ten years after his resignation as governor of Mississippi, Adelbert Ames received a telegram. It was from former US senator Blanche K. Bruce and former US representative from Mississippi John R. Lynch, who were in Washington. They had just met with President Grover Cleveland over the Carrollton incident. They would be there a few days and invited him to come for possibly a second-chance meeting.

Ames had also read of the tragedy in his own *Lowell Sun* newspaper as well as the *New York Times*. He was devastated and had collected papers from all major sources. He hoped the media attention would be the vehicle to get Congress to act.

He was traveling down on the train the next day to meet Lynch and Bruce. What he did not know was that very evening a couple of Southern heavyweights were meeting to block any support of the blacks from Mississippi. Senator James Z. George from Carrollton, Mississippi, would meet with a prominent representative from Texas, John Reagan, who had ties with Mississippi confederate leadership.

On the train headed for Washington, D.C., Ames reminisced about his years in the Civil War, followed by his appointment then election as governor. His past haunted him, not because of what he had done, but what the white supremacy mentality of his Southern enemies had done to him.

President Andrew Johnson appointed General Adelbert Ames as the provisional military governor for Mississippi following the Civil War from 1868-1870. He was the military authority for the state, to include officer-in-charge of the military districts. When the Negroes began to vote, there was still fear and lack of organization in the Republican Party to win an election.

Scalawags and carpetbaggers helped organize the Negroes and helped them exercise their right to vote. At that time, the legislature elected US congressmen and senators, rather than the voters electing them in a general election.

By then, the legislature had many black senators and representatives. After a tour as US senator, Ames won the office of governor in 1874 by vote of the people. The democratic machine in Mississippi was furious. The white Democrats committed intimidation at the polls, lynching, burning at the stake and other deliberate attempts, to unseat the Republican party.

Politicians, prominent citizens, and law enforcement personnel were most likely part of these violent groups that insisted on annihilating the Negroes. This violence would destroy the Republican Party, ensuring Democratic dominance from then on.

In December 1874, over seventy-five Negroes died at the hands of white supremacists at a Republican convention in Vicksburg. White regulators forced the Negro sheriff out of town. He had to seek refuge at the state capitol building forty-five miles away in Jackson, Mississippi.

Southern lawyers like James Z. George from Carrollton led the Democratic Party. Democrats regained legislative control in Mississippi during the election of November 1875 and took office in January 1876. The Democrats started their agenda with conducting so-called investigations targeting mostly Negro public officials. Governor Ames' running mate, the lieutenant governor, also a Negro, was ousted on what he called "trumped up charges," as was the superintendent of education, a Negro, too. Ames would follow, with the Democrats bringing up impeachment proceedings on him, forcing his resignation at the end February of 1876.

Ames, a wealthy man born in Maine, settled in Northfield, Minnesota, to start a flour milling business with relatives. In the fall of 1876, the infamous outlaw Jessie James and his band of former Confederate guerilla soldiers followed him. It was their last attempt at bank robbery. They supposedly had attempted to rob a bank there reportedly because Ames' and former Union General Benjamin Butler's investments were held there. The gang killed Robert Heywood, one of the bankers, for lying about being unable to open the safe. A shootout ensued, also leaving a Swedish immigrant bystander dead. The hail of gunfire resulted in their quick departure without learning that the safe had really been unlocked the whole time. They hated Grant's right-hand man, Butler, who was a close ally of Ames', and sometimes called him "Beast Butler."

Ames later moved to New York for a short time but settled in Lowell, Massachusetts.

He was very distraught and bitter over the actions of Mississippi legislators. He was also very disappointed that President Ulysses S. Grant refused his request for troop assistance to stop the killing of Negroes, scalawags and the carpetbaggers who helped organize them. The president claimed he was afraid a new civil war would break out, far bloodier than the last. However, Grant did not refuse South Carolina in a similar request later that summer of 1876.

Following his resignation, Ames kept up with the goings-on of what he hoped would be progress in Mississippi. He had not forgotten all the riots and useless killings of blacks. He never dreamed that he would once again be facing issues with his archenemy, James Z. George.

Chapter 40:

Meeting at Mordecai's Pub

*"These bastards who run our country are a bunch
of conniving, thieving, smug pricks who need to
be brought down and removed and replaced with
a whole new system that we control."*
-Michael Moore

Mordecai's Pub was a quiet, little, old English-style pub located on the old Washington Navy Yard. It was not one of those hot spots frequented by members of Congress and was far enough away from Capitol Hill. It had little to no business when the ships were not in for repair and stayed open only for the navy officers. The atmosphere was dark with walls and ceilings made of dark wood salvaged from old sailing ships. Also salvaged and placed in the entrance of the pub was a beautifully painted wooden figurehead, a mermaid that once adorned the bow of some majestic sailing vessel. This was a perfect place inside a secure area, not open to the public or press, and had the coldest beer in town.

Senator James Z. George had made contact with Texas State Representative John H. Reagan, a ranking member of the Railroad Committee. At about 6 p.m., the two men met privately in the back corner of Mordecai's. They were the only patrons and had to wake the bartender, whose head lay comfortably on the bar over his crossed arms. He awoke quickly when he saw the two large figures dressed in suits with vests and hats. Both had full beards. George looked a little scraggly and unkempt with tobacco stain on his lips. Reagan noticed, but overlooked crumbs and dandruff on George's dark vest and wrinkled lapel.

"I want to talk to you about three things," James George said with a serious face.

"I bet I can tell you what at least two of those things are, Mr. George," Reagan said.

"Pardon me, sir, for getting straight to business. Would you like a cigar?" asked George.

"Don't mind if I do," Reagan said as he reached across the table and grabbed the cigar, dragging it once under his nose and once in each direction through his lips, before biting off the tip and spitting it into the corner.

George lit both their cigars as the bartender delivered cold pewter mugs of beer. Conversations about the South and the Civil War began as they compared their backgrounds and service to the Confederacy. George was already familiar with Reagan's background and his close friendship with Jefferson Davis.

"I understand you and President Davis were imprisoned together, Mr. Reagan, is that right?" asked George.

"Yes, it is—no finer man anywhere. By the way, your own General Robert Lowry personally appeared before the Union to seek his release after the war," Reagan said. "He did a mighty fine job too. Even though it did not happen immediately, your Governor Humphreys got President Davis out on bail. Your present governor, Lowry, had started the wheels turning."

"Yes, that's true. Did you know West Point kicked old Humphreys out for disciplinary problems? He enrolled in 1825 as a classmate with General Robert E. Lee. I am surprised he came back to excel. I spent the last two years of the war in prison myself on the Great Lakes. Almost froze to death. I go shot in Tennessee and captured. I do not have much love for niggers or Yankees and I damn sure do not like cold weather. Speaking of niggers, Mr. Reagan, I am sure you have heard about our most unfortunate incident in my town of Carrollton, Mississippi, have you not?" asked Senator George.

"Oh, I have heard about it. Who hasn't? The press is all over it. I understand some resolutions are going to be introduced on the floor of the house as early as tomorrow," Reagan said.

"Well, the riot at Carrollton was one thing I wanted to talk to you about. Another was potential bills or resolutions arising out of this and the third is about the railroad," George said.

"What about your son?" Reagan asked. "The newspapers in New York are saying your son may have been a member of the regulator gang that did the shooting."

"I'm not addressing that and they will never prove it. They may plaster it all over the newspapers but it will not go to court. He is staying out of sight at the home of a state senator friend of mine in Jackson, Mississippi. It will all blow over. This ain't the first time this has happened. What concerns me the most right now is blocking motions, bills, and resolutions. I can handle the Senate but I need a confidant like you in the House. We have equal concerns about the railroad, which is my long-term worry. If Congress fails to take action on this deal, it will go away after a while. If we passed laws because of it, this would affect states all over the South. My greatest concern is that it could prevent the railroad from coming through our town a couple of years from now."

"You can count on me in the House. I will object to any resolution that comes up. However, the route of the railroad could be an issue. There are many people coming down there from the North. They do not want to go into a place where massacres occur or, worse yet, are condoned. These people want to be safe. Hell, many people from up North and back East think we are still fighting the Indians and that scares them enough. You may lose that route," Reagan said.

"Well, Governor Lowry is real tight with the railroad companies so I am not going to worry about that too much," George said.

"Mr. George, tell me something while we have one more beer," Reagan said, calling the bartender with a flip of his hand.

"Sure, time to relax and get business out of the way, huh?" George asked.

"I heard y'all had a real landslide for old Lowry over there in Mississippi this term. How did you pull that off?" Reagan asked with a big laugh as he pulled on his mustache.

"Probably no different than you Confederates over in Texas are doing. We are damn proud of this last election. It took a lot of work. I was just poking fun at a couple of other senators today. My constituents at home telegraphed me the results of this election. Compared to the last two…got 'em right here in my coat. Pull that lamp over here and look at this." George said.

"I see the counties listed here and how they voted. Which county do you reside in?" asked Reagan.

"Sir, I am the 'Commoner of Mississippi' and damn proud of it. My wife, Elizabeth Young, comes from rich blood but I am just a poor old boy living in Carroll County. I will tell you how we voted in a minute but let me tell you this. I know you heard of the old Union General Adelbert Ames who got the Medal of Honor at Bull Run during the war. Well, we did not go along with everything the Yankees wanted like ratifying the thirteenth and fourteenth amendments to the Constitution right away and they would not allow us representation in Congress until we did. Then the president appointed that no-account niggah-lover Ames to be our military governor during reconstruction. He served from the middle of 1868 until mid-1870. They divided us into military districts with federal forces occupying various districts around the state so they could make sure we treated the niggahs like real people. Then in 1874 old James Alcorn, a white scalawag traitor, as far as I am concerned, ran for governor as a Republican and lost to Ames. You know, because all the niggahs could now vote. He did hate Ames, though. They had served together in Congress the term before," George said, before Regan interrupted him.

"Wait, Mr. George. That James Alcorn...was he a former Confederate general?" asked Reagan.

"He was for a short time. He came from Illinois, you know, nothing but a damn Yankee in a Confederate uniform. He did not care what party he represented. He lowered himself to be a Republican and got elected knowing the plantations had ten freed slaves to every one white family member," George said.

"Ames started his elected term in January of 1874, about the time we started to regain control making sure niggahs didn't show up at the poll. That is all I care to tell you about on that subject. Anyway, we conducted investigations targeting him and his nigger lieutenant governor running mate, and his superintendent of education. We got them out of office in January 1876 as soon as the legislative session started. Then we hit old Ames with impeachment proceedings and that bastard resigned in late February 1876. John Stone, our first Democrat after the war, was president pro-tem in the Senate. Since the governor and lieutenant governor were gone, he stepped up and assumed the governor position in March 1876. It was downhill from there," George said.

"What do you mean by that?" Reagan asked.

"Get this...when Stone ran for re-election in November 1877, there were no—not one single—Republican vote cast," George said with a big, hearty laugh. "We had the same kinds of results for the legislative positions and retook our legislature from the Republicans, which also gave us control of the Congress. If that was not enough, we pulled off the Compromise of 1877, which benefited you and the rest of the South. We let them have their Republican president from the tie vote. They had to get those damn federal occupational forces out of the South and agree not to interfere ever again. Our one vote did that," George said proudly, puffing on his cigar.

"Well, sir, I didn't realize all that. You have good reason to be proud," Reagan said.

"You are damn certain we were proud but then Lowry ran the next term against a Republican named Benjamin King. Old King got 951 votes in my county as opposed to 1,131 for Lowry. It was pretty much the same in all the counties but we still were not happy that so many niggahs turned out. Lowry ended up with 77,509 total votes to 52,009 for King. Lowry took office in January 1882. We would make damn sure it would not get that close again. Those damn niggahs needed to learn their lesson. We've had more lynchings and other niggah engagements after reconstruction than we did during reconstruction," George said.

"Sure, you have, Mr. George, without the federal forces occupying your soil...until then you had to be careful because those federalists were just waiting to charge some member of the state with violating a niggah's civil rights," Reagan said. "You kicked their ass when the feds left."

"Well, the Lord was with us, as you know, because the next year in 1883, the US Supreme Court overturned the Civil Rights Act and we took advantage of that. Now you just look right here at these last results and you will see what I mean. Lowry ran for reelection here in November 1885. He got...look here at this number. He got 88,783 votes compared to Republican candidate Darden, who only got 824 votes." George laughed again loudly and slapped the table, he was so happy.

"Any chance that Governor Lowry was just that popular?" asked Reagan.

"Hell, no, the Republicans just didn't vote or were scared to vote their minds. You see the state auditor's Republican opponent only got one vote— his own; the state treasurer Republican opponent only got one vote—his own. The same goes for the attorney general and superintendent of education," James George said proudly as he began to laugh and beat the table.

"Mr. George, you had better be glad those feds were gone. Looking at your chart here, the Republicans only got votes in nine counties and Lowry got votes and carried all seventy-four counties. The feds would want to know where the niggahs were on Election Day, or how you got them to vote Democratic, you old sly dog, you. I have to leave on that note," Reagan said.

"No, no just one more thing. Lowry was, of course, very pleased. He gave his address to the joint houses of the legislature. Let me read you his opening line. I have it right here in my billfold. It will dispel your thoughts of violence and intimidation. Here it is: '*Since the last meeting of this Legislature, the people of Mississippi have enjoyed a peaceful and uninterrupted prosperity.*' Ha, ha, ha, can you believe he said 'peaceful'?" laughed George. "It is in the record!"

"At least we white folks have enjoyed prosperity. My allegiance is to the wealthy farmers," George said with a blast of laughter.

"Come on, sir, let us go," Mr. Reagan said as they walked out into the chill of the Washington, D.C., March air. "I sure am glad we have got electric lights and steam heat in the Capitol Building now. By the way, I do expect at least two representatives to introduce resolutions on the floor tomorrow that would require Congress to send out fact-finding bodies. My stance is that we have no constitutional authority and I will object on those grounds. You don't have to worry, my friend."

On their trip back, Reagan brought up another issue. It was the fact that Mississippi had the contract prisoner law and most prisoners contracted out were to either plantation owners or the railroads. The railroads were expressing concern about the number of deaths that were occurring with these prisoners under state guards. The North was of the opinion it was just another form of slavery and that the contract prisoners were literally worked to death. In one county alone in Mississippi in 1886, 104 prisoners died. A legislative committee looking into the deaths received only limited information and no explanation for eighty-eight of the dead. The committee recommended that the law should require a coroner's inquest in every case of violent death of convicts.

That's where the two men's discussion ended for the night.

Chapter 41:

Congress and the President Respond

"The oppressed are allowed once every few years to decide which particular representatives of the oppressing class are to represent and repress them."
-Karl Marx

B lanche Bruce and Hyram Revels met their former colleague, former Mississippi Governor Adelbert Ames, at the always-busy Union Station. They had served in Congress during his tenure as Mississippi governor. They explained that the president was aware that Robert Lowry, the governor of Mississippi, had not taken any official action. Further, the governor had maintained that no action would take place, as it would trench upon the authority of Carroll County.

The president showed no emotion when they also told him the massacre had occurred right across the street from US Senator James Zachariah George's office. Also, according to one of the New York papers, his son was said to possibly be one of the regulators involved in the shooting. They said George refused to discuss it or take any action when the press attempted to contact him.

Bruce and Lynch said the president had previously listened to their recitals in detail as they explained themselves as being against such affairs as "a blight" to civilization. The president commented that he was surprised the state authorities had taken no steps to have the outrage investigated and the guilty parties brought to justice.

They traveled back to the White House to meet the president again, this time with former Governor Ames, who carried a note from Frederick Douglas. The president met with them only for a short while and explained that he deplored the conduct of the citizens of Mississippi, those involved and those with knowledge who refused to get involved in an investigation. However, he said the attorney general had informed him the federal government had no jurisdiction or constitutional authority in the state matter unless the state had violated the civil rights of those injured or killed.

Bruce and company left sadly disappointed that nobody would ever know if any of the assailants were culpable law enforcement people representing the state since there would be no investigation.

The newspapers did not even mention Adelbert Ames' name as having joined his old Mississippi colleagues when visiting the president on their second trip.

Senator Hoar spent the next evening with Mr. Ames discussing the issues. Hoar was convinced and assured Mr. Ames something would be passed. He then recommended that Mr. Ames follow the action from the galleries. While Hoar was drafting a bill, he learned that other members of the House and Senate were unsuccessfully introducing resolutions.

Hoar went ahead anyway and introduced a bill on the Senate floor the same day, providing for a method of inquiry by national authority in case of murder like the recent one of Negroes in Carrollton. He told the Senate that the victims of the incident were all of one race and all from one party. He explained that the incidents were too frequent, and that their uniform result was that the political opponents of the Democratic Party were the victims and the Democrats were the murderers. His bill provided for inquests under national authority. It provided that:

Whenever any three citizens petition a Judge of the Circuit Court, in term time or in vacation, setting forth that any person within the Judge's jurisdiction has been killed or injured in person or estate, or threatened with such injury, because of his race or color, or because of any political opinions expressed by him, or to prevent such expression by him or others, or to prevent him from voting as he chooses, it shall be the duty of the Judge to hold an inquest into the circumstances. The Judge may call upon United States District Attorneys to aid him in this work. The evidence taken and the conclusion of fact reached by the Judge are to be forthwith sent to the President of the United States, who in turn must transmit to Congress.

Mr. Hoar was of the opinion that the usual political affrays were themselves apt to take on a partisan character, and he thought an inquiry by a federal judge would be more searching and its result more satisfactory. Congress referred his bill to the

Judiciary Committee, where Hoar intended to endeavor to have it favorably considered.

Mr. O'Hara of North Carolina introduced the first House resolution. Mr. John H. Reagan, a prisoner of war sharing confinement with President of the Confederacy Jefferson Davis, objected. He had been a loyal servant to the South and was already in Congress when the Civil War broke out but resigned and went home under an appointment by President Jefferson Davis as postmaster of the Confederacy.

Later that day, on March 30, 1886, Mr. Samuel J. Randall, a white Democratic representative from Pennsylvania, had heard enough. He had read accounts from the *Chester Times* of Chester, Pennsylvania, dated March 26, 1886. It included excerpts from the *Jackson Mississippi Clarion* and the *New Orleans Times Picayune*, with editorials from both, and it was clear to him that everyone condemned the incident. He immediately drafted a resolution the night before and held it in his hand as he read excerpts from his home state paper to himself:

It is admitted that these defendants were being tried by a lawful court in the very sanctuary of the law, when 100 armed men appeared upon the scene and surrounded the temple of justice and shot to death under the eye of the court, eleven citizens of Mississippi an d mortally wounded nine others. It is admitted that not one white man was hurt.

It is hard to realize that there could be found in Mississippi 100 men who could be led to avenge the personal wrongs and injuries of a friend in the heartless, conscienceless, and cold-blooded manner, which characterized the conduct of the mob at Carrollton. It is harder still to realize that the place selected for this exhibition of hideous atrocity should be the temple of justice at the very horns of the altar. It comes to this...that there is no place so sacred that the bloodthirsty will not enter to do their damnable deeds. If so, then indeed we are worse than heathens.

The people of Mississippi realize that at the door of the courtroom in Carrollton the bloody bodies of its slain citizens be heaped one upon another. They have not been removed; they cannot be removed. There they will stay a monument to the foulness and wickedness of their ruthless slayers.

Shocked by the conduct and lack of prosecution, he introduced a very similar resolution as the one previously presented on the House floor: "Mr. Speaker, I ask by unanimous consent to submit for present consideration the following resolution." The clerk read as follows:

Resolved, That a committee of five members of the House of Representatives to be designated by the Speaker, be appointed, whose duties it shall be to investigate the circumstances and causes attending and resulting in the killing, on the 17th day of March, 1886, in Carrollton, Miss., a number of colored citizens of said State, and make report thereof to this House.

Resolved, That said committee, when appointed, shall have power to subpoena witnesses, to administer oaths, and do all other acts necessary to a free investigation of the subject matter; that said committee may appoint a subcommittee to visit the State of Mississippi to take testimony and do such other acts as may be necessary in the premises, and that the expenses

of the committee shall be paid from the contingent fund
of the House, not to exceed --- dollars.

"Is there any objection to the present consideration of the resolution which has been read?" asked the speaker of the House.

"While I am aware the resolution has been offered by request of the Mississippi delegation, yet I am constrained by my respect for the Constitution of the United States to object to it. We have no earthly authority to deal with the subject matter," Mr. Reagan of Texas said.

"Then I ask to refer it to the Committee on Rules," Mr. Randall said angrily.

"On behalf of the Mississippi delegation, I ask the honorable gentleman from Texas to withdraw his objection to the introduction and adoption of the resolution submitted by the gentleman from Pennsylvania. The Mississippi delegation does not shrink from any investigation into the occurrence referred to, but on the contrary, invite the fullest and most searching examination. The gentleman from Pennsylvania has not presented this resolution in opposition to the wishes of the Mississippi delegation, but with their knowledge and consent and really at their suggestion," Mr. Ethelbert Barksdale, Democrat from Mississippi, said.

"I would gladly do anything which the gentleman from Mississippi delegation asked me to do, but I am constrained by a sense of duty in this matter to insist on my objection. There are more states than Mississippi involved," Mr. Reagan from Texas barked out.

"Why should the gentleman who objects to the consideration of the proposition insist upon arguing it?" asked Mr. William Henry Wadsworth, a Republican from Kentucky.

"I was only answering a question," Reagan said.

"Objection being made, the resolution is not before the House," the speaker of the House said assertively.

Then on motion of Mr. Springer (at 4 o'clock and 55 minutes p.m.), the House adjourned. And so came the end of the day in defeat.

Not only had the day ended in defeat in the halls of Congress, this day would be the beginning of the end of a fight for human rights, justice and the American way. Men had perished, slaughtered like cattle only because of the color of their skin. These were men much needed prior to the Civil War, albeit as slaves, but aside from occasional beatings or mistreatment from a few unscrupulous landowners, these were people cared for with food, clothing, shelter, and medical care. The South's opinion was that the war had now made them useless, low-class scum often elected to office over the white supremacist Democrats who had now grown to hate them as heathens rather than cherish them as farm workers.

As governors and presidents began to turn their backs on these people, they had no help in defending themselves. The hatred grown out of the results of war had brought us into a situation Thomas Jefferson described as "having a wolf by the ear, unable to hold onto but unable to let go of."

The white supremacists were not about to back down and the North was not about to help. The blacks were left with facing death or succumbing to the white man, just as the Indians had done half a century before. What had our nation become?

Conclusion:

The Vision

"If I have seen farther than others, it is because I
was standing on the shoulders of giants."
-Isaac Newton

One hot summer day while putting the final changes on this story, I drove to the historical Carrollton Courthouse and parked out front along the busy street. A large, red fox squirrel hopped across the wrought iron fence in front of me before I scared him away with my squeaky car door. Reluctant to leave the comfort of my cold air, I sluggishly stepped into the intense heat. Quickly struck by the extreme humidity, I walked smartly up the old concrete steps onto the sidewalk, passing war memorials from three centuries of fallen soldiers. The large oak trees out front cast a welcome shadow over the west entrance of the century-and-a-quarter-old building.

After making my way past the county supervisor's office on the left, and beyond the breezeway, I found myself beside the lower level of the giant wooden staircase. It led to the legendary and mysterious courtroom only one flight up. Across from the base of the stairs was a now-air conditioned boundary accessible only by a single, solid wooden door. Just inside, a kind and considerate gray-haired lady, one of four in the chancery clerk's office accustomed to my many visits, quickly came to my aid. With a smile, she retrieved the large metal ring holding the key to the courtroom and placed it over her wrist like a giant bracelet. She made her way promptly around the long counter to where I was standing.

Anxious and very accommodating, she walked with me, making small talk as she carefully clung to the worn, wooden banister. With me following behind, we ascended the ghostly old stairs. She knew exactly which key in the large array of keys fit the antique lock, as if she had opened it a thousand times before. Short in stature and posture slightly bent, she was barely above eye level with the keyhole as she aimed the old brass key directly into its slot. Shaking the key up and down as she twisted it with one hand, she turned the old brass knob with the other. At last, the door was open. She clung to the knob, opening the door for me proudly, as if she were a smartly dressed and highly tipped bellhop in a New York high-rise hotel.

As she quietly turned to leave and began her descent down the old staircase, I turned around before entering the perfectly preserved old courtroom. A small brass plaque caught my eye on the opposite side of the entrance. It seemed out of place, although I had seen it many times before. I was inclined to go back and read it once again, as if maybe I had missed something important, but I felt drawn into the room by a magnetic force beyond my control.

With the door open, that smell hit me, not the smell of gunpowder that had dissipated so many years before. You only detect this indescribable but pleasant odor at your grandmother's house in the closets, or in the storeroom of an old building. Once inside, I assumed my normal state of awe. No matter how many times I had visited this hallowed hall of justice, I felt humbled by its solace. My own demeanor went unnoticed when I entered alone, but quickly stood out when I had shared this experience with other onlookers during some of my many previous visits. Those acquaintances of mine who knew not the whole story carried on as if inside a local restaurant or other place of business. I, on the other hand, always felt just as I did on this day — and on this day, I was alone.

Cold chills rushed over me as the hair on the back of my neck stood out due to the distinct aura emanating from this room. It was like a tremble, or ever-so-slight jolt of electricity that hit me with that first step on those old shellacked, pine wooden boards that creaked beneath my feet. I felt a sense of reverence, forced to act as if I were walking into a church full of people, moving softly and slowly so as not to interrupt the sermon.

Tired following the long trip from Jackson, and droopy-eyed from the lack of sleep the night before, I immediately took a seat. It was on the back row, a ways away, but in direct view of the witness chair. Once occupied by who knows how many hundreds, if not thousands, of witnesses before, it sat vacant on this day. My eyes tracked to the left, where the judge had sat so many times, often talking quietly to the bailiff, a small but wiry old man dressed partially in some sort of uniform, to his right.

A thin vertical object partially obstructed my view of the judge's seat. Placed there with good intentions and an obvious useful purpose, the rope hanging from the bell tower into the center of the room above made me cringe. The stiffness of the hemp still showed an outline of thirteen circular wraps near the bottom, confirming the existence of a carefully made hangman's noose that once hung there as a reminder. "Used only as a novelty bell-pull"—so said an old sheriff over the years, but he knew…the Negroes knew….and God knew.

Out front, in the judge's direct line of sight, was a long wooden table, on the day in question and in my mind today, occupied in the center by one James M. Liddell, a cold-blooded murderer, I thought, in his own right. Surrounded by the legal minds of the day, lawyers sat on both sides of the defendant, arguing the case of innocence to the judge, as if it had not already been determined.

I cleared my mind for the moment and got up quietly, the courtroom now empty again, and walked around the front row of the long wooden pews. I sat in the front, next to the west wall where the Browns had grouped together during that dreadful day. I closed my eyes and began to meditate, trying again to imagine that scene from March 17, 1886. I got too relaxed and fell into a deep, tranquil sleep. Within seconds, out of body, I saw myself walking around, pacing back and forth from the witness seat to the lawyers' table and down to the pews. I stopped momentarily and turned to face the north wall. Trying to determine how five or six white men could be in front of that wall with 175 chunks of hot lead headed directly towards them at lightning speed and not even a scratch, I became confused. With notebook and pen in hand, I started to draw lines of trajectory in order to identify the path of the bullets, musket balls and buckshot.

As I turned around facing south to look at the back door, there stood a young black man, who also appeared to be looking around.

"I'm sorry. I didn't hear you come in," I said.

"Oh, that's okay, don't mind me. Just keep doing whatever you were doing," he said.

I continued to walk toe-to-toe towards the back door, counting the number of footsteps from the front wrought iron railing to the back. I counted fourteen, fifteen, sixteen, and so on. He looked at me without interrupting, but smiled as he saw my lips moving until I was within three feet of him.

"Hi, I'm Will McKinney," he said cheerfully, as I recorded the measurement on my writing pad.

I exchanged greetings without paying much attention, as I often do during introductions, forgetting the person's name five seconds later.

"Excuse me for a moment," I said. "I just need to walk out here to the stairwell and look at something."

"No problem," he said quietly. "Need to know anything about what happened here long ago?"

"No," I said, as I continued to walk out the squeaking door while he sat down on the back pew. I felt like I had done enough research so that I pretty much knew it all and any additional information would just bog me down.

Outside on the top step, I turned around, looking for remnants of the patches now covering ten bullet holes, which had been reported by the New Orleans press. I looked at the opposite side of the door, now closed to the courtroom. The top insert of the door appeared as though framed in gold. An image of a man, not standing but hanging by the neck from a tree limb appeared; head bent downward and blood oozing from multiple parts of his body. It was as if it had been meticulously painted by the likes of Rembrandt... Then, suddenly, it hit me like a ton of bricks.

"Who did he say he was?" I asked myself with intense frustration.

His name was rolling around my feeble brain and off the tip of my tongue. I knew it was familiar, but I felt dazed and groggy, unable to put two and two together.

"Who did you say you were?" I exclaimed as I hurried back through the door, barely even noticing that the painting had by now, faded away.

"Where are you?" I asked frantically as I paced quickly around the courtroom. He was nowhere to be found... I walked in and out of the courtroom, looked between and up under the benches. Then, suddenly, just as quickly as he had disappeared, there he was, sitting nonchalantly in a window sill on the west wall with the window wide open, back to the ground twenty feet below. He appeared to be modeling for a shoe commercial with his legs crossed, right foot pointing towards me, rocking up and down, his fingers of both hands laced together around his knee. He had a smile from ear to ear.

"Get the picture now?" he asked.

"Yes, yes I do." (Although I really didn't as of then.) "Careful, you could fall out of that window. What did you say your name was?" I asked.

Then, suddenly, my vision seemed murky as I heard at first a loud echoing sound resonating to a slight whisper: "**WILL MCKINNEY,** WILL MCKINNEY, Will McKinney…"

I heard it over and over as I seemed to be spiraling through space. I felt like I was falling through a bottomless tunnel, spinning ever so gently as a blurred vision of the courtroom appeared once again. There were black men of all ages, walking, almost marching, in an orderly manner directly out of the window, not jumping, not stumbling, but straight out, upright as if on a cloud. Looking back, they focused on maybe a half dozen well-dressed white men, lying face down on the floor inside the wrought iron enclosure. Then they turned their heads to face me with all the discipline of a military drill team marching in review, facing their commanding officer, but with a smile as they departed the window.

"What are you doing? What are you saying? What's going on?" I screamed desperately, almost in tears. But by then they were all gone. I looked back to see the white men who had been lying on the floor. They were the last things those black ghostly figures had focused their attention on before leaving the room through the window. They, too, were gone, but they did not go out the window.

They must have run past me down the stairs while my eyes were glued to the awesome marvel I had just witnessed, I thought for just a moment with a dazed, groggy mind before I found myself completely awake and alert to a feminine voice.

"Hello, hello...ready to go yet, Mr. Ward?" a middle-aged, graying lady cheerfully asked with a smile, as I turned around, facing the doorway.

There was the clerk who had let me in, with the door key in one hand, pointing at a small watch on her other. "It's after five and I have to go home," she said with a smile. "My husband will be waiting for his dinner."

"I'm sorry, I'm coming right now. I must have fallen asleep. Who were those men you passed on the stairs on your way up here?" I asked as I walked toward her at the back door.

"I didn't pass anybody coming up the stairs, Mr. Ward. Aside from being sound asleep, you must have also been dreaming. You are the only one that has come up here today," the clerk said sympathetically as she locked the door to the courtroom one last time...and, by doing so, she gave closure to the final saga of the Carrollton tragedy.

EPILOGUE

"Lord, make me an instrument of your peace;
where there is hatred, let me sow love; where there
is injury, pardon; where there is doubt, faith;
where there is despair, hope; where there is
darkness, light; and where there is sadness, joy."
-St Francis of Assisi

As my work was ending in Carrollton, I found it difficult to let go. It was the topic of discussion with my friends and family, news media and talk show hosts, in anticipation of the book's release. I spoke of characters in the story as if I were on a first-name basis with many of them. I called them by their first names and even described them right down to their habits. I had read so much about them, from family accounts to official records to newspaper clippings, that I felt I could almost predict what they might say or do in just about any given situation.

The bullet holes that scarred the walls of the courthouse served as a reminder for Negroes of the community to know and stay in their place. They remained for 106 years until the county refurbished the courthouse. The bell tower directly in the center of the courtroom would use a hangman's noose as a handle, dangling just above eye level, long after the refurbishment.

While a brass plaque on the wall outside the courtroom identifies the supervisors and contractors responsible for the work, no plaque identifies the dead men of the Carrollton Massacre. The newspapers of the day identified twenty victims but one of those (Jake Cane) lived. The murderers were never brought to justice. Some believed those who committed the murders were those supposedly responsible for seeing justice upheld.

President Grover Cleveland chose not to assist. The bill presented to Congress by Massachusetts Senator George Hoar never made it out of the Judiciary Committee. Mississippi Senator James Z. George did not support it, or any other legislation regarding the massacre. Neither of the resolutions presented in the US House of Representatives by Mr. O'Hara from North Carolina or Mr. Randall from Pennsylvania made it further than the Rules Committee.

The Mississippi Legislature did not find the incident worth discussing on the record. The Senate/House session reports do not mention it during the last week of the 1886 legislative session. They often issue resolutions to honor victims of tragedies, sports teams, retired state employees, singers, writers, and the likes of Kermit the Frog, but no action for these dead.

James Monroe Liddell, Jr. was approached by his friend about an assault. The proper course of action would have been to advise him to sign charges. Instead, Liddell took matters into his own hands with far more knowledge of the law than that of a layman. He sought out the offenders, confronted them, and used provoking language against them, even making an overt move towards them before bystanders restrained him. That was provocation enough for them to respond likewise. He then had an opportunity to walk away from it. He went to eat and somebody approached him, indicating the Browns had gathered with friends and were making insulting comments about him. If he felt threatened, he could have sought out an officer of the law. He did not; rather, he went back and again attempted to assault them. From that point on, it depends on what accounts you believe from the various papers as to who shot first, but even the grand jury did not dispute the accounts up to that point.

Liddell was the editor of the *Yazoo Valley Flag* as well as part proprietor. While examining newspapers from that week and the next six he had written, I also found a notice where Leflore County had approved H.S. "Houston" Whitworth as a contractor. Liddell probably negotiated the use of Whitworth's gang (if they came from Greenwood at all), and orchestrated the whole massacre. It would have been difficult at best for the whites in the courtroom to escape the barrage of fire without knowing or anticipating that it was coming. The vast majority of the bullet holes were in the north wall, where they stood or sat.

Liddell became a member of the legislature in 1878 while his uncle of the same name served as well. They may have labeled him with the suffix "Jr." to avoid confusion, and it stuck.

His brother, William Walker Liddell, named after their father (who served as a state representative during the civil war), should have been the "Jr." Their father also had a younger brother named Phillip Franklin Liddell, who was a colonel killed in the Civil War. James Liddell, Jr. would later marry and have one son, naming him Phillip Franklin Liddell after another Civil War hero, instead of his father. The Liddells occupied two different homes in Carroll County, based on 1880 census records. No 1890 census is available.

Ironically, around 1900, Liddell moved to another Carroll County—Carroll County, Tennessee, and married Mary L. Brantley, formerly of Greenwood.

However, two years before that marriage, he was at Fort McPherson, Georgia, in his middle forties, going through Officer Candidate School to take over a company headed to fight in Cuba in the Spanish-American War. Others from Carrollton volunteered as well, including Tandy Oury, formerly of the *Carrollton Conservative* newspaper and later town marshal. In addition, former state representative L. M. Southworth volunteered and went to the Philippines.

Their training included trips back and forth from Meridian and Nashville, but finally at a Cuban mock-up camp in Jacksonville, Florida. The war ended before most got there, but Liddell went on. On his way back from Jacksonville, Tandy Oury died of an illness near Meridian. He is buried in North Carrollton at Evergreen Cemetery.

After graduation at Officer's Candidate School, James Monroe Liddell assumed command of Company D, 29th Regiment volunteers and deployed to the small island of Cuba. Ironically, the president put General Adelbert Ames, former provisional and ousted elected governor from Mississippi, in charge of the volunteers in Cuba.

The Philippine insurrection was going on by then. Liddell and L.M. Southworth went to the Philippines as regulars with the Fifth Army. Not long after their arrival, the war there ended, too. The US government was setting up a judicial branch that included eight military lawyers and the rest Philippine nationals. James Liddell received one of the judge's appointments in 1901.

Liddell became an entrepreneur by buying a plantation of coconut trees. He also publically endorsed a tonic that supposedly cured allergies. He was promoted to temporary major but was not allowed to keep it for not staying in the grade long enough. He left as a captain.

He established himself in social circles back in the US as a big game hunter and guide for people who wanted to kill a large wild water buffalo called "Tamaro." He was also a successful photographer.

As the automobile industry began to take hold, he saw an opportunity to get in on the ground floor of a new invention. He opened the first Chevrolet dealership the Philippines ever had. His son, Phillip Franklin, worked with him.

A 1913 letter from then Governor-General Forbes to President Taft describing the "state of the Philippines" spoke of both Liddell and Southworth in a less than honorable manner. He cited improper collusion in dismissing criminal cases that eventually led to Liddell's forced resignation.

James M. Liddell died of cholera in 1915, but his place of burial is unknown.

His friend, L.M. Southworth, died of cancer years later in a Baltimore hospital but his body was brought back and laid to rest in North Carrollton.

James Liddell's brother, William W. Liddell, went on to officially become a doctor and remained in Carrollton practicing medicine, just as his father of the same name before him had done. Like his brother, who showed little regard for allowing the law to handle his personal quarrels, he killed a man. The man was the legal guardian of the young orphan girl he married, who was upset because of the marriage.

William Liddell told the New Orleans newspapers that after the courtroom shooting occurred, he stepped over wounded Negroes scurrying away without offering any assistance to try to save them. He was in a hurry to get to his excursion train headed for New Orleans. His body now rests at Evergreen Cemetery in Carroll County.

Senator James Z. George died a Civil War and agricultural hero. He is most noted for his writing of Mississippi's famous 1890 Constitution that almost totally disenfranchised the black race. His life was celebrated after his death by granite and marble. Mr. George's body also rests at Evergreen Cemetery in North Carrollton, Carroll County, Mississippi. The Mississippi Legislature further celebrated Mr.

George's life by erecting a statute of bronze in his honor in the halls of Congress at Washington, D.C.

In addition to the tomb and the brass full-size statute memorializing Mr. George, the National Historic Society has placed his home and office on the National Registry of Historic Places. The North Carrollton High School also bears his name in his honor.

The revelation of these facts is not intended to harm the reputation or ignore any good Mr. George may have done. They allow the reader to use them as a comparison to see the worth of one life over another as it was valued then, depending on what social class you enjoyed. Times were different and different things were acceptable back then. The fact that it was in Carrollton makes no difference. It could have been any town in Mississippi or any town anywhere in the South, for that matter.

The attitude of white supremacy caused this incident. The incident itself was only a catalyst for white domination in our political system. That attitude was widespread, especially after 1875 and well into the twentieth century with men like Hernando Desoto Money (James Z. George's law partner and successor to his seat in the Senate), James K. Vardaman (Hernando Desoto Money's cousin) and Theodore Bilbo. These were some of the most radical, outspoken men of the century. They treated blacks as less than four legged animals and publically referred to them by every disgusting name imaginable. Yet they were our senators, governors, and congressmen.

Governor Robert Lowry died a Civil War hero, noted governor, and received credit for bringing the railroads into the state. He went on to become a noted author of Mississippi history after teaming with retired Vicksburg newspaper editor William H. McCardle. The book was published in two versions, the first being *A History of Mississippi*, where he commented about the Black and Tan Convention, which was made up of blacks and whites to write a new constitution. His comments about the black involvement included, verbatim:

Many intelligent, respectable whites from around the state prohibited from participation while ignorant, unscrupulous Negroes knowing nothing of the elective process were made docile instruments of equally ignorant but more corrupt and worthless class of white man ever known to be none other than carpetbaggers.

These characterless vagabonds, of these bold brigands thus suddenly raised from their native insignificance to a position of prominence, masquerading as statesman and constitution writers were here only because of four newspapers in the state.

The second book had similar, somewhat toned down language; it was called *A History of Mississippi* (for use in schools) and was used as a textbook for over forty years. He called black people "imbeciles" and other names in print. He blamed blacks and carpetbaggers for most things that went wrong and praised former Confederate general, later US senator, James Z. George for many things.

None of the lives of any of the victims of this massacre has ever been celebrated publically. Somewhere in the woods of that cemetery are the unmarked graves of the victims. There are no markings for the victims of the massacre.

In 2006, a researcher from Mississippi State University described her view of the Carrollton Courthouse as having the appearance of a memorial. There is a memorial to war veterans of all wars on the southwest side of the lawn. There is a statute memorializing Confederate soldiers that stands high on the northwest corner of the courthouse grounds. Beside it is a flagpole memorializing the South with a Confederate flag that flies every day. It stands on a spot near the site where the outlaw gang hung William McKinney adjacent to Senator James Z. George's law office.

Former Governor Adelbert Ames' life was also celebrated with memorials to include his receipt of the Congressional Medal of Honor.

Carrollton's racial murders didn't stop in 1886 with McKinney or the Browns. In 1901, a black mother and her two children were taken from the old jail by an angry mob of 500 people and murdered for a crime they only had knowledge of, but were not participants.

Author Comments

"We must accept finite disappointment, but we
must never lose infinite hope."
-Dr. Martin L. King, Jr.

While conducting extensive research for this book, I started stumbling across information and facts that lead me to believe that we in Mississippi may have been misled or swayed by our history books. In some cases, I would blame that on acts of omission. Mississippi's boastful claim of being the first state to have a black US senator is one example. It is actually not something of which to be proud at all. Mississippi was under military occupation by the North and Governor Adelbert Ames was appointed as military governor. These men were there as a part of the Northern military occupation to make sure we did not abuse blacks at the polls since freed slaves' votes far outnumbered the white plantation owners.

Mississippi had black US congressional representation because the state legislature at that time selected the congressional representatives and many blacks had been elected to the legislature.

Mississippi has taken credit for having a Greenwood plantation owner and former ship's captain who is said to be the first in the nation to graciously and kindly send his slaves back to Africa. According to our history, they formed what is now the country of Liberia on Africa's west coast. President Lincoln himself campaigned on colonization of the blacks and sending them to place with which his administration had negotiated, called Liberia and Haiti. His intent was to send them all back but it failed to get congressional approval midway through the war. Lincoln's action came after the Mississippi ship captain's. However, the American Colonization Society had formed for that purpose some forty years before the Civil War and had already sent slaves to Liberia.

An enclosed Philadelphia article reprinted in a New York newspaper addresses both the Carrollton massacre and colonization but not during the Civil War—rather, over twenty years later, in 1886. It sheds light on what the blacks thought about colonization. They were not in favor of this organized deportation and raised the issue of sending Italians and Irish back to their homelands.

Back then, the Ku Klux Klan was considered nothing more than a left-wing, paramilitary group used as a right arm for the Democratic Party to "regulate" and "enforce." History does not hide or dispute what the Klan did, so where does that put the leader of the Democratic Party in the big scheme of things?

The capital of Mississippi is named after Andrew Jackson, a man who participated in and led ethnic cleansing of the Indians in Mississippi. He loosely threatened to kill them if they refused to leave. That action could possibly lead to charges of terrorism if done today.

Greenwood Leflore has often been praised for his work. This was a man who "sold out" his Indian nation to Andrew Jackson by accepting land and other compensation for negotiating the treaty. His actions, no matter how noble one thinks they were, cleansed the Indians from Mississippi. Leflore stayed to build his mansion on the land awarded to him for his achievements. He also sold out his own State of Mississippi after having served three terms in the legislature. He sold out Confederate soldiers by committing what one could compare to treason, by selling goods and supplies to the Union army, intended for use against Mississippi Confederates. Although claiming loyalty to the North, he stayed in Carroll County in his mansion and kept his slaves. After the war, his heirs filed claims at his dying request of almost seven hundred thousand dollars for war damage—that included twenty-seven slaves he provided to the Union army to fight against Confederate forces, expecting payment later. Ironically, though, Congress concluded he kept them in captivity as slaves following two executive orders proclaimed by President Lincoln to free them. When he turned the so-called slaves over to the Union in mid-1864, by law, they were not slaves at all. The Emancipation Proclamation had already been issued. Congress concluded that neither he nor, his estate was entitled to reimbursement at the rate of "$800 per head." If anybody was entitled to compensation at all, it was the soldiers who fought.

Looking beyond the slaves and back to his own Indian people, wagons showed up out front and whisked his people away to Oklahoma without notice. They had little time to gather only necessities, knowing the journey ahead would be a thousand miles on foot in severe weather. His people said their brothers would have rather died fighting for what was theirs than die in shame, regret, disease, infection, starvation, exhaustion or of a broken heart.

Most all of the men involved in all of these issues felt controlling the newspapers controlled politics. Therefore, each of them at one time or another owned a newspaper, was editor of one or more newspapers, or had close ties to newspaper offices and editors. Every single one of them had been a lawyer and/or politician. They had been state representatives, senators, congressional representatives and one had been president of our country—another, the chief of a nation of people.

I find it hard now to look a Choctaw Indian in the eyes. I find it hard to theorize how Lowry or the others could think they would have behaved if someone had snatched them from their homes at the end of a saber. How would they have acted if they had been held in captivity and oppressed to the point that their mother, father, brothers, and sisters were sold, and wives and daughters raped in front of their own eyes? If, unable to defend their families, instead they received ninety-nine lashes from a whip and were then made to work in the fields with blood pouring from the wounds, how would they have felt? If, called names like "imbecile" or "idiot," how would they have felt? What if they had not been allowed to learn how to read and write? Might they then be seen as having no spirit, no self-esteem, no education and little to live for? Could that have been the reason the Negroes acted the way they did? Would they have been able to walk around with the confidence of statesmen?

My father, who died at seventy, was as illiterate as the slaves were. He picked cotton as a child and could not go to school. He raised eight kids as a mechanic. My mother, who died in 2009 at ninety-two, picked cotton as a child. She only went to the third grade. As an adult, she made dresses for black women to supplement the family income. She went to her grave harboring blame for letting her baby brother get bitten by a snake and die. He played on a quilt in the edge of a cotton field while the rest of the family picked cotton at Forked Lake in Quitman County, Mississippi.

If it had not been for blacks, who made up ninety percent of my mother and father's business while I was growing up, we would have starved. I was raised with cotton fields all around me, played with black kids daily and watched as blacks picked cotton until the late 1950s or early 1960s, when the mechanical cotton-picking machine became widely used. My father worked constantly, mostly on plantation owners' and their "hands'" cars. He never had time to take me hunting. My elderly neighbor, a black man named Mettie Bridges, taught me to hunt and trap. When he lost his sight and could not go with me anymore, he bought shotgun shells for me. I took the game I killed back to him. His wife could make a squirrel taste better than a steak.

His parents were born into slavery. I cried when he died and for weeks thereafter. His wife and her sister that lived with them never missed my birthdays, always bringing a gift next door to me when I was a child.

I lost a child when she was sixteen, every parent's nightmare. I went through counseling. I took anti-depressant drugs for years. I experienced loss of functionality in the workplace because of it. I cannot image what the slaves must have felt when they watched family members sold, beaten, raped and killed. They could not defend them. Most couldn't even cleanse their wounds. They were not able to go to counselors. There were no support groups. Anti-depressant medications did not even exist. They had no choice but to "suck it up" and go to work anyway. Can anybody imagine what life must have been like for them? I would have looked like a zombie.

I cannot help now but see many of our former leaders in history as THUGS. Many stole the offices by violence, threats, intimidation and murder, or conspiracy to commit murder, just as they stole the land from the Indians. Some of them could be considered terrorists by today's standards. The United State Code defines terrorism as: *"the unlawful use of force and violence against persons or property to intimidate or coerce a government, the civilian population, or any segment thereof, in furtherance of political or social objectives"* (28 C.F.R. Section 0.85). You might say, "Well, we didn't have terrorism laws back then." If so, you are right. We did not, but we had laws against murder! Why did so many of these massacres go unprosecuted?

Having said all that, I do not think all is doomed. We often see in the paper where a person convicted of crimes many years ago is vindicated and pardoned. We see legislative bodies issuing proclamations and resolutions in an attempt to right a wrong or make an apology for something our ancestors did. We see markers erected from time to time to commemorate the site of a significant event or honor a person or group of persons.

Even though there were many newspaper accounts of the Carrollton Courthouse tragedy (some different), most people can conclude those people were murdered. Yes, their skin was black and, no, they did not contribute as much to society as did Mr. George or the others remembered by statues and monuments, but they were human beings nonetheless. They deserved to live. I do not believe they went there that day looking for a fight. They did what James Liddell should have done if he or his friend felt that a crime had been committed against them. They signed charges and sat patiently in court to offer testimony and allow the accused to face his accusers. They tried to allow the judicial system to work. The system was not designed for them. They were victims of an age gone by.

Our ancestors, not us, chose not to hunt down their killers. However, they have long since gone on to meet their maker and either have or will answer for their actions here. Just like the ancestors of some of the more affluent whites involved, so do some descendants of the blacks still live in Carrollton. Jake

Cain's name was on the list of those injured that fateful day. The newspapers said he would die. He did not die, and his granddaughter listened to his stories of that day. She later gave an interview to one of Carrollton's residents, Susie James, a freelance writer, about the incident. Mildred Cain Burkes had hoped one day to write a book about it. God chose to take her home before that was possible. Her descendants still live in Carrollton and today are carrying on the memories of this deep, dark secret nobody was supposed to discuss.

Would it be so hard to do something in their honor, like maybe put one more brass plaque outside that courtroom honoring those men and boys who lost their lives? It would not even have to be an apology or an admission of guilt if that offends anyone, but their names are not even honored on a headstone, much less a monument or plaque. Their descendants do not even know what part of the cemetery to visit so they can pay tribute to their dead or place flowers in their honor. It just seems to be the humane thing to do.

Maybe an act of kindness could rid the shame from some of the townspeople of Carrollton. Some current residents are direct ancestors of that day. Maybe they harbor that shame because the blame placed on a group of Greenwood outlaws may simply be that, blame alone. The Town of Carrollton was made up of about 400 people at the time of this tragedy. Prior to the tragedy the women spoke of their husbands going to secret meetings at stores, churches and lodges at night. If you subtract the elderly, sickly, women and children from the 400, you may come up with about 100 to 150 people left that could have attended meetings. Most witnesses claim that the band of outlaws was made up of 100 to 150 people. Did they really come from Greenwood at all or did the town ban together to commit this tragic act forever concealing it behind a cloak of secrecy? We will never know. Rick Ward 357

Finally, in closing, I must say that *ALL* of the men mentioned in this story did *SOME* good and, for that, I am pleased and proud. I am sure they were good family men. I have no doubt those who served were brave, dedicated and loyal soldiers, just like my ancestors, regardless of what some may think of the reason they fought. However, I am not proud of the bad they did, the institution they stood for or the mentality they shared. I accept it because I cannot do anything about something that happened that many years ago. Times were different then. We have come a long way.

Please provide any comments you may have to:
authors@springmorningpublishing.org

About the Author

R ick Ward was born in Tunica, Mississippi, on August 1, 1953. He enlisted in the US Navy during the Vietnam era and received an honorable discharge in 1975. He remained in the Navy reserves for over thirty years. He has an associate degree in law enforcement from Mississippi Gulf Coast Community College, a bachelor of science in criminal justice from the University of the State of New York, and a master's degree in educational administration from the University of Hawaii. He is a graduate of the Mississippi State Police Academy, United States Army Military Police School, and Federal Bureau of Investigations' National Training Academy.

Rick retired in 2005 with a dual career in civilian law enforcement and United States Navy law enforcement and security. His career netted him a total of thirty-four years combined military and civilian law enforcement experience as he traveled the world.

Throughout his career, he has been a municipal uniformed patrol officer, undercover state narcotics officer, county criminal investigator, state attorney general political corruption agent, Mississippi Gaming Commission division director, and Federal Employment Compensation Act fraud investigator.

Between those various positions in civilian law enforcement, Rick served on active duty as investigator aboard a battleship, and officer in charge of security for two major shore installations and an amphibious assault ship. He was a force protection officer for counter-drug operations in Central America and regional security officer for the entire Northeast coast. Rick was on site in New York on September 11, 2001, and was responsible for Navy security reactionary forces.

Rick's last assignment with the Naval Criminal Investigative Service (NCIS) led to his position at headquarters in Washington, D.C., before retiring as a lieutenant commander. He has written articles in military and civilian law enforcement journals with worldwide circulation throughout his career.

Rick's experiences have inspired him to research real-life historical events to write narrative fiction and nonfiction stories about them. *The Lawmaker* (2008) was his first, followed by *Blood-Stained Justice* (2009), both legal crime thrillers written as novels, but loosely based on his own life experiences.